Surviving Passion

Surviving Passion

Kathy Lewis

Library of Congress Number:		2004195139
ISBN:	Hardcover	1-4134-8023-3
	Softcover	1-4134-8022-5

This book was printed in the United States of America.

To order additional copies of this book, contact:
Xlibris Corporation
1-888-795-4274
www.Xlibris.com
Orders@Xlibris.com
26878

ACKNOWLEDGEMENTS

I am grateful to Lin, Ann, Jane and Henry for their love, help and patience in our busy life of family, work, cabin and travel. This book would not have been written without the life lessons gleaned growing up with my parents, five brothers and sister in metro Detroit—thanks for all of the ongoing encouragement and support.

Thanks to our many exceptional friends who encouraged my finding time to write and always had a kind word when I was struggling. My writing teacher, Pat Francisco, and my writing group read more drafts of *Surviving Passion* than I care to admit—I appreciate their patience with the material and with me more than I can say.

Thanks also to Carol Anshaw for responding to an unknown writer's plea for help and for directing me to Sharon Stark, who provided an insightful and incisive critique of the previous draft. A special thanks to Kim Dalros, my graphic artist, for her lyrical way with illustrations and copy.

And finally, thanks to my abaton.com and McKesson friends, colleagues and clients for sustaining me in our collective search for meaningful work and a decent paycheck.

CHAPTER 1

Amidst fire and water, birth came from the flood and when the flood receded, the landscape was permanently altered. Some trees, yanked up by cataclysmic wind or drowned at the root, toppled and fell. The trunks of others turned gray, then white and petrified. A few stood tall and serene above the river, denying the occurrence of the flood. The light dappled through their feathery crowns and danced off the granite. Birds gathered amongst the limbs, their young falling out of the nest en route to learning flight. In the part of the forest allowed to burn, new jack pines sprouted where the heat of the fire burst their seeds. The river flowed quietly amid its banks, dark green on calm days, gray and tinged with whitecaps during storms.

*   *   *

Therese, April, 1989
Bloomington, Minnesota

The blue glass and steel tower loomed out of the fog like a shimmering artifact from another planet. Headlights crawled toward me as I waited behind the series of gleaming red taillights turning onto the private road, which snaked toward the building complex. The dashboard clock read 7:22 AM. I sipped coffee from my silver-lidded car mug, lowered the volume on Patsy Cline's "Crazy" and sighed. Every year I mixed a cassette tape or two with favorite songs.

This year it was love gone wrong on side 1 and melancholy yet hopeful longings on the reverse.

Carepath was housed on the I-494 strip overlooking the valley of the Minnesota River as it made its sluggish way east toward the much larger Mississippi. My office on the eleventh floor of the middle tower had a view of river and marshland, a glimpse of a natural world which we completely ignored in the pursuit of stockholder dividends. The location, about ten miles south of downtown Minneapolis and close to the Twin Cities International Airport, was convenient for a small health care software company whose staff ran in caffeine-fueled packs working evenings and weekends to test endless lines of code falling off the screen like teletype.

I drew myself up as I pulled into a parking space and headed for the first of the day's four meetings, trying to remember which clinical background I was interviewing candidates for this week, as specified in the quarter-page ad in the Sunday classifieds. Four meetings was a light schedule for me on a Monday. I'd blocked off time to do actual work now and again in the afternoon.

Waiting in the freshly-bathed, curled, pressed and perfumed horde peering at the first floor bank of elevators, I saw Alan's curly hair above wire-rim glasses, his bushy beard through an elevator door as it closed and waved. Judging from his preoccupied face he was already mentally in his office, figuring out how to prevent packets of text from being dropped along network data lines before they'd been read, but he shrugged as if to say he would have held the door had there been any room and waved back.

Alan Dockman, the managing programmer, was my best friend at the company. He and our boss, Paul Enfield, the CEO of Carepath, were classmates in computer science at the University of Minnesota. Alan became the second employee of Carepath when Paul got his very first contract. Alan was a quiet man, tall and bear-like in appearance with a big chest and gray streaks in his beard but almost formal in his demeanor. He played chess and Risk, games my brother played while we were growing up that I never particularly liked. He and Paul were the techies, and I their translator.

I'd been with Carepath since it started five years ago, the third employee, hired by Paul to work with Alan on a computerized self-help book on staying mentally fit. I started out as a combination designer, technical writer and project manager. Now that the company had one hundred and twenty employees, I spent all my time in staff hiring and development, product training and project management.

I opened the door to my office and snapped on the light. Hanging my coat on the back of the door, I saw the river beneath the swirling fog, iced in along the backwater, thick with reeds and tall grass, a bridge above it with traffic stalled coming north. I turned on my computer, hearing the primeval DOS grunts, waiting for the command to select a drive. I straightened the Van Gogh print on the wall above the credenza, a field of flowers given to me by Deb, my ex-girlfriend, chosen to remind me of life outside the tower. I registered the dull hurt that was Deb four years after our break-up, the blue flower holding on in a stiff wind, and pushed my chair hard against the desk.

I stood at the window and watched an egret pick its way among the reeds. Its slender white body stood out against the gray of the river and the drifts of fog. It rose awkwardly and flew a few feet, then settled in gracefully on the water. Clumsy and elegant at the same time.

The highlights of my weekend were raking the leaves off my tulip and iris beds, hitting a bucket of golf balls with my friend Stephanie and roller-blading around Lake of the Isles where I fed the bottom of a bag of tortilla chips to the geese. Steph, a native Manhattanite, and I met in public health graduate school in Ann Arbor, and shared an apartment our second year. Stephanie was an internist interested in environmental medicine. We played close, hard-fought tennis and saw Ingmar Bergman films together. She took me to my first Seder and I bought her first Christmas tree.

I made a mental note to go to the Farmers' Market next weekend to buy arugula and spinach plants. Maybe this summer I could find a woman to invite over for dinner who'd be impressed by a homegrown salad. It was not the first time I'd told myself it was time to look for someone. And standing at the edge of the driving range in a cold wind, Stephanie said, apropos of nothing in particular, "You're overdue. And I'm not talking about library books."

I watered the Easter cactus my parents gave me two weeks ago and read the half dozen e-mails from people who arrived before I did. I straightened the six chairs around my conference table, took a file from the bottom drawer of my desk and headed out in search of more coffee.

My first meeting was easy: I sat at the back of the room, drank my coffee and rated a woman from an outside vendor who was training staff on project management. I'd grown up as the oldest of three children, so project management felt like a logical extension of big sisterhood. At age eight I organized my first group that included non-family members, to build a snow fort and hold our own in a month-long series of intense snowball fights. We understood specialization as well. My sister Carolyn, two years younger, was responsible for the snowball inventory along with her friend from down the street. My friend Jody and I handled strategy, setting up the posts we used for defense and leading the occasional daring raid on the boys' fort four doors down. My mother brought us hot chocolate with marshmallow refills in a thermos during lulls in the action. My brother Danny, aged two, was too little for combat that year, but absorbed the general excitement and myth making that went on while Mom made dinner.

My second meeting of the day was with Paul, at the long, polished wood conference table in his office. Paul was soft-spoken, tall and slender, with straight brown hair that fell over his forehead and cowlicked in the back. He was the sort of man who'd interested me while I was in college: incredibly bright, a bit lacking in social polish which he made up for in enthusiasm, fair and logical, interested in debating an issue from all sides. Smiling at him, I was again glad to be a lesbian. It kept my relationship with him on an even keel. We connected on the level of our thinking and our low-key but intense styles. I spent my first year resisting the temptation in meetings sitting next to him to reach up and smooth his hair with my hand. Once I told Paul that, a crack opened in the layer of reserve that he wore like an extra suit jacket. I lost a little bit of the awe and caution I carried toward him, and began to tease him, carefully.

"What's on your list?" Paul said. Paul started a tradition of meetings between a staff person and his or her boss called a one on one. It was the staff's job to come with a list of what they needed: guidance, a decision, a barrier they couldn't overcome without help.

"First, the status of hiring," I said. I filled him in on the composition of the ten active project teams, giving highlights of the new hires and the plan for filling vacant spots. "I found a firm to screen and reference check the IS application hires. They send me final candidates and Alan and I interview them. It's really speeded things up."

Paul nodded his approval. "How'd you talk Alan into that?"

"I told him I'd handle the hunt for oyster shells and he could focus on the pearls. So he'd have more time for the important stuff, like coding."

Paul shook his head and grinned. "We men are putty in your hands." The grin evaporated and he leaned forward. "Therese, you've got to get the diabetes project moving. We don't have a track record with this client. If we don't deliver the beta version in a month, we're toast."

I felt anxiety rise in my stomach, or coffee reflux. I breathed, reminded myself that Paul was prone to pessimism. "Paul, a month isn't possible. I need a pharmacist on the team. I've got two candidates coming in today. Anyone I hire will have to give notice. Do you want me to make an offer if one of them looks good enough?"

"I trust your judgment, Therese. Go with your gut, we need to move."

I finished my list for him, got his approval on higher salaries for two programmers and his signature on the project management instructor contract and a software purchase order. I fielded his questions about project timelines and trends in our client base and left.

I stood at my secretary's cubicle to grab a couple of carrot sticks from the five-pound bag I peeled and brought in every Monday. June had the first pharmacist candidate sitting in a chair outside my office. I saw graying hair and glasses over a magazine.

"What do you think of this guy, June?"

June shrugged. "He looks like your typical middle-age guy in Dockers. He's got a nice ass. He must do something besides sit in front of the TV."

I rolled my eyes at her. June's been my secretary since my third year at Carepath. After interviewing five candidates I hired her on the spot, because she quoted a funny statistic out of the Harper's index to me. "Did you notice anything I'd care about?"

June pushed back the bangs on brown hair which she hennaed for a reddish tint. She wore it in some kind of reverse pageboy, with black plastic glasses. The combination gave her a sort of fifties schoolmarm look, until you looked at her clothes. June favored lime green or day-glo orange mock turtlenecks, black patterned nylons and short, tight black skirts. When the chartreuses and other day-glo colors began to fade in popularity, she moved onto pastel chenille sweaters and black velour tops. She scorned Doc Martens and wore what the greasers in my high school referred to as fruit boots: an ankle high black boot with laces. Today she wore her Walker Art Center t-shirt proclaiming "Closed Mondays" under the pastel cardigan.

"His name is Jon, short for Jonathan. First things first, Therese. I'm in the market for a man and I'm not finding him at the Y or on the bus. You're going to ask him about his strengths and weaknesses and whether he's a team player no matter what I tell you."

"True," I conceded and grabbed another carrot.

June was 33, two years younger than I was, and hoped, as she put it, that the clothes shaved off five years. She walked with a slight limp, the result of a teenage car accident where the ankle hadn't set quite right. She had a notoriously miserable romantic life even for a heterosexual woman: she was married once to an alcoholic masquerading as a hip young house painter and had many dismal stories since of men she'd met in bars or at the Arthur Murray dance studio run by one of her gay male friends. She had a nine year-old girl from the house painter marriage whom she liked to refer to as June-yer, but whose name was actually Rose.

I liked Jon OK but he didn't inspire me to throw caution to the winds, abandon reference checks and hire him on the spot. When he left I looked at the blinking red light on my phone which proclaimed voicemail and heard the every-ten-minute chime of the computer announcing e-mail. I cursed the technology god for never letting me have a guilt-free moment and then smiled and wondered what I'd do with it anyway. I walked down the hall, greeting staff, asking about their weekends, chatting on the elevator down to the cafeteria. I stood in a short line at the cash machine, a longer one for the soup of the day, chicken with rice, and again at the cash register.

The fog had burned off, leaving a gray April day with naked tree limbs waving outside the cafeteria window. The egret was long gone.

I ate lunch at my desk, spooning up soup while I read e-mail, dunking a soft breadstick in the Styrofoam bowl to soak up the last drops. I munched dried apricots out of a ziplock bag. I called my travel agent to check on summer airfares to Vermont, where my sister Carolyn and five year-old niece Shoney lived.

When June hadn't brought the second candidate in by five after one I figured she was late getting back from lunch. I walked out into the hall. Sitting in the chair outside my office was a blonde woman with short, curly hair, reading a magazine so intently that she didn't hear me approach. I remembered that she had a first name I'd never heard before. Automatically I glanced at the resume in my hand. Brinnae Anderson.

"Brinnae?"

She jumped at my voice, dropped the magazine, picked it up, set it on the table and stood in one fluid motion, extending her hand. She was at least three inches taller than me and had a firm handshake.

"I'm Therese Denard, Brinnae. I didn't mean to startle you, you must have been deep in thought."

She smiled a smile that could be in a toothpaste commercial, big white teeth, eyes the color of blue morning glories and a little crinkly at the edges. She gave a brief, high-pitched giggle. I was simultaneously put off and charmed by it. She was nervous.

"Call me Brin. I was reading about Novell losing marketshare and wondering if I ought to replace my WordPerfect software with Word."

"I don't think you can go wrong with Microsoft. What kind of computer do you have?"

"We're bi-lingual. My son David just switched from a Macintosh to a PC because there are more games."

I had Brin review her resume for me, observing her long skirt and sweater ensemble, the expensive jewelry she wore: silver earrings, the metal hammered into glittering angles, and a ring and wrist watch in the same style and color. She described her first job at University of Minnesota, Duluth, where she graduated from pharmacy school, followed by a stint as an analyst of pharmaceutical companies for a Twin Cities investment firm. She must be strong analytically or they wouldn't have kept her for four years. She missed the patient contact and went to work for her current employer, a pharmacy chain, filling prescriptions, counseling patients and overseeing the daily operations of the computer system where pharmacy claims were logged and processed.

She wore a silver ring with an onyx stone on her right hand but nothing on the left.

I went through my list of interview questions and added up the answers: intense and thoughtful, a good analyst who talked knowledgeably about the pharmaceutical companies and their systems subsidiaries, a woman who understood that the health care industry was transforming itself into a data-driven business where patients would come to have nearly as much information available to them as doctors did. We talked about the fact that this job wouldn't have much patient contact. She seemed a bit reserved personally, but willing to laugh at my attempts at humor.

"What questions do you have for me, Brin?"

"I know Carepath is growing and has diversified into CD-ROM products. How would you characterize the corporate culture here?"

"We have an entrepreneurial bent but are big enough to have achieved financial stability. We want to be first to the market with our products. One of my team leaders likes to say that he's Magellan, captain of a ship sailing around the unknown world, wondering if his bright and motivated crew can identify and avoid the shipwrecks, the shark-infested waters, the dead-end products and chart the right course." Brin smiled the gleaming smile again. "We invest in the latest technology and value intelligence, hard work and having fun. And we offer stock options so that someday, when we go public, you'll see the value of your work directly."

I told her about the diabetes project and watched her interest heighten. I felt my own excitement begin to grow, my sense that I could work with this person and teach her what she didn't know: how to design software and work with programmers. She was smart and serious enough to win the respect of my colleagues. I didn't often feel that sense of possibility with someone on the first encounter, of going into the unknown with a smile. Feeling the first breath of spring when there's still snow on the ground. I took a deep breath and hoped that I wasn't fooling myself just to meet Paul's deadline. My Myers-Briggs type said I was analytical, able to drive projects to completion but prone to making serious errors where emotion was involved.

When I offered Brin the job, she insisted on giving a month's notice to the pharmacy chain. I gave her points for being responsible and talked her down to three weeks, plus coming in for three days of training beforehand on her own time. We agreed on a salary and I handed her a sheet listing employee benefits. I told myself that it was OK to take a risk, to hire her without a reference check, like the early days of Carepath. Remembering all the mistakes we made that way made my knees wobble.

I walked her out to June's desk, introduced them, shook hands with Brin and pointed her towards the elevator. I handed Jon's resume to June. "In case you want to call him. I'm sure you can come up with something."

June tossed her pageboy. "I'll tell him you save the second interview for the brains of the operation. And that we'll have to do it offsite so that I can tell you what he's really like." She looked at me for a minute and gestured toward the elevator. "You must have really liked her. I've never seen you hire anyone without a second interview before."

"Not since I hired you," I retorted, and she grinned. I told her what Paul said. "I wouldn't have done it if I didn't think she was good. I'm sure I can work with her. I'm taking a gamble that everyone else can, too."

"OK," June replied. "One more cube, computer, phone, desk and chair coming up."

CHAPTER 2

Brin, May, 1989

I watched David construct a fort out of the quarters of his half-eaten grilled cheese sandwich, with celery and carrot sticks as the cannons. Stirring my tomato soup, I took a sip, glancing at the headlines in the Star Tribune. It was lukewarm, but I didn't feel like getting up and putting it in the microwave.

"Mom, I'm going over to Jason's. We're going roller-blading."

"Finish your sandwich first, David." Scanning a full-page ad proclaiming Dayton's 13-hour sale. "And your vegetables."

"I'd rather have chips," David complained. "Dad always has chips."

"I can't help it that your father's a junk food junkie." And a liar. And an adulterer.

Again I returned to Teddy's cabin in his family compound last summer. David had gone off with his uncle and cousins early to fish. I'd handed him a pair of jeans that didn't walk by themselves, found a new fishing lure and sent him off with lunch in his backpack.

I was pouring onion soup mix over the Sunday rump roast, wishing my family were more adventurous eaters, when Teddy emerged from the bedroom. He came up behind me and slid his hands inside the waist of my pajamas. He hadn't seemed very interested lately. I managed a few squeals as he goosed me, pushing me toward the bed. After he fell asleep, I stretched out in the sunlight pouring through the window and read the paper.

I heard his light snore, saw his hairy chest, one long arm extended outside the covers. Teddy, long and lean, with large hands that he knew how to use when he felt like it. I encircled his nipple with my fingers and watched it harden, saw his slightly wolfish mouth turn into a sexy smile and the sheet over his loins rise. I reached under the sheet and began to stroke him lightly. I heard him moan. I slid the sheet back and climbed atop him, riding him. "Oh, God," he said. "Oh yes. Oh Tami yes."

"Tami?" I said and he woke up. Deflated. Scowled. "Who's Tami?"

How can I be so vulnerable to memory all these months later? I heard David yell. "Mom? Mom!" and looked across the table. The grilled cheese was gone, the paper napkin crumpled on the plate.

"What?"

He emerged from the laundry room with his skates and wrist guards. "Mom, you're in la-la land again. What time is dinner?"

"I'm sorry, honey. Have a good time with Jason. Be home by five thirty."

I skimmed the front section of the paper and gave up on the rest. I couldn't forgive him for the way I'd found out, in the midst of intimacy. Unbearable, unfinished intimacy. Hearing his confession naked, a sheet pulled over me. Making him leave the room while I dressed and packed. Then I packed for David, leaving a clean t-shirt and pair of shorts out for him to wear home. After I put David's and my suitcases in the car came the one moment of triumph: calling his mother two cabins away. "Roseanne, please come down here at 12:00 and take the roast out of the oven. Your son the adulterer can tell you why I've left." Slamming down the phone.

Smiling, then burying my face in my hands. The three-hour drive home alone, stunned and crying. Twelve years of marriage like fish guts all over the floor.

I told Therese about it yesterday at lunch, the Cliff Notes version. We sat outside under an umbrella, eating salads from the cafeteria and talking about thinning our iris and lily beds. It was a mild spring day, the kind I dreamed of in January when it was twenty below. The air held the first scent of lilacs.

"I knew I couldn't forgive him," I said. "I didn't let him come home except to pack. He stayed with his brother for a couple of weeks and then he moved in with her. The bastard."

"A therapist once told me that there were two things to look at in deciding whether to leave a relationship."

"You were in therapy?"

Therese smiled. "For the longest year of my life."

My lower lip trembled. "You're so calm and well put-together."

"Good," Therese smiled again. "Those lessons at the Guthrie Theater are paying off."

I breathed, laughed. I felt my whole face relax. "So . . ."

"The first is whether you have the same goal and the same values about how to get to the goal. If the answer to that one is yes, the second is whether the speed with which each of you can figure out what you want and move forward is at all similar."

I must have looked as puzzled as I felt.

"My ex claimed that she wanted the same things that I did: a long-term, committed relationship, honesty, tenderness, blah blah blah. But Deb wouldn't give up her lover. She would have been happy to go to therapy for years and discuss the situation. I had to know immediately, so I could deal with the pain and move one way or the other. It meant that I had to decide, because Deb wasn't going to. I was absolutely shattered to leave her, but I did."

In the distance I heard the drone of a plane, the cawing of crows. "Yes," I said. "That's it exactly. In my case, I would have been devastated if Teddy dithered and devastated if he didn't."

Therese had a pained look. It was a look I knew, the one where you're sucked back into quicksand you're trying to stay out of.

"Thank you, Therese," I said.

"For what?"

"For telling me something that must be difficult for you to talk about."

"You're the one who's brave, Brinnae. You and David, too."

I pushed the soup bowl away and leaned back in my chair, stretching like a big cat. I took a puff from my inhaler, the albuterol this time. Therese understood me. It was a miracle. Last week, after I'd blown up at Jeff in the diabetes team meeting over turning in the project status report without consulting me, Therese called me in. I expected her to yell at me and was enormously grateful when she didn't.

"What set you off, Brin?" Therese asked. "Why do some mistakes cause you to lose your temper and some don't?"

"I think the programmers live in their own world," I said. "I find them very hard to communicate with."

I was trying to master the intricacies of using "I" language in discussing the faults of others. My sister Marlys, ten years older, had been after me about "I" language since she started therapy last year. "Don't say to the other person, 'you screwed up,'" Marlys instructed. "Say, 'I feel upset when you cut me off in the middle of a sentence.'"

I replied, "I feel unhappy that you're teaching me a sentence structure that takes twice as long to get to the point." Marlys was not amused.

"Try to get to know them a little," Therese said. "I'm not suggesting that you're going to be best pals. Think about their Myers-Briggs types, how their ways of approaching the world might be different from yours."

Sighing, I cleared the dishes, loaded the dishwasher, wiped the kitchen table clean. I took two ribbed chicken breasts out of the freezer and marinated them in lime dill dressing. Therese had a way of letting me know when I screwed up without reprimanding me. Sometimes in meetings as I was talking, I got a sense that I was heading in a direction that Therese wouldn't like. It never stopped me, though. When seconds later Therese smiled sardonically, I'd grin in the middle of my own analysis. Sometimes we finished each other's sentences. Once Therese mentioned that in a meeting. She laughed and said it was scary.

I tried to remember exactly what Jeff said that sent me into meltdown. "Never turn in that report before checking with me," I'd said. With the icy tone I'd learned really well from my mother. The three other people at the table were looking at their feet.

"Like you had a better way of saying we were two weeks behind," he said.

Then he'd smirked at me. The asshole. I hate being condescended to, especially by men who think they know everything.

I checked to make sure there were waffle fries in the freezer and a bag of salad. David's favorite meal. We called it three piles. We liked to suck on the chicken bones, gleaning the meat and the marrow. I put a fresh cut in the vase of yellow roses on the table and changed their water.

Jeff shared Teddy's juvenile fascination with sports and games. They played Tetris on their computers, had fantasy baseball and football teams and bet every week in their office pools on college and pro sports. David was more like me. Not that David was uncoordinated, but he didn't thrive on running and throwing and catching or kicking. He was blond and dreamy-eyed, stubborn and serious, full of enthusiasm and grand plans one minute and gloomy the next. I felt a surge of gratitude that my son was not instinctively macho.

I sorted the laundry into whites, light colors and darks, and started the first load. I poured a box of pudding into the mixer, added water and turned it on high speed: my favorite, crème caramel. Therese and I were the same type on the Myers-Briggs scale: introverted, intuitive thinkers who liked closure. My score was actually higher on feeling than thinking, but I wasn't going to admit that at work, where we'd sat around for an hour with someone from human resources talking about our types. I guessed at how to answer a few of the questions and made my thinking and feeling scores come out even. I hated some of the questions. How could I pick which was more important between justice and mercy? Sometimes you have to temper justice with mercy, sometimes you have to steel yourself. It was part of figuring out how to be fair to a person and the situation.

I dusted the living room and the dining room. It was funny that a lesbian gave me advice on how to deal with the male programmers. That news hadn't bothered me, though I could tell that it made others uncomfortable. I'd overheard one of the trainers complaining to June, "I think it's unnatural. What can they possibly do without riding the wild weenie?"

"Plenty of things are unnatural," June replied. "I'm not giving up my Diet Coke or my Velcro. Not everybody worships the weenie the way you do, girl." She paused for dramatic effect. "If you're lucky, someday you'll find the true Polish sausage I've enjoyed." Later June told me to keep the information to myself. "Most of the guys are oblivious to it and it's better that way."

Carepath teams were like my favorite college classes run amok. I loved the software confections we created, frothy as gauze in their delicacy but solid as interlocking puzzle pieces underneath. Software was a vision made real, a genetic, physiologic and behavioral translation of how patients with chronic conditions felt and what they needed. My mother said that my single-mindedness was dangerous to me and my family, my focus on constructions of logic and data. My mother has never understood the first thing about me. I'm getting to know two of my cousins. One was a diabetic and the other had multiple sclerosis. I wanted to help them chart the course of their diseases with the scientific disinterest of a physician. Market research gone bad, my mother would say if she knew. You should be interested in your cousins because they're family.

I got out the vacuum and did the downstairs rooms. I put the whites in the dryer, the light colors in the washer. I hauled the vacuum cleaner upstairs, sat on the top stair and took a puff of beclavent. Saturday drudgery almost through. I collected David's clothes from the floor and piled them on his bed so he'd have to put them away. Last weekend I explained to my mother how the people on a project team became family. Marlys, my mother and I were having coffee. Augustina shook her head dismissively.

"You're a workaholic just like your father, God rest his soul."

I ignored her and kept talking about the pharmacy formulary team, my second project. "The pharmacy team eats together around a long table. We sit and talk in one of the conference rooms with a view of the river, while we stare out the window, looking for birds. We started a bridge club and a softball team. We take turns carrying the beeper."

Marlys snorted. "The beeper makes you live in a world of work 24 hours a day. That's healthy." Marlys still hadn't told Augustina that she was in therapy. A fine arbiter of healthy she was.

I persisted. "Therese and I ran into each other at Weight Watchers yesterday. We're going to take walks at lunch when she doesn't have a meeting. In the winter we'll put tennis shoes on over our nylons and walk through the underground tunnels that connect the towers. Toni and I are doing crossword puzzles. When it's not my turn to drive to soccer practice, Jeff and I play Myst after everyone else has gone home."

"Would these people think about you a day after you changed jobs?" Augustina asked rhetorically. "Don't let yourself be fooled. We're your family. And why are you out playing computer games with a man when you should be home cooking dinner for your son?"

I dragged the vacuum down the stairway, cleaning each stair. Jeff still deserved what I said to him. Maybe I should have talked to him privately, but he'd been in the wrong. Like family, I had to be cold to them when they didn't deliver what they promised. Didn't understand how hard I was working. Wanted to revisit the problem I'd already solved.

CHAPTER 3

Therese, June, 1989

I met with Brin and Jeff, in my office, where a month ago I stood at the whiteboard, teaching Brin to diagram the clinical process of diagnosing a diabetic patient in flowchart form, with colored markers. Today Brin stood at the board, reviewing the clinical services a diabetic person needs in a year: daily blood glucose tests, glycoselated hemoglobin every six months, an annual eye exam by an ophthalmologist checking for retinopathy, a dental check, a foot care exam. Jeff sat beside me with the pile of color printouts of rectangles, arrows and cylindrical databases Brin produced, which we pored over with the intensity of kids sharing comic books.

Normally I'd first assign a new person to a couple of projects as an analyst and acceptance tester of software to observe how he or she worked in a team, and judge the quality of output. I had Brin start immediately on the design of the diabetes tracking software. Our job was to create a diabetic education product to help patients record their blood sugars, track their insulin dosages and connect on-line with their doctors for help.

"Bottom line, where are we?" I asked, when Brin finished her list.

Jeff shrugged. "I've designed the software in two pieces: a place for the patient to track stuff like blood sugar and a format for the physician or nurse to capture what they've ordered against their care plan." He pushed his hair out of his eyes and slouched back in his chair. Shaggy-haired and bearded, Jeff wore a Butthole Surfers t-shirt and stained khakis that anyone else would have reserved for mowing the lawn. He had a huge pyramid of empty Pepsi cans in his cubicle and a desk drawer full of peanut M&Ms. When he wasn't telling mordant jokes about serial killers or passing out Calvin and Hobbes cartoons, Jeff was capable of long, intense periods of coding at his workstation, producing efficient programs with few errors.

"Sounds reasonable," I said. "Brin, can a clinician use what Jeff's designed?"

"I need screens to tell you that," she said. "It depends on how long it takes to fill in the data, how many screens they have to look at and how long they have to wait for the processing."

"So, the next step is screen design?" I queried.

"Somebody needs to tell me what the nurse is gonna do before the doc comes in the room," Jeff said.

"Do the two of you need to talk to a diabetes nurse in a clinic?"

"I thought that was her job," Jeff said, gesturing towards Brin.

"As if," Brin said. "As if you'd believe me when you hadn't seen it with your own eyes." She'd been here for six weeks and already they fought like siblings.

"Who's going to the clinic, people?" I said.

"I guess I could go with her," Jeff said. "She'd never find it by herself anyway." Brin stuck out her tongue at him.

"Our next meeting will be design review," I said. "I need to schedule it next week. Will you be ready?" Screen design would give me enough to meet with the client, to meet Paul's deadline, the month which I re-negotiated with him from Brin's start date plus the two weeks the client had key staff on vacation.

Jeff shrugged.

Brin said, "If Wonder Boy here can read my specs by then."

I stood up and waved them, still grousing at each other, out of my office. But Brin's eyes were sparkling with the intensity of the hunt. Brin left full of enthusiasm, ready to tackle any problem, sweeping out the door, headed to a meeting or a design team session. Hours later she swung back past my door, her emotions riding on her face like those of an adolescent, broadcasting her view of the meeting's outcome.

"Brin," I called, "Let me look at you and get the project weather report."

"Partly cloudy, Therese," she said, sinking heavily into a chair, glowering and fidgeting with her ring. Partly cloudy, the most frequent forecast, meant a month behind and I'd told her it was not an option on this project. The beatific smile I craved indicated we were on schedule; intense dejection and few words meant a problem for which no one had an answer, which meant a rough ride for our little kayak or the iceberg that would sink us a week hence. Cold fury signified anything from other staff's rudeness or dithering to total dismissal of the person or their approach. It was the most puzzling of Brin's emotions but so far the least frequent. I'd never seen the facial weather shift so rapidly on a woman in her thirties.

The best project teams were small and bonded beneath the surface, like ridges of molten rock shifting and reforming deep in the earth's crust. Last weekend the three of us came in our sweats and worked all day, all Saturday night and half of Sunday to finish the preliminary functional design of our software, sending out periodically for pizza and Chinese food. At one point I fell asleep on the sofa in the conference room and vaguely remembered Brin taking off my glasses and tucking an afghan around me.

I was struck by the intimacy of our work, the pleasure of teaching someone bright and eager to learn, my happiness when Brin seized an idea and took it in a direction I hadn't considered. I was responsible for organizing and leading many project teams, but right now was most at home with Brin and Jeff. We felt like an island of family in a company which was mushrooming under tremendous centrifugal force, popping up small offices all over the country, barely held together by data lines and cellular phones, electronic mail and quick plane trips.

These moments kept me going through political battles over budgets in dimly-lit conference rooms, technical nightmares which forced weekend marathons from designers and programmers and technicians wearing the jeans and polo shirts they had on when they were pulled away from their kids or yard work, the calls from Paul on his car phone flinging another rush project at me, the challenge of keeping up with technology that changed and crashed every month and made us re-evaluate weekly whether we'd have any market for our software by the time it was written, debugged and manufactured.

*   *   *

Brin

I sat at the very back of the lunchroom, with a sandwich, fruit and a garden catalogue. "Mind if I join you?" Jeff asked. He carried a cheeseburger, fries and a 32-ounce glass of Pepsi on his tray.

I smiled, shrugged and turned the page to a display of white porcelain birdbaths decorated with sunbursts.

"Looks pretty suburban to me," Jeff commented.

"Try to say suburban like it's not a four-letter word," I replied.

"How's David?" Jeff asked.

"Fine."

David would be with Teddy this weekend. Tonight I'd rent a video that you couldn't watch with a 12 year-old. Tomorrow I'd be up to my elbows in petunias, dahlias and sweet William. I'd cleared a small plot to add tomatoes and eggplant to the lettuce, peas, radishes and spinach I'd planted when the ground thawed. The radishes and lettuce were little green shoots now, promises of summer and warmth. The tulips were just dying back, their red and yellow splendor finished for another year. The irises were showing the first hint of purple.

The divorce decree came yesterday. I pulled it from the mailbox, slit the envelope open and read it, over and over as if it would make more sense the eighth time. I felt like I'd graduated from a school I hadn't meant to attend. I'd have to open a new safe deposit box.

"I'm teaching Brittany how to appreciate baseball," Jeff said. Brittany was his girlfriend, a blonde from Iowa with the sweet, vapid demeanor of a cow. Brittany, a species of dog. I tuned out the details the way I did when Teddy turned talk radio or football on in the car. Therese suggested that I try to get to know the programmers better. So I listened to Jeff drone on.

I wondered what to do with myself on Saturday night. Most of our friends were couples, more from Teddy's side than mine. His friends from St. Olaf or other electrical engineers and their wives. I must know another divorced woman who didn't have a date tomorrow night. What would the men look like who'd be dropping off the load of black dirt? Sunburned with long hair and bandanas, all of twenty-five. I grimaced at the thought of a date. I can't have a man come to the house. It wouldn't be fair to David. Maybe one of them would be a woman in a tank top, muscular, with eyes that took me in openly. At the rate I was going, I'd be signing up for adult cable.

Jeff had moved on to his Irish setter, a breed I considered stupid and untrainable. "She's catching the Frisbee in her mouth now, but she won't bring it back. She lies down and starts chewing on it. She'd rather lie down than anything. The bitch."

I gave him my most angelic smile. "Not too bright, but then dogs do take after their masters."

"Ooh, direct hit. Score one for the Brinster."

What did Therese do on a Saturday night? Maybe I should invite Therese to a movie. No, that would seem too forward. I wanted to get to know Therese better. Maybe drive by her house and hope to catch her out in her yard. Surely there was something I needed to go into Minneapolis for, lefse or krumkake at the Scandinavian Bakery on Lake Street or incense from Global Village. I could go to the Amazon Bookstore, breathe in a world of women.

Therese and I had chatted for a few minutes after a meeting yesterday. I must have said something wrong in the meeting, though I wasn't sure what it was. Maybe I'd been too insistent on the changes I wanted made to the training materials. Therese told me the theory that our best traits taken to extremes lead to problems. She talked about perfectionism and figuring out when it was appropriate and when it wasn't. Growing up, I'd heard often enough about how I'd had to have my own way and how thin-skinned I was. "I like my new faults better," I said.

Jeff stared at me. "What?"

"Have you seen the new Steven Seagal?" I recovered. Teddy was big on Steven Seagal and Jean Claude Von Damme. We'd seen two of those for every Merchant and Ivory film I wanted to watch. Maybe I should get the video about those English women who rented a house in Italy. Forever April? It would be better than channel surfing between Lorenzo Lamas, Chuck Norris and some lame made-for-TV movie.

I took the elevator upstairs with Jeff and spent the ten minutes left before the meeting reading and filing my e-mail, occasionally printing one I needed to think about. The meeting was to review the design with the diabetic software client. It would be my first meeting where Paul was present. Therese talked about Paul with admiration and familiarity. I was both curious and resistant to meeting him.

Therese said I needed to develop a second skin, a crust over my boiling emotions, before I imploded from my own heat. I visualized sunspots, the constant flaring up, my body inhabited by a glowing center.

CHAPTER 4

Brin, September 1989

I got out my new rolling suitcase and stuffed clothes into it. This afternoon I was meeting Therese at the airport to fly to San Francisco for a sales conference and trade show. We'd be gone almost a week. I held up a navy blue suit with a white blouse and a dotted Swiss print. A taupe linen pantsuit, a cantaloupe-colored silk blouse, a skirt and gauzy sweater set. Jeans, shorts, a sweater, a sweatshirt, two t-shirts. My portable nebulizer just in case. How was all of this crap going to fit?

I'd never been to California. I pictured palm trees, then fog and bridges. Therese would train the contract sales force on the strategy and features of Carepath's new product line. I would staff the booth at the trade show to talk to customers about the data tables behind the glitzy on-line formulary that allowed people to refill prescriptions by dialing in from home.

Making David's breakfast and packing his suitcase for five nights at Teddy's, I worried. David still spent the weeks with me and every other weekend with his dad. This was the longest we'd been apart. I tucked packs of raisins into his suitcase in case Teddy didn't keep fruit around.

It was my first trade show working the booth. Driving to the airport, I catalogued my fears. What if the system crashed in the middle of a demo? If I couldn't answer people's questions, would they walk away in disgust? I paced at the airport gate, until I saw Therese striding briskly toward the counter, garment bag slung over her shoulder.

I confided my worries as we buckled our seat belts. Therese laughed. "The question is not if the system will crash, it's when. Put a couple of the Carepath tote bags in your briefcase, they're a freebie we generally don't give until the sale is closed. When it crashes and won't restart, make a fuss over presenting the customer with the bag in honor of your first crash ever. That's usually good for a few laughs."

We sat close together in the 757's cramped seats. I looked out the window. Therese's arm brushed mine as she pointed out the chain of city lakes below us. "There's Harriet, where I rollerblade. You can't see it, but there's the Rose Garden. I love being able to walk to the Rose Garden from my house." Therese's arm felt hot and I shrank toward the small square of window.

Over plastic glasses of wine, we told stories of college, other business trips, people at work. Air traffic was backed up in San Francisco. I watched the sky turn orange as we circled for an hour. I felt dreamy and sleepy, suspended in mid-air.

After we checked into adjoining hotel rooms, I asked, "Can I leave the door open between them? It's just something I'm used to doing with David."

Therese shrugged. "Sure, why not?"

We sat in the bar with the rest of the Carepath group until I couldn't keep my eyes open.

In the morning I called David at Teddy's, figuring that Teddy would be playing golf. David was watching cartoons and eating Fruit Loops. I sighed. "Don't eat too many of those. They're all sugar."

I could hear David's shrug over the phone. "Mom, it's the only cereal he has."

I finished unpacking. I had cut a picture of Therese out of an annual report. Therese was sitting around a conference table with the CEO and two other men, caught in half profile, the hint of a smile on her lips as if she were amused by something only she understood. I propped the photo against a bottle of perfume on the countertop of the hotel bathroom and rehearsed with it while I dressed. I pretended

Therese was asking me questions about the product. I knew all the answers. I wandered between the walk-in closet and the window with its view of downtown San Francisco and the Bay Bridge arcing over the water towards Oakland. I'd looked in on Therese once during the night, curled up with a bare arm thrown outside the covers.

After I finished dressing, I tucked Therese's photo into my suitcase. I took the elevator to the concourse level and wandered through the maze of ballrooms. I sat at the table on the left side of the room nearest to the speaker's podium and watched Therese talk with the hotel's audio-visual man, as they conferred over the flat screen device that allowed her to project color graphics onto the large screen directly from the computer. The light glinted off Therese's hair for a moment before he darkened the room.

I watched Therese while she spoke. I smiled when she looked my way and glanced around at the contract sales force, who tapped notes into their laptops or wrote on pads imprinted with the hotel's name, aided by the glow of the low-intensity lights which illuminated the glass-topped tables from below. I listened to the rise and fall of her voice, the words escaping, the sigh of contentment from the man next to me as he imagined his commission check. I imagined Therese murmuring just to me. When Therese finished speaking and asked for questions, the room burst into applause. I felt absurdly proud, as if I'd watched David do well in a school play.

Therese introduced me to Nate Silverman, Carepath's first salaried salesman. Nate was stocky and balding with a Danny DeVito-intensity grin. He was nearly as tall as I was. He took my hand in both of his. "Brinnae," he repeated. "What a beautiful name."

I blushed. "Thank you."

"When we hit one hundred fifty employees, Paul said he couldn't be the bacon generator for that many people," Therese said.

"I told him that's fine," Nate said, "but I only produce kosher bacon."

"Nate's job is to get these sales guys whipped into a frenzy, then figure out which of them are any good and hire them."

"And Therese has certainly helped me get their attention," Nate executed a deep bow and kissed Therese's hand.

Afterwards Therese and I changed into sweaters and jeans and went to Therese's favorite restaurant on the wharf for lunch. Over cracked crab we talked about the year Therese spent traveling in and around the Bay Area while running a joint development effort.

"I liked living out here," Therese said. "I camped in Yosemite with friends I met at the company. They taught me how to cross-country ski. It was great to have snow three hours away when you wanted it and otherwise not to have to think about it."

"It's so exotic-looking here," I mused. "Imagine having a bird of paradise plant growing in your backyard. And those funny trees with the red bristles."

Therese laughed. "The bottle-brush trees."

We walked outside and threw sourdough bread to the seagulls lazing on the edges of small boats just back from salmon-fishing expeditions. We strolled around the wharf and past the old Ghirardelli chocolate factory, since converted into shops. I bought David a gray sweatshirt emblazoned with the rust-colored image of the Golden Gate Bridge.

Therese drove the rental car through the long boulevards of Golden Gate Park, past the field of bison, the Dutch gardens, and the windmill. "Paul's in New York meeting with investment bankers so I can take the afternoon and tonight off," she explained "He and his wife are going to see a play tonight. He doesn't get here until tomorrow night."

Crossing the long, narrow shape of the park, I felt as though we were traveling through another country, a country of women, of intimate conversation. At the ocean we put on sweatshirts. "Take off your shoes," I shouted, over the crashing of the waves. We walked along the beach barefoot, pointing, exhilarated by the crashing waves. At one point I grabbed Therese's hand and we skipped along like ten year-old best friends. The sand was both rough and smooth on my wet feet. The wind rushed through my hair, raising goosebumps on my neck.

In the late afternoon we sat out on the deck of the hotel bar. I talked about Teddy. "I'm putting him behind me. David and I go to movies, to his soccer games. We watch our favorite TV shows after his

homework is done. We've made our own rituals, our own routines."
Tears welled in my eyes.

Therese nodded. "That must have been hard. I'm sure it's taken
a while."

I watched her dark hair tousle in the breeze. Her face had added
color over the course of the afternoon, a blush of pink on her cheeks,
bronze on her forehead.

Therese sipped a glass of Chardonnay, a half-formed grin on her
face. "What?" I said, wanting to break the reverie or enter into it myself.

Therese shook her head.

"You have this funny little smile," I said. Like the one in the annual
report.

Therese smiled at me and leaned backward. She wrapped her
hands around the back of her head. "I'm just enjoying being here,
listening to you."

I returned the smile, suddenly feeling very shy. "I feel like we're
getting to be friends," I said. "You know, more than just survivors of
work."

"Yes," Therese said. "We are."

We dressed up and went to dinner on Nob Hill, at a northern
Italian restaurant recommended by the concierge. I wore my gauzy
sweater and long skirt. The small room gleamed with candlelight,
bronze fixtures, and sponge-painted Italian butter yellow and
tangerine walls. We sat in a dark, intimate corner over a bottle of
cabernet, with a single candle flickering between plates of veal marsala
and artichokes. I watched Therese's smile expand as we drank more
wine. Therese's wistfulness when she talked about Deb. The
loneliness of being by herself and all the extra time she spent at work.

I didn't want to feel anything for anybody. I felt my fury rise against
Teddy, against myself for being in the dark for so long about his
girlfriend. After we stumbled back to our rooms, we hugged goodnight.

In the middle of the night I gathered up all of my courage and
slipped into Therese's room. Moonlight filtered through the crack
in the drapes. I sat on the edge of Therese's bed. Therese rolled over
onto her back, half-awake. I tried to slip away, but Therese caught my
hand. "Brin, what's wrong?"

"I'm sorry. I didn't mean to wake you."

Therese sat up before she realized she wasn't wearing anything besides bikini briefs. Near naked and so innocent and sleepy. Looking at her almost stopped my heart. When Therese pulled the sheet up over her breasts, I took her hand and let the sheet fall. "Please, Therese. Can I just look at you?"

I watched the sleep careen away from Therese's face. I saw the same rush of adrenaline I felt coursing in my arms and fingers. I felt the room begin to spiral. Therese gestured me toward her pillow. Therese took my hand. I climbed under the covers and buried my face in Therese's shoulder.

I sobbed like somebody close had died. "Brin, what?" Therese said.

"I'm so scared," I said. The pictures of women together, surreptitiously scanned in the narrow aisle of the Amazon Bookstore, were hazy, inchoate. I was wearing a sheer white cotton nightgown. I knew my nipples would be visible if I weren't pressed against Therese. "Would you just hold me?" I asked.

"Of course," Therese said. She turned on the bedside light and opened her arms. I buried my face in the soft spot above Therese's right armpit and we fell backward onto the pillows. Therese stroked the back of my head as I might have consoled David when he was little. I lay on top of Therese, my weight partially on my knees, one leg between Therese's. I was in the midst of a fierce storm, torn between desire and fear. I felt every breath, every current in the room register on my skin.

I dabbed at the tears I'd left on Therese's chest with the sheet. I felt her flinch. I sensed the heat of Therese's body echoed in my own. I pulled the sheet down and sat back to look at her. "Therese, you are beautiful." Therese stretched her arms wide and flattened her stomach. I hadn't ever seen her be vain before and I almost laughed. I watched Therese look at my breasts beneath the gown. I took Therese's hand, lay it on my breast and felt both of our pulses jump.

"Whoa, Brin, slow down."

Instead, I put my arms around Therese and kissed her. I started shyly, kissing her lips and her eyelids, but soon we were tongue kissing.

Therese's hands were wrapped in my hair, bringing my face back to hers.

"Brin, this is insane," she said, between kisses.

I kissed her again, long and lingering, and Therese groaned. I stood up and pulled my nightgown over my head. I watched Therese, in shock, take me in, breasts to thighs. "Therese," I said, "I want to make love with you." I felt as if I were in a movie, reading lines written by someone else. I took a deep breath and felt the beginning of a wheeze.

Therese turned off the light and moved into the middle of the king-sized bed. "Brin, you're barely through a painful divorce. You have no experience with women. We work together. This is crazy."

The crush on the girl who sang soprano next to me in junior high. Interrupting my college roommate, bare-breasted and bouncing beneath a boy, with a turn of the key. Backing out, apologizing, wondering if her nipples tasted like baby oil. Tugging the khakis down over Therese's slim hips. Did imaginings and rehearsals count as experience?

I climbed back into bed and Therese reached for me. I kissed her and she kissed me back with equal ardor. Ripe fruit ignored will fall from the tree. "I rented a video," I said. Therese kissed my shoulders.

Therese pulled me on top of her. She ran her hands through my hair and over my shoulders to the small of my back. A current traveled down my spine with every movement of Therese's hands.

"Let me get this straight, pardon the expression."

I laughed.

"You rented lesbian videos so you'd know how to seduce me."

"Mmm hmm." I breathed into her ear and touched her nipple with the edge of my hand.

"Must have been some movie."

"It was terrible. But I'm a quick study." My shame in the video store. Hiding it under a copy of Born Free. I brushed my fingers between Therese's breasts. Therese seized my hand.

"Brin, I don't think this is wise."

"I don't know," I breathed. "But I know I don't want to stop." I wasn't at all sure of the script, but I did my best with the part. I took a breath.

"Then only this trip," Therese said. "Only this trip. We'll get it out of our systems. We'll go back to being friends."

"If that's what you want," I said. Relief washed over me. I would not have to change sides. I put my hand on Therese's belly.

"Yes," Therese said.

"OK," I said. I put my hand between her legs.

We made love slowly, fell asleep and did it again, more slowly. I felt the incredible gentleness in Therese's fingertips. Her tenderness when she touched me overwhelmed my fear. Suspended in a long, orgasmic wave, I floated above the bed. A balloon aloft, calm, then sucked into a wild draft. We slept again and ordered room service. I pulled the covers up and buried my face in the pillow when the waiter came in. Out of the corner of my eye I saw him wink at Therese. Therese laughed after he left the room, then kissed me. "It's OK, Brin. It *is* San Francisco." We sat naked in bed, feeding each other scrambled eggs and fresh raspberries. I crawled shyly back into Therese's arms.

"Is it what you expected?" Therese asked later, propped on one elbow, stroking my cheek.

"No," I said. "It's much better than I'd imagined." The part of me that was floating meant every word of it.

My Sunday passed in a haze in the booth. On a break I thought about calling David, but decided that the probability of getting Teddy was too high. Paul's plane was late, so Therese and I walked across the street for dinner. I picked at my food, held hands under the tablecloth and said little. We spent a couple of hours at the cocktail party for conference attendees, where I made mental notes on the way Therese worked the room. When Paul arrived, he and Therese and Nate headed for the bar. I rechecked my equipment in the booth, used my inhalers and went to bed.

A few hours later I awoke when Therese slipped into bed beside me, smelling of smoke and toothpaste. I slept fitfully with Therese spooned around me. The roaring inside my head stopped when Therese caressed me. I awakened to find Therese stroking my feet. Waves washed over me. I did not fight them. Therese put my big toe in her mouth and bit the underside of it gently, again and again, then proceeded north with her lips until I felt the world expand and contract around me to the size of our two bodies huddled together.

I careened between working the conference and our secret world for two more days. I was underwater, gasping, unsure of the water's depth or the way towards shore. The words nervous breakdown rang in my ears like ship's bells. I was buoyant, filled with excitement and longing, proud to stand on the surfboard without lessons. What lessons could there be to live in a typhoon?

I watched Therese with Paul and Nate in the booth, schmoozing with current clients, occasionally bringing a prospect over for me to practice my demo on. "Nobody knows the pharmacy and diabetes software better than Brin," Therese said to Paul, who watched the last demo I gave.

"She had a good teacher," Paul said, and Therese smiled.

We were quiet on the trip home. Therese sat in the window seat and caught up on a stack of journal articles. I sat next to her, reading a mystery novel where the private eye chased the villain around San Francisco and alternately mourned and celebrated his single, heterosexual status. I tried to pretend that we were just friends. The flight was full. When the man next to me got up, Therese raised the armrest between our seats, threw a blanket over us and took my hand. I stuck the postcard I'd written to David into my book, leaned back in my seat and dozed. Holding Therese's hand, I hoped we'd never land.

CHAPTER 5

Therese, Fall 1989-Winter 1990

I lived in a nether world, a place where I felt like I was sleepwalking even when I was awake. Before we left, Brin had scheduled a week off to spend with David and her visiting brother-in-law, wife and children. My appetite for work seemed to accelerate. I ran from one project to the next, specifying who was responsible for next steps, setting and resetting deadlines, supplying ideas to a team who had stalled out. I walked by Brin's cube, listening in vain for the soft tap of her fingers on the keyboard, a sound I hadn't even known I'd heard until it wasn't there when I walked down the corridor. I even peeked around the corner to see a photo of David, a child on his way to being as tall and unathletic as his mother

Then, a half hour before the third game of the World Series was to start at Candlestick Park, San Francisco was hit by an earthquake. I glued myself to the television in horror, as though the heaving earth had obliterated any trace of the few fragile days and nights Brin and I had shared. I felt selfish and guilty harboring these thoughts in the midst of tragedy but I was powerless against them. I called a TV station and pledged $100 to an earthquake relief fund to make amends. I watched the coverage all weekend, reassuring myself that despite the cars crushed on the Nimitz Freeway and the closing of the Bay Bridge,

Nob Hill, Fisherman's Wharf and Golden Gate Park were still there. That Brin, somewhere up north, was OK.

During Brin's first day back at the office, I became aware that I was listening expectantly for the rustle of her skirts in the hallway. Over lunch, I waited in vain for her to appear in my office. At the end of the second day, after everyone else had gone home, she stood in my doorway. I beckoned her in. She closed the door. She sat in the armless chair she always took, on the same side of the table at the other end.

I watched her as she stared out my window, happy to be in the same room with her, afraid of what either of us might say. When she spoke, her voice trembled. "Therese, I can't bear the thought that you don't want to touch me again."

Before I knew what I was doing, I stood behind her with my hands on her shoulders. I dropped to my knees and wrapped my arms around the chair and her. "Does this speak to the part about what I want?" I heard myself say.

She raised me up and pulled me onto her lap, straddling her. She drew my face to hers and we kissed hungrily. "The cleaning people," I whispered.

"They've already been for the wastebaskets," she said.

"They'll be by again in an hour or so to vacuum," I said.

She kissed me, long and lingering. "I locked your door."

"They have keys, you know," I responded, returning the kiss, caressing her shoulders.

She put her hands on my knees and pushed my skirt up. "They have keys, you know," she mocked, as she unbuttoned my blouse. I removed her sweater and put my head between her breasts. We made love beneath my conference table, nesting between the chair casters in little piles of our clothes. We left before the cleaning people returned. I asked her to dinner but she had to get home to David, who was waiting to be picked up at a friend's house.

And so we fell quickly into a routine, where once a week Brin arranged for David to go from band practice to his friend's house for dinner. I didn't know what she told the other mother about her weekly

Tuesday commitment, but Brin hosted David and his friend at her house on Thursdays. Every week Brin and I left work and she followed me home in a two-car caravan. Once inside, we fell upon each other with the hunger of two lovers who'd been within fifty yards of each other all week and unable to acknowledge or touch the other. We made love on pillows in front of the living room fireplace, sprawled on cold tile against the bathtub, stood up in the kitchen until our knees buckled and we crumpled softly onto the linoleum. We stretched out in my leather recliner in the den and finally, christened each of the three bedrooms.

Sometimes her mood was dark when she arrived, and the first kiss inside the door was distracted or remote. Asking what was wrong or how her day had gone proved fruitless. I soon learned to point to the sofa, where she stretched out face down, one arm trailing on the rug. I lit a candle and put on quiet music, then sat on the edge of the sofa and stroked the back of her head. After a few minutes, she began to make little purring sounds. I gave her a brief head and neck massage, then suddenly she began to speak about whatever was worrying her: David's mood, a tense conversation with Teddy, whatever hadn't gone well at work.

Other times I led her into my bedroom and stretched out beside her on the bed, an infinity of six inches between us. She wouldn't speak at all, but turned over and reached for me wordlessly, stretching me out on top of her while she ran her fingers through my hair and sighed. Eventually she told me, in a small voice, how much she loved me or how good I was to her when she was moody and pulled me into a long, deep kiss. On those days our lovemaking reached new heights of ferocity as she endeavored to please me in every way she knew how. I was a parched tree soaking up a language made of rain.

I was shocked and totally enthralled by the intense eroticism between us. I'd been a slow learner in the field of sexuality. I'd dated a grand total of three boys in high school, going with one to a school dance, skiing a few times with another and his family, going to a couple of movies with the third who didn't know how to kiss. A boy named Dean who I'd met in my dorm at the University of Wisconsin was my first lover. We lived together as juniors in a decrepit five-bedroom house in Madison with three roommates. Kim, one of the other two women, was a lesbian. I remembered studying her at the dinner table over the brown rice and cheddar casserole she'd make on her night to cook, as though she were an exotic plant. Kim had a faint fuzz above her upper lip, which she did not bleach or wax. She had frizzy black hair and wore a black leather vest to the bar on Friday night. She played softball and introduced me to Virginia Woolf's novels. We weren't really friends, but we could sit in the two rockers in the living room and talk for a half an hour without discomfort if no one else were home.

I joined Kim's softball team that summer, a pack of bronzed women who came braless to practice in tank tops and gym shorts, muscular women who didn't shave under their arms or their legs, except for a couple who had to wear nylons to work. We'd go to the bar after games, where I saw for the first time women kissing on the dance floor, running their hands over each other's hips clad in pinstriped baseball pants. With Kim's encouragement, I went out a few times with the pitcher, a tall, lithe, olive-skinned woman named Leslie. Dean had gone home for the summer to help out on his father's farm. Kim told me that Leslie had a lot of girlfriends, which made me feel safer.

Leslie taught me a dance called the funky chicken and to play miniature golf. She took me to the drive-in and put her hand on my thigh. "I've been seeing this guy named Dean," I said.

"That's cool," she said, leaving her hand where it was. "I used to think I was bisexual."

On our last date, a week before she was due to transfer from her junior college to Mankato State, I followed her upstairs to her bedroom in the house she shared with three other women. She lit a candle, put on a Chris Williamson tape, "The Changer and the Changed," and poured me a big glass of wine in a jelly jar. We played our own version of strip poker wrestling: whoever could pin the other rolling around on Leslie's water bed got to take an article of clothing off the other. Once Leslie had me naked, she was happy to let me win. She seduced me with massage oil, a vibrator and a fast pair of hands.

After the softball season ended, I began volunteering at the Women's Center as a phone-line counselor. One of the other women on my Thursday night shift, Paula, became my first real girlfriend. Paula was short, dark-haired, stylish in an East Coast, preppy sort of way and intensely verbal. We could debate whether God was dead or whether Holly Near's lyrics were more feminist than Cris Williamson's with equal fervor. A month after we started dating, I told Dean I wanted to break up with him and why. He was furious and moved out. I felt guilty and confused, but spent two nights a week with Paula through the rest of my senior year. We moved into an apartment after graduation and lived together for five years before I moved to Ann Arbor to go to grad school in public health.

I met Deb after I started working at Carepath. She was a contract programmer who worked one job for Alan and then decided to specialize in the banking industry. Deb was a star volleyball player, moody and intensely private. I lived with her for three years, until I discovered that two of the three volleyball practices a week were private lessons with Deb and her coach in the coach's apartment. After Deb and I broke up, I didn't sleep with anyone until the San Francisco night with Brin four years later.

While my relationships with Paula and Deb were physically satisfying, they had not been ruled by wordless hunger. When after a couple of hours of intense lovemaking Brin dressed hurriedly and left to pick up David, I wandered around the house in a fog, trying to decompress. I took a bottle of spring water from the refrigerator and loaded or unloaded the dishwasher. Sitting on the living room sofa, I counted the roses on the matching chintz-covered armchairs in front of the fireplace. I looked at the sterling silver candlestick holders atop the built-in wooden buffet and the antique beer steins in the china cabinet in the dining room as though I'd never seen them before.

I plucked an old Anne Tyler novel out of the bookcase and thumbed through it idly or switched on the computer and stared at the screen. I collected the bills and magazines from the mail slot on the front porch and checked the answering machine for messages. Inevitably I returned to the bedroom and sat on the edge of the bed in my robe, holding the sheets with their faint remnant of warmth in my hand, as though I could grasp the future in them.

Sitting amid the musky sheets in my logy, twilight state I pondered the question I couldn't ask anyone. It was the question that every lesbian feared most with a first-timer: would she go back to men and heterosexual privilege when the road got rocky? Underlying the question was one horrific likelihood: if and when our love affair went up in flames, one or both of us would have to leave Carepath.

Brin didn't want me to tell anyone at work about our relationship because somehow the news might find its way back to Teddy. I didn't mention that I'd already told Stephanie. In combat you don't have to say who else is in your foxhole.

"You've got this little smile," Steph said, Saturday morning at the bagel shop. She leaned back, rocking her chair onto its two rear feet, her small wiry frame in black tights and a long-sleeved black t-shirt. She ran her hand through short, black curly hair and pushed her hip, red-framed glasses back on her nose. She'd just finished telling me about a patient who'd been a dentist, and had become allergic to the adhesive compounds routinely used in dentistry. "A smile untouched by your complaining about fifty-five hour weeks and dealing with roofers."

"Must be an especially fine bagel," I said, my grin widening.

"Don't insult my intelligence. Who is she?"

I described Brin and made an oblique reference to being unavailable on Tuesday nights.

"I'd like to see you on a Wednesday morning," Steph said. "I've never seen you drool before."

I made the three-point shot with my empty coffee cup into the trash and we did our standard goodbye. "Have a nice day," I said.

She gave her best New York attitude, hands waving, shoulders back. "Hey! Don't tell me how to live my life."

I wanted to tell Alan because he was my other best friend and I felt dishonest keeping it from him. Brin and I argued about it for weeks.

"It's not fair to me, Therese. I have to work with people in IS. If Alan knows, it could affect who he assigns to work with me on projects."

"If Alan knew, you might get better people to work with."

"Because he's your friend, not because I'd deserve having his best analyst."

"Brin, Alan's my best friend. I want him to know I'm happy. He's asked me several times if I'm seeing anybody."

"What did you say?"

"I said I wasn't ready to talk about it yet, that so far it was just friends. That I need to get a sense myself of whether I want something more to develop."

"That was a good response."

"But it wasn't honest."

"Do you want the word out all over Carepath?"

"Of course not. Are you saying Alan can't be trusted to keep a secret?"

"You can't tell him, Therese."

"But I have to tell someone."

"Why? I haven't told anyone."

"Because I'm not ashamed of being a lesbian. Because I want people who care about me to know I'm in a relationship."

Finally, she agreed that I could tell my sister, Carolyn. The fact that Carolyn lived in Vermont, did not keep in touch with her old friends in Minnesota and had a child somehow made it all right. Carolyn left home while I was in graduate school and moved to New York to be a free-lance photographer. She and her ex-husband, a half-blooded Iroquois, shared custody of my niece, Shoshone. Unfortunately Larry's tribe had dwindled to the point that Shoney could not look forward to casino earnings. Carolyn scraped by teaching photography at a community college, taking school graduation pictures and filling in for a catering company.

I was curious about Brin's house, her life away from the office and from me, but I waited her for her to do the inviting. One night when David had an overnight with his friend, I followed her home to the suburbs. We met first in a restaurant in Hopkins that she picked out of the phone book.

"Why didn't I just get take-out and follow you home?" I demanded, after she arrived fifteen minutes late.

"I had to give you the garage door opener here," she said.

"But I'm following you," I said.

"In case you get there first."

"Ah," I replied. "No cars overnight in the driveway or parked in front of the house. Someone might talk."

"You don't know my neighbors, Therese. We have to arrive after dark."

"It's already dark, it's February for God's sake. I feel like I'm in a spy movie. If I'm caught or killed, the Secretary will disavow any knowledge of my actions."

We'd joked about my innate discomfort with long swatches of green lawn without sidewalks, but I felt it mount as I pulled into the circular asphalt drive in front of the two-story colonial. The house reminded me of the one my parents moved to while I was in college, with the back screened porch and the den off the kitchen. I wandered around the downstairs. Brin appeared in a silk kimono.

"Where do you keep David's report cards?"

She pulled open a drawer in the dining room hutch and handed me the neat stack. All A's and B's.

A large terrarium sat on an end table in the den. A hermit crab scuttled away as I approached. I saw a flash of lizard green. "It's a chameleon," Brin said.

"How appropriate," I said and she wrinkled her nose at me.

That night I absorbed the dimension of Brin that I knew the least about, the ex-wife in the suburban house, the mother of a young boy. I was inordinately thrilled to use her favorite of my lovemaking techniques in her marriage bed, bringing her to orgasm with my tongue amid queen-sized flowered sheets and an oak headboard, her kimono thrown onto the wall-to-wall carpet, our clothes draped on both sides of the walk-in closet. I held her all night, barely sleeping with the novelty of it.

In the morning she made me scrambled eggs and mushrooms while I read her little snippets of the news. I followed her into the laundry room. She put bras and little boy underpants into the dryer. "Therese, you're making me nervous."

"I'm an anthropologist," I explained, backing her up against the washing machine. When she left to pick up David, I pinned her against her car in the garage for a final embrace.

I looked forward to my long-awaited chance to meet David, at the office picnic. Brin introduced me as her friend and her boss. He gave me a weak handshake. "I hear you've got a chameleon," I said.

"Yeah," he said. "He's getting scaly. He's getting ready for his fall change."

When he left to go roller-blading along the bike paths which ran beside the creek, Brin and I sat on a park bench and talked about him, how he wanted a dog more than anything, the sullen, hopeful look he got when Teddy's name was mentioned, the way he was outgrowing his clothes and becoming particular about his jeans and shoes.

The boundaries of our secret world sustained me through the sense of foreboding I felt about the fragility of our relationship, the fear of discovery surrounding us at the office. I was a camel whose weekly stop at the oasis gave me the wherewithal to travel through the desert that was the rest of my life. I came to life solely in the world of physical sensation, Brin's touch, my skin against hers, the ecstasy of bringing her to orgasm, the surrender of my body to hers. I worried that I was losing my edge at work, even though I worked as many hours except for Tuesday nights. I counted the hours until I could be alone with her again, which appalled me. The last half hour of her visits, having to let her go, became agony. We consoled each other with I love yous, and vague promises about a day when we would be together. Sometimes as she dressed, I hurriedly made us scrambled eggs or grilled cheese sandwiches, which we bolted at the kitchen table before she went home to David. After she left, I sat listlessly in my recliner, channel surfing, or reading a magazine which lay open on my lap, unattended for long stretches of time. I slept badly on the nights she was here.

*   *   *

Brin, June 1990

I lived in my head growing up. Marlys left for college when I was eight. My mother worried that my few friends didn't come to our house. I preferred to play with Legos and lie under the bed surrounded by my dolls.

My father was my protector, the lap I crawled into when my mother spanked me. He taught me to count during a breath, to help me calm down when I got too excited. Daddy read me the weather reports from other cities, absent-mindedly rubbing my curls. "Houston. Yesterday 65, today 68, tomorrow 72 and rain."

"Daddy, where's Texas?"

"Due south. If you and I started walking straight toward the noon sun, we'd get there in about two months."

My father, Gunnar Anderson, was a research scientist who worked for Eli Lilly in Indianapolis conducting drug studies on mice. He'd become interested in animal physiology and after marrying Augustina, returned to Minnesota to work for the University extension service. He'd encouraged me to go to the college of pharmacy at the University's Duluth campus. I loved Duluth, the huge iron ore boats sailing from the harbor, the lift bridge, the cobblestones and red brick buildings downtown, the stiff breeze off the lake. Duluth seemed Victorian to me. I wore velvet blazers and dark skirts during the long winters and lived in a house where the gaslights had only recently been converted to electricity. I was good at science and languages.

My asthma started while I was in college. I'd been staying up half the night working on papers and caught a cold that turned into bronchitis. By the time I got around to going to the health service, I had asthmatic bronchitis and pleurisy. After two rounds of antibiotics and a course of prednisone, I got rid of the pleurisy and the croup. The asthma never left.

I met Teddy at a party in Northfield when I was a senior. He lived in a basement apartment in the house where my friend threw the party. When I introduced myself, he leaned back and surveyed me. "I'm Teddy," he said and gave me a rakish smile. I wore a long flowered dress. My blonde hair curled around my bare shoulders. I felt ready to take my place in the world in that dress. Teddy was tall, finally someone who was taller than I was, good-looking in a fullback sort of way, with dark hair and a full mustache.

"Do you know anyone here?" he asked.

"Just the woman who brought me."

"So no one will be offended if I ask you to dance?"

"It depends on whether you step on my feet."

He laughed. "You've got spunk. I like that." We slow-danced to an Eagles song. He smelled good, a little musk mixed with his aftershave. After an hour he asked if I wanted to go downstairs and see his room.

"I bet you say that to all the girls," I teased.

He smiled. "Only the ones I want to kiss," he said.

I liked the Picasso print he had on his wall and the suits, which hung in his closet. He was two years older and working for IBM in Rochester. We sat on the edge of his bed and kissed. I let him push me back onto the bed and climb on top of me, but I held his hands at his sides. I wouldn't sleep with him until we were engaged.

As a teenager I felt like an outsider. I was too tall, tongue-tied in the presence of boys, prone to sudden tears. Marrying Teddy made me feel for the first time that I was doing what I was supposed to do. My mother started to treat me with respect, asking about my husband's opinions on food and politics. Living in that certainty was like standing in a pool of warm sunlight. I began to relax, to feel like I fully inhabited my own clothes. Teddy's adultery threw me back into the cold wind of self-doubt. Feeling love for Therese multiplied my questions a hundredfold. I stood in a blinding rainstorm, the wind howling in Turkish.

I finger-painted as a child, pushing my fingers into the bright, wet watercolors. I still loved to paint, splaying color onto the page, big white sketchbook paper, then throwing clumps of clay against the wet paint to mar it, blur it, shade the sharp contrasts. I hung one of my favorites, "Abalone," in my office.

Every week I rearranged the surface of my desk, pushing the magnetized array of circus acrobats on a stand behind a crystal paperweight. David's photo sat in front of two sets of elaborate metal files which held folders captive like the plates on a dish rack. My smallest treasures moved from the base of my monitor to sit in front of my technical manuals: a green Gumby six inches high which Therese gave me for acceptance testing the Coumadin flowsheet; an eraser shaped like a miniature Bigfoot from David, a seashell and a piece of yellow agate from Lake Superior. If I could put the pieces in the right order, life would start to make sense again.

I was afraid that Teddy would find out about Therese, that he had a private detective following me. I knew it made no sense. He was the adulterer. He was living with Tami, he didn't care what I did.

I'd talked to Teddy last week, to arrange the drop-off time. "Who's this Therese?" he said. Out of the blue, before I could get off the phone.

"Oh, she's just a friend from work."

"Well, she must be over there a lot. David's mentioned her several times."

"I've got to go, Teddy. Bye."

I couldn't tell David not to talk about Therese. But if Teddy were to find out, I could lose David and my life would be over. I'd have to disappear with him, move to a foreign country where there was no extradition, like a story on "60 Minutes". I couldn't live without David. As long as I could keep Therese and David apart, David couldn't find out and let something slip to Teddy. Teddy had David every other weekend; that was often enough to see Therese along with Tuesday nights.

David had my analytic side but not the passion. He could be a scientist like my father, following a research agenda, relentless and methodical as a chessmeister. He didn't look like Teddy at all. Living with only David, I forgot about the third leg of our triangle, the point of difference I struck sparks against, defining what I was and was not. Loving Therese was completely different, like swimming in warm honey. Some times it was too much. I needed the taste of something salty or bitter or hot to push my tongue against.

When work was going well, a piano composition played in my head: my own translation of Beethoven's Moonlight Sonata, sharp, melodic strokes building momentum, rhythm, purpose. Therese laughed at me when I confided this, and called me the human jukebox. Chewing on the end of a ballpoint pen, sniffing a magic marker, tapping on a keyboard. When the ideas slacked off, a repetitive pop song arose, my brain spinning in circles on the same hook. Work was consuming. It invaded my dreams at night, processed batch jobs at 3 AM of the problems I hadn't solved during the day. Thinking of a new angle to share with Therese. Writing it on a piece of paper in the dark, squinting the next day to make out the words.

I moved to the pharmacy group at Carepath, so I no longer worked directly for Therese. When a position came open, Therese said, "It will be better for us if you're not working directly for me. And you'll still be on the diabetes team so we'll still be in meetings together." I missed her so much the first month that the lining of my stomach hurt. I'd walk by Therese's office at least every other day just to see if she was in, to get a glimpse of dark hair, of the mole under her lip. Then I decided if I weren't working for Therese, I'd be able to keep her at a distance when I needed to.

The Monday I started in pharmacy, a young African-American woman named Roxanne Hamilton joined the group as a technical support specialist. Roxanne also had a ten year-old son, Darren, bright-eyed and exuberant in the photo on Roxanne's desk. On Tuesday Roxanne stopped at my cube.

"You're a pharmacist, girlfriend?"

"Mmm hmm," I said.

"Explain to me what is a formulary, please?"

I went through all of the insurance terms, drugs that were covered, drugs that were preferred, drugs for the same condition which had a higher or lower copay, depending on the employer's wishes.

Roxanne took notes, shaking her head in disbelief. "Who made all this up?"

"Companies called pharmacy benefit managers. They're like specialized HMOs for drugs."

"Don't you mean *on* drugs?"

I laughed.

"OK, Brinnae, you come see me next time you need to know the difference between a server and a router, OK?"

*   *   *

Fretting about Jeff, who'd asked me every week of the last nine months if my divorce were final. Finally, one snowy March day walking in from the parking lot, I said yes.

The next day he stood at my table in the lunchroom. "How about coming over for pasta tonight?"

"Jeff, I have a son. I can't just drop everything and eat rigatoni with you."

"Well, when's the next time he's with Teddy?"

"I don't know. Next Friday, I think."

"Great. Let's go hear Marshall Chapman. She's playing at the Cabooze."

"Jeff, you're a really nice guy, but I don't want to get involved with someone at work." I crossed my fingers under the table as I said it.

He didn't let up, so I told him I needed to be alone to figure out what I wanted. When that didn't work, I said I was dating one of Teddy's brothers.

"Cool," Jeff said. "That's got to really grind him."

I sat with Therese and Jeff, in Therese's office, planning the new release of the diabetes tracking software. Software is never done, I thought, you have to fertilize it every quarter or at least every year. I looked out the window, thinking that David would be done with school next week, while Jeff droned on about the snag he'd run into during program testing. "It's taking too long for the program to call the care plan. The docs will scream if the response time is more than two or three seconds. We're going to need to cut down on the number of data elements the program's looking to update or create a summary database or something."

"Which approach do you recommend?" Therese asked. She looked so intent that I shook my head. I was so bored that I did my long cat stretch and gave her a slow, sexy grin. I saw Jeff look at me in the middle of my stretch, but it was too late. I barely managed to avoid licking my lips.

Jeff finished his sentence and looked at his watch. "Sorry, Therese, I've got to go."

"Thanks, Jeff. We'll pick this up next week."

I got up to follow him out. "Brin, sit down," Therese commanded. She got up and closed the door. Her face was red and furious. "What in the hell is wrong with you?"

"What?" I said.

"Don't play innocent with me. You gave me a look like you were about to take off all my clothes and Jeff saw it."

"I couldn't help it," I replied. "He was boring me to tears. I didn't mean for him to see it."

"God damn it, Brin, where is your head? If it gets out that we're involved, one or both of us could be fired."

"It would probably be me," I said. "You're too valuable to Paul and Alan."

"That's not the point. We have to be extra careful, extra discreet every minute of every day. You go find him and tell him you were daydreaming about Tom Cruise or something."

I looked for Jeff all afternoon but couldn't find him. The next day I saw him at the copy machine hands in pockets, slouched, aggrieved, muttering to another programmer. I walked up to him, smiled at the other man and said, "Could I borrow Jeff for a moment?" I put my hand lightly on Jeff's shoulder and he smiled sullenly.

"We need to talk, Jeff."

"What for?"

"Are you free for lunch?"

"What's the matter, your girlfriend can't meet you in the john today?"

"Jeff, that's enough. You pick the place, I'm buying."

At lunch, I pleaded. "Jeff, I'm going crazy. I need you to respect my confidences and my confusion."

"How can you just turn into a dyke? You were married for what, ten or eleven years?"

"I haven't decided that I'm a lesbian. I just have feelings for Therese. You have to admit, she's wonderful."

"She's OK, for a boss. Lesbos aren't my type."

"She's not my boss anymore. Please don't call either one of us a lesbo."

"Why shouldn't I talk about it?"

"Because we're friends, Jeff. Because you don't want to hurt me."

"Well, yeah."

"We'll be better friends now that you know. I need you to listen to me, to help me."

"I can't make any promises." But his face softened. After lunch we lingered in the vertical June sun, the breeze forecasting days on the beach and weekends at the cabin. I didn't really miss Teddy's family compound but it would be nice to rent a lake place for a week. I gave Jeff a full-body hug and felt him harden against me. I didn't pull away too fast.

Therese was apoplectic when I admitted I'd confessed to Jeff. "You confirmed that we were lovers?! I can't tell Alan and you tell Jeff? You might as well put it on e-mail to the whole company!"

"Therese, I didn't tell him. He figured it out. That's different."

"I can't believe you told him."

"Come on, Therese, he's not stupid. I couldn't take back what he'd already seen. If I cry on his shoulder and tell him how confused I am, he'll be more sympathetic and he won't be gossiping."

"Fine. I'm having Alan and you over for dinner and you can moon over me then."

"All right, damn it, you can tell him, but nobody else at Carepath."

When Therese came over that night, I made her repeat the whole conversation."

"What conversation?" Therese complained. "I said, 'Alan, you know the woman I've been seeing?' He said, 'The one you've been so mysterious about?' I said, 'It's Brin.' He said, 'That would explain why you've been so mysterious.' End of story."

"Surely there was more to it than that."

"He made sure you didn't still report to me. He said that you can't be too careful about sexual harassment these days."

"Good," I said. "We can stop fighting about that and move on to what's for dinner."

Competing fears circled my brain like race cars speeding around the track. Jeff saying that the program logic was still too complex, that the patient wouldn't wait for the minute it would take to cycle through the past medical history and then call the program. Teddy ringing my doorbell, showing me grainy black and white photos of Therese and me in bed. David waving goodbye as Child Protective Services put him in the car. The worries collided and spun into more elaborate anxieties, sending me bolt upright in bed, the sleeping pill fog clearing to a brilliant starry sky.

CHAPTER 6

Therese, New Year's Eve, 1989

Three months after our trip to San Francisco, I turned into Brin's subdivision, onto her street and into her circular driveway. Teddy and his new wife, who was pregnant, took David for the New Year's weekend. I rang Brin's doorbell with a bottle of champagne, a rented video and a jar of her favorite bath oil from the Body Shop, gardenia. She opened the door in her bathrobe, coughing and smelling of Vicks vapo-rub. "I'm sorry, Therese. I'm not feeling well."

I sighed "I'm sorry, too," and followed her in. I'd looked forward to this weekend with a hope that far surpassed reason. Brin wouldn't let me come to the house when David was there. I could count the number of nights we'd spent at my place on one hand. I felt like running out the door, getting in the car and driving to another state, say Montana, where no one knew me, the wind howled miserably and I could sit in some bar getting plastered until the handful of taciturn men in cowboy hats sitting on stools around me acknowledged the TV midnight revelers in Times Square with total and stony silence.

Instead I felt Brin's hot forehead, then took her temperature, which registered 101 degrees. I put her in bed with the vaporizer and the TV remote control, thawed a whole chicken in the microwave and made chicken soup with plenty of garlic slivers spooned from a jar, celery, carrots, onions and egg noodles. I brought a bowl of soup in to her and a bag of oyster crackers and sat in the rocking chair beside the bed with my own bowl.

"Your soup is wonderful, Therese," she said.

"An old family recipe," I replied. "Passed from one generation of snifflers to the next."

She managed a croupy laugh and gestured me toward the bed. "I have to be careful. If it turns into asthmatic bronchitis, it gets really ugly."

I put the video in the VCR, and climbed in with her. I fed her more acetaminophen and handed her the inhalers. She fell asleep in my arms, her head resting on a pillow propped on my chest, her hot little hand clutching mine. While Brin slept, I watched the video with headphones, a French farce with subtitles about an executive who fell in love with his cleaning woman, his only ally during a hostile takeover attempt. I stayed attentive to Brin's raspy breathing, brushing the damp curls back off her forehead.

When the movie was over, I rolled her gently onto her side into a nest of pillows, put on a pair of her flannel pajamas and poured myself a glass of wine from her refrigerator. I toasted her sleeping form, drank the wine and spooned myself around her. Drifting off to sleep, I felt her stir, take my hand and put it on her belly. "I love you, Therese," I heard her whisper.

"I love you, Brin," I mumbled and fell asleep.

After three months, I could no longer ignore the fact that our weekly Tuesday night rendezvous was not enough for me. Sometimes after she left, I crawled back into the sheets, hung on to them the way I wanted to hang onto Brin and cried. I'd given up so much to love her. I could have been with someone else, a woman more comfortable being a lesbian, whom I could talk about and be seen with more publicly, at least outside the office. I'd given up the pleasures of being Brin's mentor, for the chance to be equals in love. I was leading a life so claustrophobic that I woke up suddenly in the night with my heart pounding. Last week I began to cry even before she left.

"I love you too much for my own good," I said.

"You have as much of me as I can give right now," Brin replied, as she dressed.

"I need more," I said, reaching for her as she sat on the edge of the bed.

I felt her body stiffen. "I'm doing the best I can."

I sighed. "I know, sweetheart. I know."

I was afraid that if she knew how much I needed her, she'd leave me. The goddess of passion does not mete love out with an even hand.

The next morning Brin's fever had broken. I made tea with lemon and honey and raised the blinds in her bedroom. A foot of snow had fallen overnight. Snow continued to stream from a sky the color of a child's flour paste.

"We're snowed in, babe," I said, glad that Montana had passed me by.

"Good," she said. "We can drink hot chocolate and watch bad movies on cable." We watched a sappy movie about a lost dog and cat finding their way back home, which made Brin cry, and then the Rose Bowl parade.

"Will you shower with me?" she asked. I watched her gulp the steamy air as I soaped her gently. We held each other close as the water streamed over us. I felt as if I were recording every moment to play back in super slow motion during the nights I was alone and sleepless. We climbed into bed, clean and naked. "I don't want to get you sick," she whispered, as I lean over to kiss her.

"I'll risk it," I whispered back.

After we made love, she gave me a wonderful smile full of sleepy contentment, her eyes rheumy as an old dog's. "Thank you for taking such good care of me," she said. I felt a stab of wild hope, which I shoved down below the surface, telling myself not to push my luck.

We ate more soup. I watched a little football while Brin slept again. By dinner time she had an appetite. I cooked some cheese ravioli from her freezer and opened a bag of salad. I found a box of crème caramel mix in a cupboard, whipped it with milk and put it in the refrigerator to chill. I coaxed her out to the kitchen table, complaining of imminent bedsores, seeking and winning the big Brin smile.

At dinner I told her Nate Silverman stories. Nate was just promoted to vice president of sales. I'd been going with him to talk with big clients, hearing what they do and don't like about the software and our services. For the last two weeks we'd sat in his office listing solid accounts, accounts with growth potential, accounts in jeopardy. Nate was the only one allowed to call me Terry because I'd been unable to make him stop.

Nate was Paul's and my emotional counterpoint, a voluble guy, with a constant smile that took the sting out of his sharp tongue and his play-by-play commentary on clients, company finances, world news and gossip of any kind. He was a couple of years older than I was, divorced, with two kids who lived with his ex-wife. He had lunch once a week with a group of the secretaries, who alternately babied him, mothered him and flirted with him. He was smart enough not to get involved with any of them, which allowed him to have an adoring harem and we introverts in the office to soak up the camaraderie they generated. Nate treated me like his little sister, alternately teasing and consoling me when things got rough. We were rivals for Paul's attention and affection, but generally in a good-natured way. Carepath had become large enough that others now traveled in our orbit around Paul and Alan.

"I said to him, 'Nate, you love gossip so much I'm surprised you're not a secretary.'

"He said, 'If you kept up with your Harvard Business Reviews, Terry, you'd realize that I'm keeping the informal channels of communication open. Giving you shy people the informed workforce and high morale you don't deserve.'

Brin laughed and put water on for tea. "What does June think of him?"

"June likes him. She says all the other secretaries are after him, calls them check-chasers, but she never turns down a chance for lunch with the group if she has the money to go out."

"June was wearing a green velour shirt yesterday. She looked almost holiday-ish if it weren't for the fruit boots," Brin said.

I laughed. "Yeah, she had Rose with her. Rose was wearing little Christmas tree earrings. I can't believe that nine year-olds have their ears pierced."

I paused. "Do you think June has figured us out yet?"

"I don't think so. I don't ever go to your office, I just leave you sexy voicemails."

"Thank God for voicemail," I said. I was testing Brin's paranoia. I knew that June knew because when she asked me if I were sleeping with Brin, I said yes.

We were eating a quick lunch at Wendy's the week before Christmas, having run out for office supplies and chocolate Santas. "I've been really careful, I thought," I said. "How did you know?"

June guffawed. "Honey, I have a nose for romance. It's my only body part involved in romance, unfortunately."

"I'm serious, June. Having this be public at Carepath could be a career-breaker. At least one of us would have to leave."

"She has a picture of you in her dayrunner. It's the one from the annual report a couple of years ago. She was standing at my desk asking about a meeting with you, and I saw it peeking out."

I groaned even though part of me was very pleased. "She's even more paranoid about discovery than I am and she carries a picture of me around the office?"

"That's Brin," June said. "That girl can't help but wear her heart on her sleeve. So I asked her how she liked working with you and her eyes lit up. She told me how smart you are and how fair, how you listen to everyone before you make up your mind."

"The things you learn," I said, "when you have lunch with your closest ally. Thanks for letting me know."

"You're welcome, boss," June said. "Now, you were asking about my Christmas list . . ."

I laughed.

"Be careful," June said. "You're not leaving Carepath without my say-so."

"I know," I said. "Unless I want to be one dead squirrel."

I poured chamomile tea and put the flan on the table. I thought about Alan while I did the dishes. His wife Marina told him on Christmas Eve that she was having an affair with her tennis instructor. At lunch yesterday he agonized over whether he should ask for a divorce and what the impact would be on Jill, his 8 year-old daughter.

"You should ask her to end the affair and see what she does," I told him. I couldn't imagine Alan asking for a divorce. He'd hang in there until Marina kicked him in the balls and filed herself.

Brin felt well enough at bedtime for us to unbutton each other's flannel pajamas and make slow, rhythmic love. After she blew out the candle, she turned to kiss me again. "I could get used to this," I said, caressing her face.

"It's nice," she said. Again I stuffed hope under the covers. Live in the moment, I told myself. I looked at the ceiling for awhile and went to sleep.

The next morning I heard a key turn in the back door lock and felt Brin spring out of bed. I buttoned my pajama top, pulled on the bottoms and yanked the covers up to my neck, awaiting inspiration or instructions. I heard Brin's voice as she and David made their way up the stairs. "You remember my friend Therese?"

"Yeah."

"She came over to take care of me because I was sick. Then we got snowed in so she stayed over."

David walked into the bedroom and surveyed me in his mother's bed.

"Hi, David," I said.

"You're wearing my mom's pajamas," he said.

"I didn't bring any of my own," I responded. "I didn't expect to need them."

He looked at the pile of my clothes on top of the rocker. "How come you didn't sleep on the couch?"

"Too lumpy," I said. "Too far to keep an eye on your mom."

"I didn't expect you until after lunch, David," Brin said. "Are you hungry?"

"I skied home," he said. "I got tired of being around Tami. I could hear her in the bathroom throwing up."

"Some women have morning sickness when they're pregnant," I replied, feeling stupid the moment I said it.

"Yeah," he said. "Mom, did you throw up when you were pregnant with me?"

"No, David," she said. "I was lucky. How about some pancakes for breakfast?"

So the three of us trooped downstairs where Brin made pancakes, I fried bacon and cut up fruit and David opened a can of frozen orange juice and stirred it around in a pitcher. Outside the sun shone brilliantly on the snow piled to windowsill height, weighing down the boughs of the blue spruce trees in the back yard. We talked about David's hockey team and about how much the Minnesota Timberwolves stunk. When David got up to get more pancakes, I winked at Brin. She frowned, then shrugged. She tried to smile.

After breakfast I cleared the dishes and David put them in the dishwasher.

"How about giving me a hand with the snowblower?" I asked. "I think your mom's still too sick to be outside."

"OK," he said.

"Do you have any gas for it, Brin?" I asked.

"Maybe. I haven't used it yet this year."

"I'll go out and look, Mom," David said.

When I heard the garage door close, I took Brin's hand and we climbed the stairs. I fluffed her pillows and tucked her into bed. After I put on sweat clothes, I sat down beside her and gave her a long kiss. She clung to me and I fought back tears, reminding myself that it was only 56 hours until Tuesday night.

"Mom," David yelled. "The gas can's empty."

"I'll go to the Super A with you, David," I yelled back. "I'll be right down."

"He's a nice kid, Brin," I said. "You've done a good job."

"I hope so," she said.

"Do you have your dayrunner at home?" I asked. "I need to look at a calendar."

"It's at the office," Brin said. "There's a new calendar in the kitchen. Twelve months of Michael Jordan. You'll never guess who gave it to me."

"What'd you do for New Year's Eve?" I asked, on the five-minute ride to the gas station.

"Me and my dad watched the Die Hard movies. Tami puked. We like Bruce Willis."

"He's pretty good," I said. "Though I prefer the Terminator movies."

"What'd you and Mom do?"

"I watched a movie myself. Your Mom slept. It was pretty quiet."

"Terminator 2 rocked. That one guy just kept coming."

I gassed and fired up the snowblower and let David move the mountain of snow on the driveway. I shoveled the back steps, the front steps and the areas around Brin's bird feeders. I refilled the feeders and looked up to see her watching us from the bedroom window. She waved. I blew her a kiss, a cold vapor trail in the frosty air.

I showered, changed clothes and came downstairs to find the two of them on the den sofa watching the Minnesota Vikings on TV, Brin wrapped in an afghan reading the Sunday paper, David totally absorbed in the game. I felt a stab of loneliness followed by envy for these two people who had each other. "Bye, David," I said. "You take good care of your mom."

"I will," he said, looking up long enough to wave.

Brin walked me to the front door and gave me a long hug. "Thanks for taking care of me," she whispered into my down jacket.

"Thanks for letting me stay with you."

"It was wonderful," she breathed.

"Yeah."

I drove off into the fresh snow and the new year, thinking about turning 36 in the spring, feeling familiar longings and hope mixed with sadness.

CHAPTER 7

Therese, February-June, 1990

During my sixth year at Carepath and Brin's second, the company reached two hundred employees and annual revenues of $50 million. We leased another floor of the building and invested in another data center in Chicago for disaster recovery. Paul and Nate began to relax enough to spend an occasional Friday afternoon on the links with a prospective new customer or a client from a large account. Alan's complaints that the company was getting too big intensified.

"It was bad enough when we hit 100 employees," Alan said. He and Nate and I were having a drink after work at a Greek bar and restaurant on Highway 13. Snow fell and the north wind rattled the window. I moved a little closer to Alan, who radiated furnace-quality heat. "Then we had to spend money on a human resources department and formal policies and all that crap. Now Paul wants me to have a tracking system on each person to see what projects they're spending time on. Christ, I'm lucky if I know half the programmers anymore."

"Alan, I hear you," Nate said. He lit a cigarette and blew quizzical smoke rings. "I can't afford to take the secretaries to lunch, there are thousands of them now. But if you don't have a tracking system how are you going to argue with the client when they challenge your bills? And if I start slacking off on new accounts, how will you pay Marina's alimony once she decides to divorce you? Ms. Denard here would have to give up Godiva chocolate and her CD club and flying off to visit her relatives at the drop of a hat."

"Let's talk about Pro Heart, speaking of new accounts," I interjected. I poured myself a second glass of beer from the pitcher on the table.

Paul had assigned me to a new client, Professional Heart Care Inc., a smart and ambitious group of 25 cardiologists and cardiac surgeons who had contracts with all of the major HMOs in town.

"The joys of market research," Nate said. "In Pro Heart's last survey of their patient population, they discover that 40% of the households have personal computers. So Mike Nelson calls up Paul, his old college buddy, and asks him to develop something to appeal to his computer-literate patients."

Alan snorted. "It's like our surveys of doctors—40% of them have computers, too, but only their children use them more than once a month."

"It's a $200,000 contract now," I said. "Half from Pro Heart, half from one of their HMOs." We all fell respectfully silent. Nate beamed as if he were responsible for bringing it in.

"Hell," Alan said, "a hundred grand is a quarter of a cardiac surgeon's annual salary. I guess they're serious."

Having met twice with Mike Nelson, who was as tall and slim as the Marlboro man with a full head of distinguished graying to white hair, I had a plan. I told Paul we should look at some kind of customized patient profile. Something that looked at the patient's cholesterol and EKG results, maybe their family history of heart attacks and printed out a diet and exercise plan developed especially for them.

I looked at Alan. "OK, big guy. We're talking a blitz team here. Let's figure out which of the usual suspects are on it."

Alan sighed, refilled his glass and ordered another pitcher. "Let's figure it out fast. I'm on vacation next week."

"Anticipating this situation," Nate said, "I've graciously ordered a decision-making tool for the both of you." He gestured to the waitress and lit another cigarette.

"Can't you change your trip?"

"Marina, Jill and I have plane tickets to the Bahamas. Non-refundable."

The waitress re-appeared with the beer. Behind her a waiter bore a life-sized Egyptian mummy doll.

Alan said. "I've always wanted one of these. How'd you know that, Nate?" He began punching the mummy, ducking and feinting like it was going to hit back.

"I know all but tell only some," Nate said.

"Then prepare for a long lunch tomorrow," I retorted. "And change your schedule for Thursday and Friday."

"My secretary's out sick." He threw a flurry of punches at the mummy's head and crowed, "The Mummy is up against the ropes. The Mummy is down and is not getting up. The ref is standing over the Mummy and starting the count . . ."

"Give me a crack at old Ramses the third, will you?" I put my arms around the mummy and began head butting it. "June will be only too happy to help you. If you're sweet to her."

"I'll bring her a large box of June-yer Mints."

"Good enough."

Like all medical systems projects, an idea that seemed simple and straightforward turned out to be mind-numbingly complex. We had to write three custom interfaces to put cholesterol, EKGs, and prescription drugs into the electronic record. I convinced Brin's boss that Brin had to be the project leader for the pharmacy piece so I could feel confident that it would be done right. Plus I'd get to see her at the weekly team lead meetings.

The interfaces turned out to be the easy part of the project. Mike Nelson wanted to use the patient's family medical history of heart problems, hypertension and strokes to predict the likelihood that the patient could have, as he put it, a cardiovascular event. But when Mike gave us copies of the dictated notes, we discovered that all of the physicians used different terms to describe medical history.

Alan was angry. "This is a complete tower of Babel."

When I proposed that the transcriptionist type the patient and family diagnoses in special fields, Mike frowned. "It will take more time. It'll raise my transcription costs."

Alan rolled his eyes at me with the look that said Nelson was a hopeless troglodyte.

"Let me watch your transcriptionist work," I said.

A month later when we met with Paul, I reported our progress. "We've got diagnosis coding figured out."

Alan chimed in. "Yep, it only took a month to get three doctors to agree. Then after we code it and test it, they'll change their minds and we'll re-code it and re-test it. The group has twenty-five doctors, so we'll have to re-code it and re-test it oh, say, eight more times. At this rate, Mike Nelson will have his system fully implemented three years after he's dead."

I glared at Alan and smiled at Paul. "We had Mike sit in on the sessions with the three docs. He understands he has to tell all of them that they're going to use the same terms. Period."

Paul smiled back. "Mike and I played racquetball last night. He mentioned that gosh, this was a lot more complicated than he thought."

"Gosh," Alan repeated. "I'm sure that was an exact quote."

"Alan," I said, "will you shut up and start bragging about the interfaces coming in a week early?"

I couldn't get too aggravated with Alan. He came up with the idea to put the patient profile onto a CD-ROM, and have the physician introduce it with an audio-video segment. We started calling Mike Nelson "Doc Hollywood" and he loved it. The CD-ROM opened with a shot of Mike in a white lab coat standing in the coronary care unit at the hospital, zooming in on the graphs measuring pulse and respiration, the nurse running down the hall with the crash cart when "code blue" was called and all the digital beeps and blips in the background.

I decided I needed a full-time tester on this project, someone who could check actual medical records against the data coming in through the interfaces. I got a recommendation from a recruiter and hired a woman named Karen Fisher.

"How are we going to update this?" Alan demanded, after we demoed the prototype for Paul and Nate, five months after my first meeting with Mike Nelson.

I sighed and coughed into my sleeve. I'd had a cold for weeks that I couldn't get rid of. Except for Tuesdays, I hadn't been home one night before ten o'clock in weeks. I could barely haul myself out of bed in the morning. I missed lingering over breakfast on the porch, missed my walk to the lake to see the orange and purple tulips popping up through the edges of a late snow.

"Right now, we're looking at having the patient print e-mail from the physician. Eventually we want to have a version which can send data both ways over the Internet, but there aren't enough people using the Net yet."

"OK," Paul said. "Clean up the bugs so we can show it to Mike and the rest of the group."

June scheduled the meeting a month out. She hired a catering company to serve dinner: parmesan chicken, twice baked potatoes and French green beans. I'd learned that the first key to working with doctors was to feed them well whenever a meeting was required.

All the team leads were lined up in the back of our conference room. Brin sat next to Karen Fisher, chatting away. Karen wore a navy pinstriped suit, the first time I'd seen her in something besides pants. She was brunette and extroverted, probably a couple years younger than Brin. Alan reported via his team leads that Karen wasn't pulling her weight. I hadn't had a minute to do anything about it. I sighed and made a mental list of people to ask about her performance.

After dinner, Alan brought up the system and promptly got a network error. I remembered a recent conference in California where a competitor's demo crashed in front of a thousand people and the VP's staff couldn't bring it back up. I coughed and cued June to serve coffee and dessert, her famous homemade blonde butterscotch brownies, while Alan and his staff frantically worked over the console and the projector. When the coughing escalated, I ran into the bathroom to take a slug of codeine cough syrup from the bottle stashed in my purse. I stood next to Brin for a minute in the back of the room. "Therese," she whispered.

"What?" I said.

"Don't worry. The system will come back up."

"Easy for you to say," I scoffed, but I smiled, suppressed a cough and had a moment's hope.

Midway through June's chatty excursion around the conference table, the network connection kicked in. I held my breath until Mike Nelson's face appeared, and the jokes about his haircut and the brilliant white of his lab coat started.

Later, after Mike had shaken Paul's hand and mine and the cardiologists had headed for their BMWs, I stood with Brin, Alan and June in the back of the conference room. The catering staff cleared away the detritus of dinner and Alan's staff packed up the equipment.

"How does it look from the top of the Eiffel Tower?" June asked me.

"I've never worked so hard in my whole life," I yawned, which made me start to cough again.

"Let's not count our chickens," Alan said. "At least not until we see how many patients try to use their CD-ROM players as cup-holders."

Brin laughed, that lilting sound I'd heard far too little of lately. "It's almost July, Therese. Though I don't suppose you've noticed."

"I wondered why I hadn't had to shovel lately."

Brin and I walked out to the parking lot together. The night was starry and clear, the Big Dipper hanging above our heads. We sat in my car and cracked open the window. The warm air and the night chatter of insects and airplanes filtered in. I held her hand in the dark in the vast expanse of the empty parking lot. I felt pleasantly sated, slightly virtuous about how hard we'd worked, and very tired.

"What I really like," I said, holding her hand, fingering her love and life lines in the center of her palm, "is that we're building a neighborhood of software. Every piece builds on the one before."

"I'm proud of you," Brin said.

"I'm proud of you, too," I replied. "And of everybody. We worked our butts off."

"Karen Fisher's a lesbian," Brin said.

"Really?" I said. Keeping my voice casual. "How did that come up?"

"She was telling me about their long weekend," Brin said. "She and her girlfriend Cindy are going to Palm Springs to play golf."

"Did you say anything?"

"Not about you."

"Good."

"Why? Wouldn't it be nice if we could be friends with them?"

"Wouldn't it be complicated?" I responded. "Brin, she works for me. Besides, I thought you're the one who doesn't want anyone to know."

"It all depends on who it is."

"Alan's group says she isn't getting the job done," I said. "Go slow."

CHAPTER 8

Therese, August 1990

After the Pro Heart project, Jeff and Brin both complained about having to move from the excitement of new system development to the drudgery of support. I realized how tired I was of the people management part of my job. While I still liked teaching my staff how to do design, I'd spent too many years in too many conversations listening to them bitch about their career paths and how the next phase of a project wasn't in line with their personal goals. I'd stopped believing my own rhetoric that these were good, conscientious people who were inevitably having trouble with change.

I sat down with Jeff and gave my standard team-building speech about how project teams must be aligned in their purpose and work for the greater good of the project. I told him that the maintenance part of the project would look good on his resume even though he already knew how to fix bugs and build reports.

"Fuck that noise, Therese," Jeff said. "I can move to a company in St. Paul that will let me use the absolute best in OLE technology and make five grand more."

I sighed. "Jeff, you're the only one who can decide whether this is the right place for you to be." I hoped he'd have a religious experience a week from now and get with the program. But instead he worked for a couple more weeks and quit.

I was so discouraged that when Stephanie called me up to play hooky for an afternoon Twins game at the Metrodome, I agreed.

"I'm shocked," Steph said, offering me some peanuts.

"Well, I won't let it happen again," I said.

"You must be coming off the adrenaline of some big project," she said. "You seem depressed."

I watched Kirby Puckett go after a ball that was low and outside and send it screaming into right field. "I'm not bored exactly. I'm tired and restless."

Two innings later, Stephanie said, "I don't get why this job is so important to you."

"I'm really in trouble if a doctor can't understand it," I said.

She snorted. "Yes, I appreciate that you're bringing me clinical data while the patient is in front of me. But why the grappling hook in your heart?"

"I'm idealistic—so shoot me," I said. "Not only are we building something important for patients and doctors, we're trying to do it in a way that lets the staff contribute the best they have to offer. Where it feels like family."

Steph rolled her eyes. "I'll try to rescue you from the asylum more often."

The next week I had to fire an employee for the first time: Karen Fisher. After her mediocre reviews on the Pro Heart project, she'd been unable to stay focused on her pediatric asthma flowsheet workplan, though for the last four of our bi-weekly meetings I'd coached her on how she was spending her time. She wandered off and generated ideas for research projects or got hung up following tangents from a conversation with an allergist. The final straw was when a test plan she'd promised to have done was in such poor shape a week before the user test that I had to give it to Brin to spend evenings on.

I was up all night the night before worrying about what I'd say and whether she'd cry. The next morning I had June call her and tell her I needed to see her at 1:00. It was Friday, and several people had taken the day off to play golf. The trees swayed in the hot breeze along the river. June had brought me a bouquet of roses and I inhaled deeply. I beeped Stephanie and asked her if she'd ever fired anyone before. "Sure," she said. "What's the big deal?"

"Don't go macho on me, Steph. How do I keep my stomach from doing flip-flops?"

Steph laughed. "Put on your Teflon suit, girl. If a sensitive manager like you is ready to can her, I know she's screwed up big time."

Karen came in, wearing a pair of linen pants, a peach-colored blouse and a paisley vest. "It's a beautiful day, Therese. Got plans for the weekend?"

"Nothing special. How about you?"

"Cindy and I are going to ride the Cannon River trail on our ten-speeds." I winced. Karen was always making references to her partner around me, as if the fact that she was a lesbian too meant that I should cut her some slack.

I sighed and indicated that she should sit down. "Karen, I have some difficult news. I'm letting you go."

She looked shocked and stricken. I felt my stomach seize. "Therese, no!"

"Karen, we've been talking for months about your difficulty in following your workplan and what you need to do to correct it. Your failure to finish an acceptable asthma test plan on time was the final straw. I had both the business and technical project leaders in here yesterday telling me that your procrastination has put the project in jeopardy."

"You know that Nancy's never liked me. She's a born-again Christian who can't handle my sexual orientation."

"Nancy's not the only one who's had trouble with your lack of production. This is not a case where one person is out to get you."

"How much severance are you giving me?"

"A month."

"A month! How am I going to find another job in a month?"

My stomach began to cramp. "Karen, you haven't even worked here six months. I'm being generous in giving you a month. You can always apply for unemployment."

"This really sucks."

"I don't expect you to be happy about it. It was not an easy decision for me to come to." The little voice in my head came from the woman in Human Resources I called to figure out how to handle the firing. Hang in there, she'd said. This is the worst moment in the life of a manager. I felt like some lame parody of the pointy-haired geek in the Dilbert cartoon. I wanted to throw up.

"What kind of a reference am I getting?"

"We'll release your dates of employment and leave it at that."

Karen stood up, her eyes flashing. "I'd expected better treatment from another dyke. Maybe it's your own internal homophobia I'm seeing."

"Karen, this is not about sexual orientation. This is about on-the-job performance. I hope after you cool down that you'll take a look at your own behavior rather than blaming everyone else for what happens to you."

She looked at the roses. "Just which of your many girlfriends gave you these?"

I looked at her, struck speechless. She stalked out of my office and slammed the door. I walked out to June's desk. My armpits were clammy. I took a deep breath to steady myself. "June, would you go sit in Karen's cube while she packs? Don't let her take any project stuff."

"Yes'm, heartless boss lady," June said. I frowned and tried to produce a grin, but when she began to whistle Randy Newman's "It's Lonely at the Top," I cracked up. I went back to my desk and filed, grateful to do something relatively mindless. The closeted lipstick lesbian crack kept running through my head. I didn't go out of my way to advertise my sexual orientation but I didn't deny it. And I hadn't worn lipstick since I was fourteen. And what the hell was that shot about the roses? Just what had Brin said to her anyway?

Two weeks later Paul called me into his office and asked me to sit down.

"We're being sued," he said, in lieu of a greeting.

"By whom?" I asked.

"A woman named Karen Fisher."

I sighed. "I had to fire her. She couldn't get the job done on the asthma flowsheet. Her test plan was a paragraph long. I had to give it to someone else who worked nights and weekends to keep the project on track."

"That would explain why I didn't hear about it at the time." Paul rocked back in his chair and pushed his hair back from his face. "Therese, there's no easy way to tell you this. She said she's suing Carepath for sexual harassment. She said you fired her because she wouldn't sleep with you."

"What?" I shrieked. I leapt to my feet. "Paul, there's not an ounce of truth to that. Not one." I was so stunned I could barely string the words together. I started pacing back and forth in front of his desk.

"Therese, take it easy," Paul said. He reached out and patted my hand. "Sit down and listen to me. We got an outside attorney to check her out. She pulled this once before when she was fired and it didn't fly. But I would need you to testify if, and it's a longshot, this suit goes to court. They'll ask you a lot of questions about your private life. It won't be pretty."

I sat down heavily. "This wasn't quite the calm and cool conversation I'd envisioned when I would reveal my sexual orientation to you."

"Therese, I guessed that you're a lesbian. It doesn't make any difference to me."

"Well, I'm grateful for that."

"Nick thinks she'll settle."

"We shouldn't pay her a cent. I should sue her for defamation of character."

Paul smiled. "That's my feisty Therese. She has another job, it turns out, because you did the right thing and didn't release any more than the dates of her employment. Nick sat down with her and laid it on the line. If she doesn't drop the suit, we go to her present employer and lay out the whole ugly picture."

"What did she say?"

"She said she'd think it over. I think she'll come to her senses, so I don't want you to worry. But I did feel I had to tell you about it."

"OK," I said. I stood up.

"There's one another thing," Paul said.

I sat back down. "As if this weren't enough. I can hardly wait."

"I want to promote you."

"What?"

"Alan says you're restless," Paul said.

"Alan's got a big mouth," I said. Paul raised his eyebrows. "But he's right. I was planning to talk to you . . ."

"It's OK, Therese. I've been doing a lot of talking with Nick and see a new opportunity for Carepath. I want you to head up an area I think of as strategic contracts. You'd be in charge of analyzing the competition, then look at the company and help me see where the holes are in our product line. Together with Alan, we'd decide if we should make the product or buy a company that's already doing it. You'd identify the companies we could buy and go off and make deals to acquire them."

"Paul, I don't know anything about negotiating contracts."

"You'll learn it. You're very bright, and very credible. People trust you because you listen to them and your ego doesn't get in the way." I perked up. Praise from Paul was as rare as orchids in snow.

He continued. "Nick will write the contracts and all the legal mumbo-jumbo and help you figure out the negotiating strategy for any given company. And you can hire a director to take over the management of the project teams. I want you to continue to lead product development from the business side because then you'll stay in touch with the things we do well and the things we don't and should look to buy elsewhere."

"This stuff with Karen must have made you think twice," I said.

"I won't deny that it shook me up," Paul said. "But I didn't believe it. I consider myself a good judge of character." He smiled. "Besides, you're an attractive woman. I'd expect you'd have men and women knocking on your door. You wouldn't need to look for it where you weren't wanted."

This was as personal a conversation as Paul and I had ever had. I couldn't wait to get out of his office. Brin's face flashed through my mind and I changed the subject as fast as I could. "What are you going to call me in this new position?"

"I'll still call you Therese and Nate will call you Terry. Everyone else will call you the vice president of strategic contracts."

"Huh." I tried to be non-committal. It sounded scary and great. "What would such a vice president's paycheck look like?"

He named a figure in the high seventies. I tried to pick my jaw up off the table. "You're one of Carepath's stars, Therese. I want you to be happy." He sat back in his chair. "Of course you'll have to travel more."

I saw Brin's face again. Maybe she'd appreciate me more if I were around less.

"If you'll give me an underground parking spot, I'll do it."

"You've got it."

I looked for Alan and couldn't find him. I went back to my office, called Brin and got her voicemail. I went downstairs and bought myself a double latte with whipped cream. Then I went back to work.

When I talked to Brin that night, she said, "It was a test."

"What was a test?"

"Paul's telling you about Karen's complaint. He knew she wasn't going to sue. He just wanted to see if you'd tell him the truth about yourself. If you did, he moves forward with the promotion."

I thought about it. "You might be right."

"I wonder how much else he knows," Brin said. She took a puff from her inhaler. "You keep an eye on Paul. He knows how to push all your buttons."

"We have to be very careful," I said.

"Now who's being paranoid?" Brin asked.

I sighed. "Being gay and paranoid is like a green sky and tornadoes—one almost inevitably follows the other."

CHAPTER 9

Therese, September, 1990

When David went to computer camp the last week of August, Brin and I rented a cabin in northern Wisconsin. Every evening we drove around the lake in the boat, scouting loons' nests and bald eagles. On Wednesday it rained all day. We padded around the cabin in long t-shirts and stayed in bed 'til dinnertime. I read an entire mystery novel and Brin thumbed though a stack of magazines, showing me recipes and pictures of gardens. We finished two crossword puzzles. We made love and napped, bears in hibernation.

One night we drove to Duluth and met my brother Danny for dinner. Through the window I watched a red-headed hulk of a man wearing a t-shirt and jeans climb out of his truck, look warily around and walk toward the restaurant.

"Brinnae, this is Danny," I said, allowing them to shake hands before I seized him for a scratchy beard hug.

He let go of me and smiled at Brin. "I'm glad she's found somebody to put up with her," he said.

Brin smiled back. We talked about loons and eagles, baseball, the cabins he was caretaker for an hour and a half north. We ate chicken wings and pizza, drank beer and finished with cherry cheesecake.

"He's lovely," Brin said as we watched the red truck drive away.

"He's a sweet man," I said.

I suffered acute loneliness the next week and was quiet and withdrawn during our Friday night card game with David. School started on Monday. Christie, the golden retriever puppy we found David for his thirteenth birthday in April, bounded around the table to lick our ears and be gushed over by each of us in turn. David knew we'd gone to a lake. "Did you and Mom have a good time?" he asked, shuffling a deck of cards.

"We had a great time," I answered. Brin nodded her agreement.

"You seem sort of grouchy tonight," he said.

"I am. I like being with your mom." I looked at Brin who was looking out the window. "I like being with you, too. I'd like to spend more time here."

David offered me the cards to cut and began to deal. "Dad asked about you," he said.

"What did he say?" Brin asked.

David sighed. "He said, 'who's that lesbo your mom hangs around with?' I asked him what a lesbo was. He said lesbos were women who were queer for each other." He picked up his cards and began arranging them into suits.

Brin looked as if she'd been stabbed through the heart. I sighed, set down my cards and plunged in. "Lesbo is kind of a nasty term, David. Like calling a black person a nigger."

"I know," David said. "Terry told me that. His father is gay."

"Who's Terry?" Brin asked. I looked at her without expression. Knowing she was worried about some guy who might be queer for her son. Hating the necessary conservatism of parents. Feeling like the room was suddenly a hundred degrees hot and all of the windows were closed.

"A friend of mine from school. He's starting eighth grade."

"David, your dad is right about one thing," I said. "I am a lesbian."

He nodded. I willed myself not to look at Brin.

"I don't know what he told you, but being a lesbian means I love women. It doesn't mean I hate men. I love my dad and my brother and I've grown to love you."

"Do you love my mom?"

"Yes, David, with all my heart. If it were legal, I'd ask her to marry me. That's how much I love your mom."

He looked at Brin, who was caught between stony and trembling.

"What's wrong, Mom?"

"How dare your father say that to you!" Brin burst out. "He has no right to ask you a question like that, to use that word."

I steeled myself for David to ask Brin one of the next obvious questions. Mom, are you a lesbian. Mom, do you love Therese. But he didn't. Instead, he pushed his chair back from the table and sighed. He said, "Mom, if you want to have Therese sleep here some times, it's OK." Then he excused himself and went upstairs to his room.

Brin stood up, went to the kitchen and began unloading the dishwasher. I picked the cards up off the table and walked around the downstairs, listening to Brin slam cupboard doors and sling silverware into its drawer. I sat in the recliner in the den and began shuffling the cards. After I'd played an entire round of solitaire, I went in search of Brin.

Climbing the stairs, I saw that the door to David's room was closed. He was growing up right before my eyes. Brin lay on her bed, face down in the pillows. I closed her bedroom door and stretched out beside her. As the pillow shook with her soundless sobs, I stroked her curly hair. I folded myself gently around her and put my arm across her stomach. Finally, she turned and rolled into my arms and let me hold her while she cried. I cried too, from fear and from sorrow at the world's view of my kind, and from anger at the intricate web holding me outside of what I wanted.

Eventually, Brin pushed herself up on one elbow and said, "Why did I have to fall in love with you?"

Stung, I replied, "Because you're a masochist?"

"It's not funny, Therese. I don't want to be a lesbian. I just want to be normal."

"I, on the other hand, have always loved being a freak," I retorted. I stood up. "Since when would you give Teddy so much power as to accept his view of us?"

She remained propped on one elbow, her face a cold mask, regarding me, I felt, as though I were a buzzing fly. I sat down on the edge of the bed, put on my shoes and tied them, feeling the blood boil inside my ears. "Fuck you, Brin. I'm going to take Christie for a walk and hope that you come to your senses."

I slammed the door hard on my way out of her room. Christie was ecstatic to see the leash and licked my face when I clipped it to her collar. I slammed the back door for good measure. The air was as hot and humid as the inside of my brain. Being dragged along behind Christie, I tried to become as mindless as she was, but fear and anger churned my stomach and made me seasick inside. We walked until the sky turned orange, then midnight blue, then black.

* * *

Brin

I was sitting in the den when I heard the key in the lock and the scrabble of dog feet on linoleum. I took a puff of albuterol. When Therese stopped in the bathroom, I let out a long sigh. I felt my neck and shoulders unclench, my feet uncurl. A stream of colors poured through my head, blues and greens, ocean waves. Thank you, I breathed and counted a slow five on each breath. Therese sat down on the sofa across from me, shuffled the cards and began to deal out a hand of solitaire. I did my best to set my face in granite. My lower lip trembled.

Ten long minutes later, I put my hand on Therese's shoulder. I sat down next to her and put my arms around her. I felt the first wave of sobs in my stomach, an icy breath trapped in my lungs. I hated having to apologize more than anything else in the world. I knew I couldn't get by without it this time.

"What?" Therese said.

"Therese, I'm sorry. I didn't mean it."

"You didn't mean what?" she asked, holding herself stiff.

"I didn't mean to hurt you. I do love you, and I'm not sorry that I do."

Therese held herself erect as I stroked the thick hair over her shirt collar. I could feel the pulse pounding in her neck, but her posture said she wasn't going to be her normal marshmallow self and let me off the hook. Last week Therese said that she was sick of being the incredible pretzel woman at my beck and call.

"Brin, I can't go on sneaking around, watching you be afraid of your old world and feeling like I'm doing something wrong. I've spent too much time in closets already. If you act ashamed of us, David will pick that up and it will be a self-fulfilling prophecy."

"But Teddy . . ."

"Don't but Teddy me. Teddy knows. He's moved on. He's got his own life and it's your job to convince him that you won't give up either me or David. That is, if you want me in your life."

I pulled Therese close and gave her a long hug. I clung to Therese, and to my surprise, tears slid down my cheeks. I started coughing.

"Then help me," I said, into her neck. "Help me find a counselor or a group or another lesbian mom or something." I took Therese by the shoulders and looked her straight in the eye. "Don't tell me you weren't confused when you first fell in love with a woman and the world started calling you names."

"Do you want me in your life?" Therese repeated.

"Yes," I heard myself say. "You're the only one I want." I coughed and coughed. I couldn't catch my breath.

"Even though I'm a woman."

I nodded. "Would you really marry me if you could?"

"Yes," Therese said.

"Come to bed," I said. I envisioned taking off Therese's clothes, the daring act of making love to her with David asleep in the next room. But when we reached the top of the stairs, I doubled over coughing.

"What's wrong?" Therese said.

"Get my nebulizer," I said. Therese went to the linen closet and got out the portable nebulizer and the liquid solution that I added to it. I put the mask over my nose and mouth and breathed through the tube to calm my lungs. I went to the bathroom and coughed up gobs of mucus. I walked slowly to the bed and stretched out, completely spent.

That night, curling around Therese as I slept, I realized that I was no longer merely crossing Antarctica. I was going to live there.

CHAPTER 10

Brin, Fall 1990

Hardly anyone said a word at the first meeting. The counselor, Nancy, made each of us introduce ourselves, talk about our children, what our greatest fear was. When it was my turn, I said, "That the other kids will ride David so hard, he'll feel like a freak." Another woman nodded her agreement.

At the second meeting the new women fired questions at Nancy like rifleshots.

"My son won't do anything my partner says. What do we do when I'm not home and she needs to discipline him?"

"When she's at her dad's, my daughter goes to her room and cranks up the music. How do we get her to stick around and interact with us?"

Some nights were the stuff of women talking about blended family tensions over coffee at work. I could start to breathe.

But other nights there were stories of pre-teen boys who were called sissies and faggots, of "AIDS lives here" scrawled in red magic marker on their lockers, of calls from teachers about fights that started with the word 'queer' or 'homo.' I felt sick at heart and guilty when I heard these stories. David wouldn't run the risk of having to deal with this if I'd stayed straight.

Do I have a choice, I wondered? Falling in love, for better or worse, wasn't irrevocable. Perhaps in time passion would run its course. Yet lying in bed luxuriating in Therese's softness, the clove scent of her hair, I prayed with all of my heart we'd stay together.

When I came home and told Therese the stories, Therese gave a tight-lipped smile. "Make sure Teddy teaches him how to fight. Make sure he knows we're not doing anything wrong so he's not ashamed."

I asked Roxanne if Darren got racial taunts. "Oh, yeah," she said. "Kids are mean."

"What do you tell him to do?"

"I told him, if somebody calls you a nigger, use your words. What are you going to say if somebody calls you that?

"And he said, 'that's a racial slur. Only somebody mean or ignorant would use a word like that. So which one are you, mean or ignorant?'"

"That's good," I said. I tried to stifle a feeling that said racial prejudice is worse, that somehow I deserved to be punished for what I was doing. Roxanne and I were becoming friends. I'd never had a black friend before. I felt lucky to have a glimpse of a world that had previously been closed to me.

I told Roxanne about the support group, though I referred to it as a group of single moms. "It's just nice to compare notes," I said. "You know, how many hours of TV should he watch a week? How to get him to say more than "fine" at the dinner table when I ask him how his day was."

Roxanne shrugged. "I can't ever get Darren to shut up long enough to get a word in edgewise. My thing is how am I going to keep him from turning out like his daddy?"

"Husbands who father children with other women," I said. "Next on Oprah."

"Least yours bothered to get a divorce first," Roxanne said.

Meanwhile Therese was gone almost every week, Monday through Wednesday night. When she came home, she brought what I derisively referred to as the lesbian find of the week. I pictured Therese in a women's bookstore or at the airport, looking for tapes for me of how to speak Portuguese. Despite my sarcasm, I was always curious. One week it was a kd lang cassette, the next a book on making lesbian relationships last. I skimmed the book, which had two chapters about the partners' sex drives falling off and what to do about it. If your girlfriend travels enough, I thought, it's not a problem.

The newspaper set me off on a regular basis. The judge in Florida who awarded custody of a girl to her father, a convicted murderer and accused child molester, rather than to her lesbian mother, put me over the edge. I raged in my car, to the mother's group and finally, to Therese.

Putting away groceries, slamming cans into the pantry, I ranted. "Why would anyone come out of the closet in this country? Why should I put myself at the mercy of people who don't know me, or you, or David, so that they can destroy our lives?"

Therese stacked packages of meat in the freezer, calm as always, and for a brief, intense moment I hated her. "In Minnesota we have a state law, which I worked for, which prohibits discrimination on the basis of sexual orientation. We aren't at that same kind of risk."

Screaming and ripping up the grocery bags felt so good. Therese followed me out to the trash. "You're right, Brin, it's not fair. It's not the whole world that feels that way, but the people who do always get publicity." Therese followed me back inside. "What is Teddy saying to you?"

"Nothing," I gasped. "I don't want to talk to him."

"If you get even one hint from him that he's going to fight custody . . ."

"I know. We'll tie him up in court for the next five years, until David goes to college and it doesn't matter anymore." I began to cry. "You don't understand how powerless I feel about all of this." I started to cough.

"OK," Therese said. "You're right, I don't understand. Because we're not powerless."

"Just let me be by myself for a while," I said and climbed the stairs. I sat on the bed, used my inhaler, tried to stop gasping long enough to breathe. I ran into the bathroom and coughed up mucus.

The next week, while I was reading about Newt Gingrich and the rise of the Republican right, the phone rang. It was midnight. David was asleep, I'd talked to Therese earlier and I couldn't imagine who would be calling. When I answered, I could barely grasp that it was Roxanne. Roxanne was hysterical.

"He called me a nigger bitch," Roxanne said.

"What? Who called you that?"

"I don't know who. I'm sound asleep when my cell phone rings, that's how they page me. I answer it, this man's voice goes 'Nigger bitch.' I think I must be having me some nightmare, I go, 'Who is this?'

"And the voice goes 'Nigger bitch, we know where you live.' And then there's the sound of a bolt sliding back on a rifle, you know that noise that you hear in the old Westerns when John Wayne or somebody racks his gun? And then he hangs up."

"Jesus Christ," I said. "Have you called the police?"

"Girl, I have called everybody. I called my mama, my sister, Cindy Wooten the affirmative action lady, the police."

"What did he mean he knows where you live?"

"Well that is the very worst part. Cindy called the police and she came right over to my house. They came over, talked to us, filed a report. Said there wasn't much they could do. Darren woke up in the middle of it, came downstairs to find these big men with guns in his living room, started crying his eyes out."

"Roxanne, I'm so sorry."

"Who would do something like that? My sister said call that white girl who's your friend and see if she's got any ideas."

I thought. "As far as I know, only Carepath employees have your cell phone number."

"That's what I said. We don't have no caller ID on a cell phone, if there is such a thing."

"This wouldn't be Ronell's idea of a sick joke?"

She snorted. "The only place he'd be this time of night is a bar. He wouldn't be thinking about me, I can guarantee that. Besides, he doesn't have the number."

Roxanne started to cry. "My mama, she keeps telling me, you think you're living this corporate life, good money, nobody can touch you. Someday we'll see what Whitey has to say about that."

"Oh, Roxanne," I said. "The world just isn't fair. It's not anything you've done. You can't let this get to you."

We talked for another 15 minutes, until Roxanne agreed to have her sister come over and spend the night. The next morning I called Therese at her hotel in Denver.

"That's unbelievable," Therese said. "You're right, it would have to be a Carepath employee. Or maybe an ex-employee."

"I've been racking my brain," I said. "I can't think of anyone who'd do something that evil."

"Evil is the word," Therese said. She sighed. "I suppose I should tell Nick about it."

"Why?"

"I hate to even have this thought at a moment like this. Carepath may have some liability here if Roxanne wants to pursue this."

I exploded. "You're such a corporate toady. Maybe for once in your life you could stop thinking about Carepath and start thinking about my friend who's scared out of her mind. And me, I'm scared, too. This is exactly the kind of thing that makes me want to be completely invisible."

"Brin, this is some isolated wacko, it doesn't have anything to do with you and David and me."

"You're such a know-it-all," I said. I slammed the phone down.

A month later, Roxanne quit.

*   *   *

Jeff and I had lunch at a Mexican place. He'd adopted a new look, with his hair cropped above his ears and a little tail in the back. Instead of the grungy t-shirt, he wore a light blue shirt with a Nehru collar. I complimented him on how handsome he looked.

"Yeah, Brin, sure. Well, it's because of my boss. She's got breast cancer and I'm having to go to client meetings in her place while she's at radiation."

"Is she going to recover?"

"Probably. They think they got it with the chemo. The radiation's like a ten percent insurance policy."

"How long has she been out?"

"Oh, she hasn't missed hardly any time. She took three-day weekends while she was on chemo, but otherwise I swear she's working harder. Every morning I've got e-mails from her that she must have done at home. I told her if she wanted to spend more time with her kids, I could probably cover some stuff. She says it's hard for them to talk to her about it. I guess it's easier to be at work."

I shook my head. "How's your girlfriend?"

He grinned. "She wants to get married. So I guess we're going to do it."

I felt a stab of panic. "When?"

"This fall some time. We haven't set a date."

"Congratulations," I said.

On the way back to the office, I kept seeing Jeff's grin, his excitement. I should have asked to give away the groom. I felt like I was losing an insurance policy I hadn't realized I'd bought.

*   *   *

I stood up from the table, knocking a file folder onto the floor. "This project is beyond repair," I declared, scooping the file folder and flinging it toward the corner of the room, paper raining down on the steel-blue carpet. "Dr. Sullivan is right—we don't deserve to have any customers until we can bring them a product that's textbook-perfect."

The new engineer raked his hands through his stringy brown hair, then put them over his eyes.

"Another Brin melt-down will certainly get us on the road to perfection," Toni said. "Don't you ever get sick of your drama-queen routine?"

I stared at her. "I thought you agreed with me, Toni," I said.

"You're my friend, Brin," Toni said, "but sometimes your behavior sucks." She looked across the table toward the engineer. "Todd, what do you have to say?"

Todd stood up. "I'm outta here. I don't need this bullshit."

Toni laughed as he left the room. "Another great moment in team-building history."

CHAPTER 11

Brin, October 1990

When Teddy said he wanted to take David up north for a long weekend, Therese suggested a trip to celebrate my 35th birthday. I didn't hesitate long. "Let's go to Vermont and visit your sister."

"You're kidding," Therese said. The smile lit up her whole face. "I'd love to see Carolyn. And Shoney's going to be seven next month."

"Call them," I said. "Tell them we've got this brief window while David's away."

Flying to Boston with Therese reminded me of our trip to San Francisco a year ago. I shuddered, thinking how little I understood about where my fantasies of sleeping with Therese would lead. How difficult it had been to admit Therese into my life with David. How cautious I was even now in my interactions with Teddy. I didn't tell him we were going out of town. I never mentioned Therese's name, and usually he didn't either, except when he wanted to provoke me.

David seemed to have adjusted much more quickly than I had. I'd overheard him on the phone with one of his friends before he went up north, acting blase. "Well, if I told her every time somebody at school called me a faggot . . . But my dad's going to pay for karate lessons." I shook my head and flashed on Roxanne's face.

I felt Therese look up from her newspaper. "You're looking awfully sober, Birthday Girl."

I smiled. I'd vowed that I would not be held captive by my fears, that we were going to have fun. "So, have you picked out our seafood restaurant yet?" We'd stay overnight in Boston and drive to Burlington the next day.

"Good idea," Therese said. "Look through the guidebook with me."

We drove from the airport through the Callahan Tunnel along Storrow Drive, Therese talking about East Coast drivers and rotaries and waving her hands. I looked out the window, watching the crew boats pull long silvery strokes up the Charles River. We checked into the hotel, ate lunch and went for a swan boat ride in the Boston Public Garden. Boston was thoroughly charming: the accents, the cobblestones and Revolutionary War headstones, our walk around Faneuil Hall and Quincy Market, the sense of distinct neighborhoods in the North End and Back Bay.

We ate dinner on the wharf, starting with the best clam chowder I'd ever had. "Tell me about Carolyn," I said. "Is she like you?"

Therese refilled their glasses from the bottle of sauvignon blanc. "Carolyn's more extroverted, more opinionated, more dramatic than I am." Therese smiled. "In some ways she's more like you. She's also more overtly political than I am. She kept refugees from El Salvador during the sanctuary movement. She spent the night in jail for protesting during Vietnam."

"Before Shoney was born?"

"Oh, yeah. She would never put herself in that position now."

The waiter brought our fish.

"How's June?" I asked. June's father had died after a long bout with lung cancer. Therese had gone to his funeral on Wednesday.

"She's doing OK. She can't believe all of her siblings are still smoking. And there they were, puffing away outside the church before the service."

I grimaced.

"I never met Mickey," Therese continued. "In the casket he had this sort of wry expression, like he'd seen the undertaker coming. He had June's pushed-in nose and his face had a lot of wrinkles. I was standing there trying to imagine this guy's life when June's sister

Rosie came over and started telling me a story about a woman in her company who barricaded herself in her office and threatened to drink lye. She just went on and on about this woman, who'd lost custody of her son to her ex-husband and quit taking her Prozac. They called the fire department but the ladder couldn't reach up to the eighth floor and the windows didn't open anyway.

"People talk about strange things at funerals. I didn't know how to respond to this story, so I said, "at least she didn't shoot up the place or hold her co-workers hostage." Rosie agreed with that. Eventually the police psychiatrist talked the woman out of it. Can you imagine going back to your job after pulling something like that? She's off on disability now."

"Therese, why are you telling me this story?" I asked.

"I don't know. You asked me about June."

"You don't think it's strange to tell me a story about a woman who loses custody of her son and goes off the deep end?"

Therese stared at me. "Brin, don't overstudy here. This isn't connected to your life at all."

I shook my head. "You tell me a story about someone who experiences my deepest fear and loses everything. Her son, her composure, the respect of the people she works with. How am I supposed to react?"

"For Christ's sake, Brin, don't start. I didn't know it was your deepest fear, or of course I wouldn't have said anything."

"How can you not know that? How can you be so close to me and not know what I'm afraid of?"

Therese stared at the slice of Boston cream pie they'd ordered, which sat untouched in the middle of the table. "Let's go," she said. She paid and we took a cab back to the hotel in silence.

At the hotel, I showered. Therese filled the ice bucket, changed into her pajamas, and read all of the hotel materials except the Gideon Bible. She turned down the covers on one of the two double beds. When I emerged, Therese said, "What else are you afraid of?"

"What?" I stared at her. She sat on the other double bed.

"I want to know what other areas of life I'm not supposed to mention or tread lightly around."

"It's very simple. I'm afraid of losing David. I'm afraid of losing you."

"Aren't you forgetting a few things? Being afraid that someone at the office will know about us. Being afraid your mother or your sister will find out. And the big one, being afraid to think of yourself as a lesbian."

"Don't you take that tone with me. I'm not afraid to be a lesbian anymore. Now I'm just afraid of the consequences. You'd have to be an idiot not to be."

"Brin, of course we have to be cautious. We're not going to walk into a fundamentalist church service and ask to be married. But there's a difference between being cautious and having your life overrun by fear."

"Don't tell me how to feel, Therese."

Therese expelled a long sigh, a tire going flat. "I'm not telling you how to feel, Brin. I'm just asking you to give me a break. I'm not a mind reader. I'd like to able to talk to you about anything. If I can't do that, then at least tell me what to stay away from."

"There's no point in continuing this conversation now," I said. "I'm going to bed."

"Fine," Therese said. "Great. When the going gets tough, the tough clam up."

"You're the tough one, Therese, remember? I'm the one who's ruled by her emotions. Good night." I shut off my light and climbed into the second bed.

In the middle of the night I awoke to the sound of crying. I sat on the edge of Therese's bed. "What's wrong? Are you sick?"

"You're breaking my heart, Brin. That's what wrong. I envy you. I wish I could just fall asleep after a conversation like that."

"Therese, in my family we don't cry unless somebody dies. And maybe not even then."

"Just hold me, OK? Don't say anything, just hold me."

I sighed. I climbed under the sheet and gingerly put my hand on Therese's arm. Therese pulled my arm around her. When Therese's breathing became regular, I got up and took my magazine to the bathroom. When I got cold, I climbed back in beside Therese. Eventually I fell asleep.

The next sound I heard was a lawnmower outside the window. We'd missed the breakfast buffet. Therese bought a candy bar from the vending machine, which we split, eating as we packed.

After checkout we got on the interstate. Therese spotted a Denny's at an exit on the outskirts of Boston. We ate a silent breakfast behind the newspaper. After we got back in the car, Therese said, "Let's just call a truce, OK?"

"OK," I said.

Therese started the car and got on the interstate. Eventually she reached her hand across the shift column to me. We drove in silence, holding hands.

Carolyn was a slender woman an inch taller than Therese. She had graying strawberry blonde hair that fell to her shoulders, silver hoop earrings, alert brown eyes and a big grin. "Brin," Carolyn said, "it's so good to finally meet you."

Therese hauled our bags up to the attic bedroom. Shoney led us on a tour of the apple orchard, the old barn which housed the goat, Maybelline, and a fenced forty by forty foot plot behind the house which had the front eighth planted in fall lettuce, spinach, onions and snow peas. "We've got a ton of tomatoes," Shoney announced. "And we're going to have pumpkins."

"And we've got beans and corn and broccoli and potatoes," Carolyn added.

"And next year we're going to have watermelon," Shoney said.

"This year the frost got it," her mother explained. "In June."

We sat in the living room. Therese and Shoney played Monopoly and Therese told the story of how many nights and weekends we'd worked to bring the ProHeart project in on time.

Carolyn shook her head. "That's horrible, T. I don't understand what you get out of working in corporate America. Though you've always been a true believer."

"True believer?" I interjected.

"Let's just say Therese has more faith in whatever system she's in than Danny or I ever did."

Therese smiled at me. "I'm attached to the people. The best thing about being in a leadership position is that I get to set the tone for my staff. June can be wacky and we can celebrate Groundhog's Day and give out prizes for the ugliest tie on Tacky Tie Day."

Carolyn shrugged. "Must be some weird oldest kid thing."

"I'm buying Reading Railroad," Shoney announced. "I've got all the railroads. Now you have to pay me $200 when you land on any of them."

"If I land on any of them," Therese corrected. "I'm going to be lucky and miss them. Otherwise I'm going to go broke."

Carolyn and I talked about the life of single mothers. The reciprocal deals made with other women to take our children for an evening. Teaching the kids to set and clear the table, load and unload the dishwasher. Car pools and overnights and soccer tournaments. Therese and Shoney played hide the thimble, then left the room for a rousing game of Bear, where Shoney hid and Therese roared through the house trying to find her.

"This is great," I said. "Therese doesn't get this boisterous around David. She's turned into a big kid."

"Shoney loves it," Carolyn smiled. "I bet Therese is pretty serious with all of this job stuff. Pretty responsible."

"Yep," I said. "We need to have more fun."

"I'm with you on that," Carolyn said.

"How's your photography business?"

"It was good this spring, with school pictures, and graduations and weddings made summer busy. It's dying down now and and should pick up about a month before Christmas." She talked about cash flow problems, Larry's lack of regularity with child support. How she hoped to build the Christmas tree grove into a cut-your-own-tree business to give her some cash for holiday bills. "It seems like there'd be a market for it, with sleigh rides and hot cider and holiday decorations. Of course I haven't gotten a quote for the insurance yet."

Shoney burst into the room. "Mom, look what Aunt Therese gave me for my birthday." She held out badminton set with four rackets, shuttlecocks, a net and stakes.

"We're recruiting for players," Therese said. "How about it?"

We played on the front lawn until Shoney began to whine that everyone else could hit further than she could.

"Why don't you and I go in and read a story?" Therese asked.

"I just happen to have something right here," I said. Therese looked at me quizzically. I pulled a copy of "Aladdin" out of my carry-on bag. I saw Therese give Carolyn a look.

"We don't normally do Disney around here," Carolyn said.

"Mo-om!" Shoney cried.

"But today we'll make an exception," Carolyn concluded.

Shoney dragged Therese toward the house.

Carolyn sighed. "I really don't mean to be rude, Brin. I hope you won't take it that way." She went on to talk about poor role models for girls and the cost of brand name toys.

"It's OK," I said. "I understand."

Later Therese and I took a walk through the apple orchard. "I should have warned you," Therese said. "I didn't know you were going to get her something. I don't get Shoney anything with a corporate trademark."

I sighed. "I guess I can see why she feels that way."

"But you were still hurt," Therese said.

I sighed again. "Mmm-hmm. In my family, even if someone felt that way, nothing would have been said. Or maybe after the fact a newspaper clipping about what kind of a role model the little mermaid is would come in a letter. Mixed in with a whole bunch of other clippings."

"Carolyn knows you were trying to be nice," Therese consoled.

I winced. Therese was trying to put a band-aid on a heart bruise. I flashed on an image of Italy, driving the narrow Tuscan roads, climbing past vineyards and olive trees to the hilltop cities surrounded by walls. I'd never been there.

"Brin, would you sit with me a minute?"

"OK." We found a bench in the densest part of the orchard. I wondered how the apples had enough light to grow in the midst of summer.

"Shoney's not the only one who gets presents," Therese said, drawing a small white box out of her pocket.

I pulled the bow off the box and drew out a ring. It was silver with a setting that held a small sapphire, my birthstone, and a small diamond. I felt warmth pulse through my hand. "Therese, it's absolutely stunning."

"Try it on," Therese said.

I hesitated, then slipped it over her left ring finger. "It fits. It's lovely."

"It means we're going steady," Therese said. "Do you still want to wear it?"

Tears gathered in my eyes. "Yes. Because I'm yours. Even when we fight I'm still yours. Lucky you."

"I am lucky," Therese said, taking my hand.

I put my arms around Therese and gave her a long, deep kiss.

"Mmm," Therese said. "I'd like another one of those, please. With extra mustard."

We wandered back to the house, and asked Carolyn to pick a place for dinner.

Carolyn chose a country inn with vegetarian specials. Over dinner she exclaimed over the ring. "Isn't it beautiful?" I said. "A birthday present from your sister."

Carolyn smiled at Therese. "You have good taste. In rings and in girls."

"We're going steady," Therese said. She looked at me. "She's not ready to marry me yet, but maybe some day."

When Therese took Shoney for her bath, Carolyn looked at me. "This must have been a big change for you. To get involved with a woman."

I nodded. "It's hard. Therese is wonderful but it's still hard." I told Carolyn what I'd overheard from David on the phone.

Carolyn nodded. "It's tough to go from thinking of yourself as normal into something other people regard as wrong or marginal. You have to rebuild your mental map of the world. And find new friends."

"I guess that's what I've been doing," I said. I felt gratitude in my shoulders and breathed deeply. I coughed. I described the lesbian moms group and the books I'd read.

"I give you credit," Carolyn said. "A divorce is difficult enough on your self-esteem and the life you feel you owe your kid. Adding in a change in sexual identity must take it to a whole new dimension."

"Thanks," I said. "It's nice to have someone else acknowledge it. Therese has a hard time seeing it." I puffed on my inhaler.

Therese and Shoney returned. "They got serious on us again," Therese informed Shoney. "What do we do when people get serious on us?"

"We tell them a joke," Shoney said.

"I'm listening," Carolyn said.

"What did the mayonnaise say to the icebox?" Shoney asked.

"I give up," I said.

"Close the door, I'm dressing," Shoney said and clapped her hand over her mouth.

"There's a family heirloom," Carolyn said. "The first joke Therese ever learned. I can't believe you're still telling that groaner!"

"At least update it, Therese," I suggested. "Nobody knows what an icebox is anymore."

"It's a great word," Therese said. "I'll have to keep telling this joke just to keep it alive."

Therese presided over Shoney's bedtime story. Carolyn and I sat in the kitchen over orange spice tea.

"Does Therese want kids?" Carolyn asked.

"I can see why you'd ask," I smiled. "We talked about it once. She said David was enough. And, obviously, being an aunt." We talked about David and great card games of Therese and Carolyn's youth.

Therese rejoined them.

"How about a round of three-handed hearts?" Carolyn said. "I'm getting nostalgic hearing about all the games you've taught David."

They heard Shoney from the bedroom. "Mo-om. Come say goodnight to me."

"OK, Shone. For the first and last time, here I come."

Therese took my hand. "Carolyn likes you."

"How can you tell?"

"She told me. She thinks you're good for me."

"I like her, too. Why am I good for you?"

"She says you bring out my sweet side."

I reached to tickle her. "Would that be the right side or the left?"

Therese groaned. "That sounds like something I'd say."

"You're rubbing off on me," I said. "I'd better be more careful."

Therese sighed. "I'm beat. That kid operates at 200 megahertz."

When Carolyn returned, we played a few rounds of hearts and ate popcorn. When Therese fell asleep in the middle of a sentence, we headed off to bed.

As we snuggled in, Therese said, "Thanks, Brin."

"It's fine," I said. "Though I'm going to go into Burlington tomorrow and let the three of you have some time." I sighed. "Your family's more fun than mine. At least since my dad died." When I closed my eyes, I saw the deepest part of the olive grove, the shimmering sage-colored leaves.

"I'll be the judge of that," Therese said. "When you're ready."

"OK," I replied. "Don't hold your breath."

CHAPTER 12

Therese, Fall, 1990

Autumn started with cool nights and warm days. Home from work on a rare sick day, I woke up to the long whine of the cicadas rising and falling. Geese gathered overhead, in their honking airborne v-shaped cab stand, and headed south. Over the past week, the corner maple tree had added a solitary streak of bright orange to an otherwise green hair-do. My bedroom window, open a hand's width for some fresh air, admitted the dull roar of a plane descending and the moldering scent of dying alyssum and larkspur. Through the window I watched the kids jump off the bus, in their sweaters and school jumpers, carrying bookbags.

I imagined Brin: a girl with long blonde curls, a frilly dress, a Swedish Christmas with lingonberry jam and lutefisk. Brin's mother a cooler, more dispassionate Brin. Her father, a quiet man who read to her, a refuge in the storms between her and her mother. Her sister Marlys, ten years older. The solitude that enveloped a girl raised from the age of 8 as an only child. Even now Brin could amuse herself alone for hours.

She'd go to visit her mother in the immaculate Cape Cod house that her mother inhabited. They'd sit on the porch across from each other in rocking chairs, Brin knitting an afghan, her mother crocheting a blanket for Marlys' first grand-child. I couldn't wrap my mind around the thought of Brin as a great aunt. It was too funny. I pictured Brin with granny glasses and a double chin.

The mystery of another person, the shared dream we inhabit with them. Occasionally the clouds part and we get a glimpse, the pout of a five year-old, the ten year-old twirling a curl around a finger absent-mindedly while reading the newspaper. What did I really know about Brin? She was three years younger than I was, inhabited a different emotional planet, was passionate and sexy, could make my heart stop by fixing her blue eyes upon me. Already I was describing her effect on me, not who she was. With David she was the thoughtful, worrying mother; with her own mother she was slightly wary. Watering the plants she gazed out the window until the water soaked through to the roots, ran over the lip of the pot holder and dripped onto her feet. At work she strode out of a conference room after a meeting, not waiting for anyone else to walk with back to her floor. She marched down the long hallway and dumped a pile of training manuals onto her desk, the intensity of her feelings spilling into the aisle, sending a humid wind through the cubicles around her.

* * *

I met Brin's mother, Augustina Anderson, on the day after Christmas. Brin and David had ridden out to her mother's the day before, with Brin's 22 year-old niece, Jessie, for an early Christmas dinner. Brin called to ask me to pick her and David up. "Have you already eaten the lutefisk?" I asked.

She laughed. "It's all gone. It's safe for you to come out."

The faint winter sun was dropping below the horizon as I got the car out of the garage. On the drive from Minneapolis to Waseca the wind came up, and a fine, stinging snow like white pine needles began to fall. I rang the front doorbell and David bounded up to the door to let me in. I wiped my feet carefully on the furry mat on the front steps and again on the throw rug inside the cold porch. He led me to his grandmother, who held court in a big, stuffed armchair in the living room, her feet in slippers propped on a pillow atop the ottoman. Augustina was built like Brin, tall and solid without being fat. Her thinning white hair had been recently curled and sprayed at the beauty parlor. Her blue eyes were a bit imperious, her smile more from habit than warmth.

"Therese?" she said, shaking my hand with arthritic fingers. "David says you've taught him to play cards. I could never get Brin interested in cards."

"I played hearts and poker with my father and brother when I was growing up," I replied.

"A woman who plays poker," Brin's mother said. "That would have been unusual in my family." I stifled the urge to tell her about sitting on my four-season porch last weekend with my golf buddies, watching the snow fall, playing poker and smoking cigars.

"Have you got time for a game of hearts?" Augustina asked.

I looked over to the sofa at Brin and Jessie, who were telling each other pregnancy stories. I shook hands with Jessie, a blonde so fair her eyebrows were almost white. She was four months along and beginning to show. She wore her hair pulled back into a ponytail and had a sort of exuberant shyness in the way she confided in Brin. Brin shrugged.

"Sure," I said. David helped his grandmother up and we moved slowly past another overstuffed chair, the Christmas tree glistening in plaid red and green ribbons and tinsel, and a mantle full of Christmas cards and family photos. I caught a glimpse of a black and white shot of a beaming blonde four year-old on a tricycle. Beside it stood a family portrait, apparently taken at Marlys' high school graduation. Marlys, her blond hair in sausage curls, was smiling in her cap and gown, her parents on either side of her looking solemnly proud. Brin was standing in front of them in a floral print dress with a big lace collar and a straw hat, gazing dreamily at the camera, a million miles away.

David showed me his presents, which were stacked neatly under the tree. A blue denim shirt, a v-necked sweater, three computer games. The pile next to his had to be Brin's: a cookbook, a red and green plaid skirt and white blouse with matching plaid collar, leather slippers and a pair of gloves. The middle boughs of the Scotch pine sagged under the weight of glittering glass ornaments with engraved names and dates. The globe that said Brinnae, 1956 was winter white with silvery glints and had an almost heart-shaped dip at the bottom. The stockings were handmade, red or green with velvet ruffs, and hung in little family groupings, Marlys and her children, Brin and David, and off to the right by themselves, Augustina and Gunnar. Gunnar died when David was four, and Brin mourned the fact that her son had had so little opportunity to know his grandfather.

I supposed Teddy's stocking was lying at the bottom of a box in the basement, for some just-in-case future. The look of Christmas in Augustina's house was much more formal and composed than what I'd grown up with. We'd hung simple red stockings with name tags on the living room mantle, and decorated a tree with the crush of ornaments we made at school or collected during cross-country vacations, the little sleds and gingerbread men haphazardly hung by us kids struggling to reach the branches or crowd someone else's out of a desirable spot. I remembered my father on a ladder, stringing lights across the front of our St. Louis Park bungalow while my mother hung the Christmas cards in the stairwell that led to the large attic bedroom my parents shared. Carolyn and I cut out the tree and star-shaped butter cookies and covered them with red and green sprinkles. My mother shoveled the cookie sheets in and out of the oven while Danny clamored to lick the beaters.

I joined my card partners. The three of us sat at the dining room table under the light of the chandelier. A bowl of oranges sat in the center of the table. David shuffled the cards, flexing them to shuffle forwards and backwards as I'd taught him. His grandmother nodded approvingly at me.

"I play the first hand you pass three cards to the left, the second hand you pass three cards to the right and the third hand you hold what you're dealt."

"That's the way I play, except I pass to the right first," Augustina said.

"Then we'll pass to the right first," I said. "House rules. Got that, David?"

"Got it," he said, dealing the cards. "We play fifty-point rounds. Do you shoot the moon, grandma?"

"You bet," she said. I suppressed a laugh and looked toward the sofa, where Brin and Jessie had moved onto episeotomies. Brin winked at me. I made fun of her whenever I caught her saying "you bet," "you betcha," "OK, bye-bye now," or any of the Minnesota Scandinavian-speak she grew up with.

We played the first hand in silence, concentrating on our cards. As I dealt the next hand, Augustina looked at me. "Do you know Teddy?"

"I've met him a couple of times," I said.

"Dad dropped me off and Therese answered the door," David said.

Augustina looked over at the sofa and lowered her voice. "She doesn't seem to miss him. It's a shame."

"Brin seems happy," I said. "Most of the time. How's Marlys?"

"She's in Phoenix, visiting her son and his family. I understand you've met."

"On Labor Day," I said. "Brin had a barbecue." I wondered if I'd said more than I should have. Did Augustina know about the barbecue? If she didn't, was she wondering why she hadn't been invited? Somehow I'd walked into a game in progress without a scoresheet or knowing who the sides were.

After the third hand, Jessie came over and said goodbye, mentioning that the snow was starting to accumulate. We played another round and David insisted that we play a fifth, since his grandmother was ahead.

David got up to make us instant hot chocolate and microwave popcorn. "So, is there anyone special in your life?" Augustina asked me.

"I don't have a boyfriend," I said. "I'm kind of wrapped up in my job," and began to tell her about Carepath. I described the presents I gave to my project teams at the annual Christmas lunch I had for all my staff. "Just little things—Christmas ornaments, candles, picture frames. To let them know I appreciate the good job they do." Augustina nodded but she didn't seem interested.

David returned and we resumed play. I was vaguely aware of the grandfather clock in the hallway striking nine. Time at the holidays seemed to dip and bend. It could morph into two hours later or twenty years earlier. Augustina won the fifth round and was still ahead after eight. I glanced at my watch and over at Brin, who was stretched out on the sofa under one of the numerous afghans, lost in a book.

Augustina hobbled over to the window and pulled back the drape. "It's snowing pretty hard," she said. "Brinnae, turn on the television so we can see the weather." I joined Brin's mother at the window. The snow had drifted up and around the spirea bushes on the side of Mrs. Anderson's house. I remembered last New Year's Eve with Brin and wished that she and I were alone at her house.

"Did you bring your toothbrush?" Brin's mother asked me.

"It's not something I carry around with me," I said, wondering what she knew and what she suspected.

"Well I've got several new ones if all of you decide to stay over," she said, letting the drapes drop.

"There are six new inches on the ground, Mom," David reported from TV central. "And another six predicted."

"You're welcome to stay," Brin's mother said.

"Thanks," I said. "Brin, what do you want to do?" She had not stirred from the sofa, didn't hear or pretended not to hear her mother's request about the TV.

"What," she said, looking up at me, slightly bewildered. I smiled at her, lost in whatever time-out she was taking from all of us. I glanced toward the hallway, wondering how many bedrooms there were. I looked at David, who repeated the weather situation.

"Your mother's invited us to stay over. Do you want to stay or go?" She thought for a moment. "David?" she said.

"It's fine with me, mom."

"Well then I guess it would be safer to stay."

"Good," Brin's mother said. "David can stay in Marlys' room. Therese, you can stay in Brin's room. Or on the sofa, if you'd rather."

I looked at Brin, who'd already gone back to her book. "David, why don't you show me your aunt and your Mom's rooms?" I asked.

The house was laid out with the living room, dining room and kitchen opening one into another in the front and a hallway leading to the bedrooms in the back. We walked out of the living room toward the beige carpet of the darkened hall. To my left I could see a large bedroom lit by a night light, presumably Mrs. Anderson's. "Does your grandma have her own bathroom?" I asked David.

"Uh huh," he said. "This is Mom's old room," he said, pointing to the nearest doorway. I stood in the entrance and flipped on the overhead light. I didn't expect bunk beds, particularly glossy maple bunk beds with frilly pink floral bedspreads. The bedspread from the top bunk hung down over the lower one, creating a canopied effect. I could almost see a young Brin hiding under the canopy. A nightstand sat next to the beds holding a lamp, an alarm clock and a transistor radio. To my right were the closet and a set of bookshelves, with a full set of Nancy Drew mysteries and the Bobbsey Twins series. Across from the beds was a big maple double dresser with a mirror that ran its full length. The dresser scarf was covered with jewelry boxes and antique dolls.

Brin had told me that after she went to college, her mother restored her room to the way it looked when she was ten. The dolls were arranged in groups, broken up by the jewelry boxes. One group was costumed like prairie girls from a hundred and fifty years ago, in long floral dresses and plain shawls and hats, identical triplets sitting with their backs propped against the mirror. Two stood like ballerinas in formal pink ball gowns, gazing into a world which only dolls could see. Another group included five bridesmaids and a flower girl in blue chiffon, gathered around a veiled Barbie in white satin and tuxedo-clad Ken. To the far left sat a Chatty Cathy with the telltale string to make her talk. Along the front of the dresser were dolls from around the world, their feet hanging over the edge. A big Raggedy Ann and Raggedy Andy completed the tableau. I'd always found dolls depressing, but I liked the Raggedys.

David walked up to the center of the dresser and opened one of the jewelry boxes. It began to play slowly a tune I could not name but recognized from childhood, short and tinkly, repeating itself after four bars. It played twice and then fell silent. David turned the crank underneath and it played again, more briskly, a half dozen times.

Marlys' room had been updated and decorated more neutrally as an all-purpose guest bedroom. It held a double bed covered by an old-fashioned quilt, a nightstand with a lamp and clock radio, and the same dresser and mirror minus the dolls. A toy chest stood in one corner beneath Minnesota Twins and Vikings pennants, next to a rolling cart with a computer. "Nice," I said.

"Yeah," David agreed, seeing only the computer. "It's got Doom on it." He hit a button on the keyboard and sat down to play.

The echo of the music box repeated itself slowly in my ears. Time slowed to a waltz beat.

I returned to the living room. "I'm guessing that the bottom bunk is yours," I said to Brin.

She looked up from her book. I repeated my statement. "Yes," she said. She gave me one of her full-throttle smiles.

"Are you tired?" I asked.

She shrugged. "A little." I sat down on the edge of the sofa, avoiding touching her. I could hear Augustina in the kitchen, putting our hot chocolate mugs in the dishwasher.

"What are you reading?"

"Hans Christian Andersen. I loved this book when I was growing up."

I took the book from her and looked at the table of contents. I remembered the story about the snow queen, who put the sliver of ice in the boy's heart, and the girl with the red shoes who could not stop dancing and danced herself to death. "I remember his stories being, well, not scary exactly. Disconcerting."

"The characters live in worlds of their own," she said.

"Maybe that's what was disconcerting. How unconnected they seemed."

Brin smiled at me, looked to be sure her mother was still in the kitchen, and squeezed my hand. "That's because you're the queen of connectedness."

"Whatever that means," I said.

"You're the kind who doesn't ever let the sun go down on your anger. You want to have everything sorted out."

I shrugged. "Life's too short. I don't thrive on conflict."

She laughed. "I know. You're still such a good girl."

I took the slipper off her foot and began to massage the bottom of her arch. "Good at some things."

She stifled a moan as I pulled each toe apart and rotated my thumb in the crevices. "Good at driving me crazy."

"Why don't you come to bed?"

"Soon. Give me a few minutes with my mother."

"OK."

Mrs. Anderson had laid out towels, washcloths and a toothbrush in a little cardboard box for me in the bathroom. I looked in Brin's closet and found two pair of flannel pajamas. I left one set on the bottom bunk, donned the other and climbed the ladder up to my crow's nest with a Life magazine I found in the bathroom.

I lay in the narrow bed and thought that this was the year of meeting family for each of us. Brin had driven up to Duluth with me to my brother Danny's the day before Christmas Eve. Danny rode a snowplow for the public works department and was seeing a lot of action. My parents flew in from Tucson and were staying there.

Dinner with my family had been cordial. My mother exclaimed over Brin's pictures of David and told stories of her volunteer landscape group decorating Tucson park cacti with red and green chile pepper lights. My father, a retired civil engineer, told Sven and Ole jokes and was charmed when Brin knew some he hadn't heard. Brin and Danny led us on a walk to see the neighborhood Christmas lights. We called Carolyn and spent a long time on the phone laughing with her and Shoney. The evening had gone better than I expected, given the normal pitfalls of families and holidays.

I must have drifted off to sleep. I sat up suddenly at the sound of the door closing behind Brin and banged my head on the railing. Rubbing my head, dazed by the brightness of the overhead light that I hadn't turned off, it took me a minute to realize that Brin was crying. "Brin, what's wrong?"

She sat on the lower bunk sobbing and did not answer. I rose unsteadily to my knees and put my feet on the ladder. I backed down cautiously. Sitting down next to her, I took her hand in mine. She buried her face in my shoulder and we fell back onto the bed. I stroked her hair and listened to her cry. Eventually the sobbing subsided. She was still crying steadily. I knew from experience that she'd talk when she was ready, but I still worried when she cried. I rubbed the back of her head and her neck. I stroked her back, still in its Christmas blouse with the red and green piping at the collar. Brin was big on Christmas outfits; she had at least a week's worth. Now I knew the source.

"I don't know why I let her get to me like this," she finally muttered into my shoulder. I rolled her away slightly so I could look at her, though I could barely make out her expression with the overhanging bedspread blocking the light.

"What did she say?"

Brin took a puff from one inhaler, then the other. She waited sixty seconds and did it again. "How selfish I am. That I was ignoring her, ignoring David. I never get any time to myself. I don't like cards. Why can't I lie on the sofa and read without having to pay for it later?"

"Did you say that to her?"

"Yes."

"How did she respond?"

"That I should have plenty of time to myself when David's with Teddy. That it's rude to come here and read. And that she doesn't understand why my generation is preoccupied with having time to ourselves. It's vastly overrated in her book."

"I suppose she gets plenty of it. Is she trying to tell you she misses you?"

"If she does, she's hiding it well."

I held her for a while, stroking her. I looked at the door, reassuring myself that it was firmly closed, wishing it had a lock. I heard the clock strike midnight. When Brin began to stroke back, it was no longer comfort she had in mind. She unbuttoned my pajama top and began to lick my nipples.

"I'm not sure this is a good idea," I said.

"I want you, Therese," she said, her tongue in my ear. My pajamas were actually men's, I discovered, when she slipped her fingers through the open fly. I spread my legs and put a hand over my mouth. She mounted me and brought me to a slow, rolling orgasm. When my muscles recovered from rag doll limpness, I undressed her slowly and made love to her, trying not to bang my head on the wiry underside of the top bunk.

When I curled around her, spreading my unbuttoned pajama shirt over us, she whispered. "You're the only one that understands me, Therese. I'm so lucky to have you."

"I try, Brin. I may not always understand you, but I love you completely."

"I know. You're my anchor."

Drifting off to sleep, the notion that it would be prudent to crawl back into the top bunk crossed my mind. But I didn't have it in me to be an inch further from Brin than I had to be. I slept heavily until the sound of the door clicking shut woke me up. I opened my eyes slowly. Brin was rolled over against the wall naked, tangled in the bedspread. David would still be asleep. I lay in bed, suddenly wide awake, and listened to the grandfather clock in the hall strike six.

*   *   *

I squirmed in bed for a while, then read the entire Life magazine by flashlight before I finally woke Brin and told her what happened. Brin was much calmer than I expected. "If she's going to interfere with my privacy, that's her problem, not mine."

The atmosphere at breakfast was as cold as the air outside. Augustina put buttermilk pancakes and sausage on the table next to the bowl of oranges, then proceeded to read the newspaper. Breakfast conversation was David reading bits and pieces aloud from the sports section. I drank a cup of coffee, put food on my plate and ate it. I couldn't remember tasting anything. When Augustina went into the kitchen, I palmed an orange and put it in my pocket. Brin took her time eating, conversed with David, asked her mother if she wanted more coffee, queried Augustina about a recent trip to the doctor. Augustina answered all questions "yes," "no" or "he didn't say."

I helped Brin clear the table, then rinsed the plates and put them in the dishwasher. It was a relief to be in the kitchen. I wiped down the counters and stood at the window, watching a pair of cardinals at the feeder. I peeled the orange and ate it two sections at a time. I could hear Brin telling her mother the saga of how she'd had the snowmobile repaired. In some strange way, I realized, Brin was enjoying her mother's silence, was throwing it back at her. Maybe she'd wanted us to get caught.

I tried to slip back through the dining room but Brin stopped me, grabbing my arm, asking if I want more coffee. I moved out of her reach. "No thanks. I'm going to shovel out the car."

Mrs. Anderson stared at me, then said, "At least you know you've done something wrong." I forced myself to meet her gaze. My heart was beating hummingbird fast. I could feel Brin reddening next to me, the air being sucked out of the room.

"Mrs. Anderson," I enunciated, slowly, "I'm sorry if you're upset. But I'm not ashamed of anything I've done." I took a deep breath. Augustina was looking at her daughter, shaking her head. "House rules," she said. I left the dining room as quickly as I could without bolting.

Snow continued to fall softly. I found two good shovels in the garage next to a Republican candidate lawn sign. David came out to help me. He told me his grandmother had a plowing service. I said I was in a hurry to get home. The snow was wet and heavy. It came off the driveway in clumps. I pushed the snow across the long driveway, clearing an escape route the width of my car. "My mom and grandma fight a lot," David volunteered.

"Did they fight when your Dad came here?"

"No," David said. "Grandma liked Dad. But he didn't come very often. Usually it was just me and Mom."

"Your grandma must have been upset when your Dad left."

"Oh yeah. She told Mom that women have to put up with a lot, but that it's the way of the world. Mom told her that she wasn't going to put up with Teddy whoring around."

"You heard her say that?"

"Yeah. I was confused. I thought only women could be whores."

"Either sex can be unfaithful, David. Do you know what that means?"

"Yeah. Being unfaithful is sleeping with someone you're not married to."

"Yes. If you're married, you're not supposed to sleep with someone else."

We shoveled for a while in silence. The wind whistled over the driveway, whirling little eddies of snow across the cleared space.

"You and Mom aren't married, but you sleep together."

"Two women can't get married, David."

"But you said you love Mom."

"I do love your mom. Can't you tell?"

"Yeah. You're nice to her. You make her laugh." He hesitated. "You don't kiss her in front of me."

"I don't want to make you uncomfortable."

"But she kisses me in front of you."

"That's different. You're her son."

"But she loves you, too.

"Yes. She does."

Brin emerged from the house, in down coat, gloves and dress boots, carrying a big garbage bag. "We're leaving. David, go say goodbye to grandma."

"What's in the bag?"

"David's presents."

"What about yours?"

"I left them in my closet. Except I'm wearing the Christmas outfit. I didn't want to put on the one I wore yesterday again."

I stifled a laugh. There was no way she would have left it behind. Somehow Brin would hang onto her version of Christmas. "I feel like I should have washed those pajamas or something."

"I hung them up in my closet. She'll probably burn the sheets." She laughed.

"I'm sorry, Brin."

"Don't be. We would have found something else to fight about."

"I feel like I should go in and say goodbye to her."

"You don't have to. It's up to you."

David came careening out of the garage and began to roll a large snowball. I gathered all my courage into my shoulder blades, walked into the house, wiped my feet and stood in the kitchen entryway. Augustina looked up from the crossword puzzle. "Yes?"

"I came to say goodbye, Mrs. Anderson." I hesitated. "I'm sorry if we've caused you pain."

Augustina pulled herself up by the arms of her chair to her full height and glowered at me. "My daughter was a married woman, a girl from a small town. You took advantage of her when she was vulnerable. You ought to be ashamed."

I felt all the air go out of me. "Mrs. Anderson, you of all people should know that no one can make Brinnae do something she doesn't want to do."

She clenched her cane like she wanted to hit me with it. "You'll burn in hell for this."

"Goodbye, Mrs. Anderson," I said and walked out. I stood outside the garage for a moment, trying to collect myself, feeling the tears well up in my eyes. Of course she blames you, I told myself. She can't believe it of her own daughter. But it didn't help.

Brin switched on the car radio once we reached the highway. We were quiet on the trip home, listening to a public radio recording of Truman Capote reading his story "Christmas Memories." I'd never heard it before, this achingly tender story of a small boy and his aunt, outcasts together in their own family, gathering pecans and their assorted nickels to buy a bottle of whiskey for soaking the Christmas fruitcake. Halfway through, Brin began to sob. I'd wondered when her bravado would give way. I took off my gloves and put my hand over hers. David sat in the back seat and played Tetris on his Gameboy with headphones.

I drove and held Brin's hand until she sighed and curled up against the passenger door to sleep. The snow fell onto the windshield and became liquid crystal, tears blown sideways across the glass for all of the cast-off fruits on the highway.

CHAPTER 13

Therese, 1991-1992

I predicted that the year leading up to Carepath's public offering would be the hardest we'd ever worked.

"It will be fun," Paul said, "because the challenge is clear."

"Every year has been hard and will continue to be hard," Alan retorted.

I spent hours on weekends with the investment banker from our board creating the public offering strategy, building and reviewing the prospectus, undergoing the inspection by the Securities and Exchange Commission of every document, every transaction, every contract, every bonus. I worked late on weeknights to do my day job: going over status reports, coaching my direct reports on team dynamics, figuring out how to stretch our thin staffing a little further. Brin complained that even though I traveled less, I still was never home.

Nate presided over the arguments about the employee stock ownership plan in staff meetings, the development of rules governing stock price, the number and classes of shares which various types of staff would be eligible to buy, the circumstances under which they could be sold when employees left the company. Paul led the public relations effort, the courtship of Wall Street analysts, the breakfast meetings with the advisors to large pension funds, the creation of mythology for the newspapers and regional business magazines, the networking at national trade shows and chamber of commerce meetings.

Alan formally took over the reins from Paul as chief technology guru, selecting which of the competing databases our products would utilize, the technology migration plan for customers who could afford to keep up and for customers who had to make do, the strategy to run the products on operating systems which were evolving even faster than chip capacity. Alan hired and trained a whole group focused solely on Microsoft products: the DOS, Windows 3 series and early beta versions of Windows 95 operating systems as well as the conventions of Word, Excel, Project and and Powerpoint software. He created another group to monitor the international growth of the Internet and early use of the World Wide Web.

We met in Paul's conference room at night for pizza, sharing the day's events and arguing over what they meant. Collectively we lived in a four-dimensional matrix, a river of simultaneous equations, an ocean of exploding technology and hungry sharks.

When Stephanie called on Tuesday to invite me to a ballgame, I declined. "You're disappearing on me, you obsessive creature," she chided.

I sighed. "I know. I'll come back."

One Friday night, after David asked me to take him to the driving range the next day and I told him I had to work, he asked me why I was working weekends so much.

"It's the stage Carepath is at," I said. "It has to grow or die."

"Why?"

"When a small company is growing, you have to build on that growth or your customers will go somewhere else. The public offering will give us money to expand, hire more people, provide more services to our customers."

"I know what Carepath is doing. I've seen the explanation and the list of products on your Web page." He laughed. "You're selling this stuff about how to reduce your stress, exercise more, eat right, do meditation, and you and Mom aren't doing any of it. Especially you— all you do is work."

I sighed. "You're right, David. But I'm thinking that this is temporary.

Once we're through the offering, I can take some time off. I'm thinking about the long-term, all the jobs we're going to create, interesting jobs, work that requires people to think and be creative, not just stand in front of a cash register. The software they're going to build, which is going to help little kids manage their asthma and old people keep track of their Coumadin levels so they can have just enough clotting factor and stay out of the hospital. And I like what I'm doing."

"Mom says you're good at it."

"How about if we go to the driving range one night next week?"

"Which night?"

I pulled the paper copy of my electronic calendar out of my purse. "How about Wednesday?"

"Wednesday I've got soccer practice. How about Thursday?"

"Thursday I've got a meeting. How about Friday?"

"Friday I go to Dad's."

"How about Sunday afternoon after you get home?"

"OK. But you better write it down or you're going to forget."

I laughed and reached for a pen. "OK."

Nate and I became good friends. He invited me to lunch one day to see what I thought of the plan for distributing stock to existing staff and stock options for new employees. After we went through the materials explaining the program to staff, he sat back in his chair and played with an unlit cigarette.

"I suppose next time we should sit in smoking," I said. I wrinkled my nose and grinned.

"No, Terry!" he protested. "It's good for me. Tell me, are you finding any time to have a life?"

"Not much," I said. "Fortunately my partner has a child, so she has lots to occupy herself with." It was the first time I'd referred to Brin as my partner. It felt weird.

"Do you and your partner live together?"

"No. I wish we did," I said. "She's paranoid about her ex-husband. We do have to be careful. She could lose custody of her son. It's complicated."

Nate nodded. "That's got to be hard." He leaned over and said in a conspiratorial half-whisper, "Can you keep a secret?"

Kathy Lewis

"Secret's my middle name," I intoned.

"I've started seeing a woman," he said. "Her name is Sherry."

I sang in a falsetto voice, "Sherry, Sherry baby. Wait a minute, I know a Sherry. Sherry Nederman. She works for 3M in, of all things, one of their software divisions."

"Now you see why it's a secret," Nate said.

"It's a matter of national security," I said. "I'll put secure red telephones in each of our offices. That's the only way I can talk about my girlfriend either."

"My lips are sealed."

"Her name is Brinnae."

"Now there's a common, everyday name," Nate said. "Workplace Romeos and Juliets, next on Geraldo."

"Isn't this where we stick each other with pins and swear our undying loyalty?"

Nate broke his cigarette in half and shook the tobacco onto the bread plate. "We'll make an offering to thank the Great Spirit for our secret lovers." On the way back to the office, he cued up an old Four Seasons tape and we sang along with Frankie Valli at the top of our lungs.

As part of the pitch to Wall Street, Paul beefed up the management structure so that the investors could be convinced that Carepath had depth in management. Alan was promoted to Chief Information Officer. I took him out for a drink to celebrate and asked him about Paul's expectations.

Alan shrugged. "Paul says the CIO's job in a company like ours is to understand the needs of the business for information, manage the executives' expectations about what's possible and kick butt to make it happen. I say that while it's important for me to interact with the other VPs, what he really needs is someone who keeps up with the technology. If he's not going to spring for a Chief Technology Officer, then that someone had better be me."

"We can't afford a Chief Technology Officer, Alan. Our challenge with the offering is to have strong management but not so much of it that overhead is a drag on earnings."

Alan snorted. "You're such a capitalist tool."

"Well, I don't see you donating your stock to widows and orphans. Paul's view is going to be a stretch for you, big guy. Mr. 'I'm in love with technology and the politics of the business side aren't important.'"

He laughed. "That's why you're my translator. You'll tell me when something is critical enough for me to pay attention."

The day we went public was a Friday in February. It was the coldest morning of the year so far, 18 below. Ribbons of exhaust whirled through the intersections like darting fish. Clouds of carbon monoxide billowed above the cars lined up at the freeway entrance. The cold was bone numbing, the kind where cats crawled up into car engines seeking warmth. Where people awoke at three in the morning and fought the temptation to go running through the house shouting the weather report and out into the snow, as if the cold were a magnet that could draw them to their deaths.

I came home late again that night, exhausted from the hoop-la, the press conference, the bottles of champagne in Paul's office, the previous twelve months. I shut off the phone, drew the room-darkening shades and blinds, took a sleeping pill and tumbled into bed in my underwear. I got up at noon the next day and took a shower until the hot water ran out. I boiled water for tea and declared the contents of the refrigerator a failed science project.

The snow fell steadily, vertically. The cold white flakes suspended in mid-air and then hurtled toward the ground. A gust of wind drove the flakes backward, horizontally, slowing their progress until the force of the wind compelled them sideways in a fury of sleet.

I munched on dry cereal and raisins as I read the business section. I checked the NASDAQ index for Crpth and the stock price, the 52-week high and low columns still blank beside it. I stared outside, something I hadn't done in months. The snowflakes nearest the window seemed to fall more slowly. A latticework of vines grew over the window, delicate thorns with a few oval brown leaves still clinging to the stems which arched gracefully upward, climbing beyond my reach. The window was half iced-over in a delicate filigree of individual ice crystals, as if each snowflake, seduced by the warmth of the pane, had flattened itself like winter's fingerprint against the glass.

Gazing at the snowflakes stenciled onto my window by the storm, I realized how much I loved my house. Why didn't I spend more time here? I looked at the dust bunnies on the hardwood floor in the dining room, and resolved, again, to clean the place. Soon, then I'd hire a cleaning service. I checked my answering machine, which held messages from Brin proposing a date, my parents, Danny and Stephanie offering congratulations, my bank increasing my monthly checking account fee unless I went to automatic payroll deposit and automatic mortgage withdrawal, the phone company informing me that service would be shut off if payment wasn't received by tomorrow, college friends I hadn't heard from for fifteen years inquiring about stock, and requests from every charity I'd ever given money to, any magazine I'd ever subscribed to and all of the telephone companies inducing me to switch long-distance carriers.

I fumbled through the pile of mail on the desk, found the phone bill and wrote a check for twice the amount. I left a message for Brin, stuck the check in the mail slot for the carrier to pick up and went back to bed.

The snow had stopped when I woke up. On my way over to Brin's for dinner, it was frontier weather, twenty-five below zero. I picked up barbecued ribs and chicken, craving anything spicy, messy, not white.

"The Indians did not arrive here in winter," I announced. "They came when there were blueberries, a river the color of root beer, a meadow of wild mustard."

"Imagine winter in a teepee," Brin said. "The smoke rising in a thin stream from the fire inside. The woman huddling in the pile of buffalo skins, her newborn suckling at her breast. Her husband tracking the snowshoe hare on foot. Bears dreaming underground, breathing slowed to a trickle."

"Let's hibernate," I said. We climbed in bed and watched a video after dinner, then slept in. We stayed indoors all the next day, staring at white walls, reading, seeking a sunny spot, luxuriating like cats in the light streaming in. Looking out the window at white snow becoming gray, the color of experience made visible, despairing over the short life of pristine innocence. I wondered what would come next but in my exhaustion, my mind could not hold the thought. I channel surfed, restless and unable to concentrate, unwilling to brave the stinging wind of the outer world. Dreaming of a turquoise sea, warmth, sensation. Settling for a glass of burgundy.

The six month stretch after Carepath went public was no less long or exhausting for all of us in management. After the public offering, atop this traveling four-dimensional circus of a would-be global enterprise, came the pressure of the daily stock price in the newspaper, with instant updates on the newly-emerging World Wide Web and in the computerized Wall Street models which could send the street reeling with programmed trading, pressure broadcast hourly on CNN and repeated in the weekly TV and radio finance shows.

In March Paul hired a new finance VP, a woman named Sandy Cimmer, who instituted an intensive process for managing quarterly earnings and their communication. Sandy was a lean size eight who favored plain or herringbone-checked suits in blues and grays with matching pumps. She had collar-length brown hair which she had frosted once a month to hide the rapidly-invading gray. When the weather got warm Sandy started a management group called the Financial Information Team, or FIT, which consisted of Paul, herself, Alan, Nate, five other vice presidents and me.

Since all of the breakfast and lunch slots were taken and the sales leaders were expected to be on the road the first three days of the week, the FIT meeting was held every Thursday night. My Thursday night golf league attendance had been spotty during the public offering. Now I had to give it up completely.

Stephanie was pissed. "You're taking your friends for granted, Therese."

"You think I enjoy sitting in a conference room on a beautiful evening? When you've had some big influx of new patients, I don't see you for months."

"But I take some time back when the hubbub dies down. I don't see you setting any limits."

"Let's play this weekend," I said.

I could hear her shrug over the phone. "You find another pair and we're on."

Sandy's meetings were well organized and I knew that Carepath needed discipline of a sort it had never had in order to compete and thrive as a publicly-traded company. Still, I began to feel as if our whole focus had shifted to quarterly earnings and the price of our stock. And Alan started to erupt in meetings, feeling he couldn't get enough resources or management attention directed to technological innovation.

*　　*　　*

When Nate, Alan and I arrived for the Financial Information Team meeting, the box dinner du jour was oriental chicken salad with snow peas. I stifled a groan when I saw it, since June had ordered the same thing twice this week for lunch meetings. I was already on edge because Brin was presenting. Suzanne, the pharmacy division leader, was on vacation. Brin was pleased that she'd been picked to give the update.

"They should put the menus on the master meeting calendar, so we'd have a chance of some food variety," I said.

Alan smiled sardonically. "You're assuming the secretaries would want to be nice to us in that way. A master calendar might make things worse."

"You're projecting, Alan," said Nate.

"Probably. Which of the four prescribed financial meditation practices are we doing tonight?"

I checked my watch. "Month two of the quarter, week three. The update on next month's product rollouts. Brin said pharmacy and guidelines are up tonight, one on time and one late."

"Let me guess—the formulary is OK, the new diabetes release is late." The pharmacy formulary was a product bought by health maintenance organizations and other managed care plans. Formulary releases were pretty straightforward except when major new drugs hit the market and their promotion screwed up demand forecasts.

I smiled. "You rocket scientist, you."

"And what does Brin say about who's at fault on diabetes?"

"Put on your Kevlar vest. Brin says IT."

Alan groaned. The Information Technology department was often blamed for projects behind schedule by people who didn't understand the intricacies of the hand-offs between a business project leader and the technical designers and programmers. But if Brin said it was IT, Alan knew that his shop was in trouble.

"Where are they hung up?" Nate asked.

"Database redesign." The problem was a more elaborate formulation of the dilemma Jeff described when he wrote the original software. The diabetes program supported a practice guideline on diabetes mellitus, which outlined the decision processes physicians and diabetic patients were expected to follow. The software collected data on blood sugar levels, which patients were supposed to enter, and a whole variety of lab results and clinical findings, which the physicians and nurses were supposed to document. For complex patients of doctors who'd used the software for a few years, the amount of data to be managed was so large it dragged down computer response time for both patients and clinicians. The database redesign involved figuring out which data was used less frequently and could thus be indexed or archived and how to access the archived data efficiently.

Alan grimaced. "Thanks for the warning. Why did I ever agree to be CIO?"

"I know, all you really wanted was to be Chief Technology Officer."

"Where's Brin? Isn't she first on the agenda?" Nate said.

"No doubt pulling the slides out of the copy machine as we speak."

Sandy called the meeting to order and I picked up the pace of my lettuce chewing. I heard a chair squeak behind me and looked over my shoulder to catch a smile from Brin. I'd thrown my coat on the chair to save it for her. She hung the coat on my chair and I felt her fingertips brush my shoulder. We exchanged whispered hellos.

Sandy whipped through her recap of last month's actual revenue and expense results, which were off by about two percent compared to budget. She looked over at me during her third slide and I automatically flashed her my supportive-of-other-women-in-management smile. She was probably the most efficient person I'd ever worked with, but I wondered what motivated that efficiency, how much was personal ambition and how much reflected warmth or caring or idealism, virtues to which Carepath had vocally subscribed during its first eight years of existence.

Sandy introduced the division leaders whose projects were on the agenda tonight, who in turn introduced their project team leaders. The division leaders sat interspersed among the vice presidents at the long oval conference table or behind them in the chairs arranged along the walls in a horseshoe shape. When it was their turn to present, they marched to the overhead projector at the head of the table. I thought of this ritual as the perp walk, the corporate equivalent of Timothy McVeigh in his bright orange jumpsuit being paraded by the federal marshals for the media after the Oklahoma City bombing.

The VPs on the committee could get a pretty good sense of how the session was going to go, based on the slant of the shoulders, the cast of the head and the nature of the glances thrown the division leader's way. The project team leaders, one from the division and one from IT, sat in the chairs against the back wall of the conference room, in case any questions came up which required actual knowledge of the project. Tonight's division leaders represented pharmacy, lab, health promotion and clinical practice guideline projects.

Pharmacy was first on the agenda, based on the leadership theory that advocated celebrating small successes first to get some forward momentum going. Brin and I had talked several times about the perp walk, and she did it well tonight, smiling and making eye contact with each vice president, carrying her broad shoulders high in the two-piece autumnal print dress she wore. She started out a bit softly on the first slide and I pointed my index finger upward to indicate that she should raise the volume. She finished her ten minute presentation on trends in formulary management and the status of the new release, answered three questions herself and deferred another to her project leads, and sat down to a brief round of applause.

"Nice job," Alan said.

"Thanks," she murmured, flushed from presenting.

"You did great," I whispered.

She gave me her biggest smile and I felt it warm me all the way down to my shoes. I winked at her and turned to face front again. Nate smiled at me and winked. I smiled back, took a deep breath and let the tension slide out of my shoulders. She'd practiced the presentation for David and me last night, and had been tense and distracted then.

Brin picked up her box dinner, untouched save for the breadstick, gathered her project leaders and left the conference room. I hoped she'd still be awake when I got to her house.

The general feeling of well being didn't last long. The diabetes project was up next and the questions were pointed, designed to identify and hang blame on someone in the room. Alan's project leader came off as defensive and could not provide an answer to something he should have known. Paul frowned at me from across the table. I saw the flush creep upward on Alan's neck as he attempted to turn attention away from Jim. When the presentation was over, the two of them left the room together.

When Alan returned, his face indicated that his blood pressure had gone up another 20 points. After the meeting ended, we walked out to find our cars in the underground garage. "What's Jim's problem?" I asked.

"He's from the old school, that IT runs these projects for the ignorant users. He can't or won't change his world view to see Shana as his equal, his co-leader on the project."

"Change or die," I said.

"I told him he either gets a new attitude about this or he's gone. Plus it doesn't help that Shana came from Chronicom. Most of them think that IT people are gorillas, who can't speak English or do anything that doesn't involve a keyboard."

Chronicom was our most recent acquisition. I'd spent the better part of six months in Chicago, negotiating in their windowless suite in Evanston or sitting in the Northwest Airlines lounge at O'Hare to close the deal. It had a staff of 300, had been in business ten years longer than we had and the staff resented that Carepath, a smaller competitor, had swallowed them up. "Can you talk to Shana's boss?"

"If I can find out who it is this week."

I started to laugh. "Ain't life grand?" 'Ain't life grand' was the latest saying of Alan's ten year-old daughter, Jill. Jill picked it up from the janitor at her school, the janitor who had become her confidant since Alan's divorce from Marina a year ago.

"You betcha," Alan said, knowing I collected Brin's Scandinavian jargon.

I got into my Honda and watched Alan roar away in his Mazda Miata convertible, the top down though it was dark and the temperature about fifty degrees. As I waited for the garage door to lift itself completely, I stared out into the evening gloom. I could barely see the sliver of new moon under the scudding clouds.

During the twenty-five minute drive to Brin's, I concentrated on slipping the bonds of the day. Waiting in the garage, I'd written three items on the notepad on the dash to call my staff about on the drive in tomorrow. I glanced at my calendar and made a mental note of what I'd say at the two meetings I had to chair in the morning. I left a voicemail for June so she could type the morning agendas. I'd figure out the afternoon meetings on the way in.

I called Stephanie but got her answering machine. "Hi. I miss you, party girl. Hope you're drinking a beer with my name on it." I flipped on the radio and listened to an interview broadcast on the public radio channel with a Wyoming rancher who'd been spending time with a wilderness group tracking wolves via radio collars and was becoming sympathetic to the wolf preservation cause. During the companion piece with the group's female leader, I decided that the rancher was sleeping with her. Still, I enjoyed the group's imitation wolf howling at the end of the piece. All religious conversions should include a ritual howl, I decided, an expression of anguish over the life left behind, the former friends who felt betrayed and of apprehension about what lay ahead.

CHAPTER 14

Brin, November 1992-Winter 1993

I sat in the team meeting, fiddling with a paper clip. It was the same old boring agenda, where we were supposed to start by reciting our accomplishments in order to create a sense of momentum. Maybe if we got enough momentum, we could manage to retch collectively instead of just individually. When Suzanne got to me, I said, "My accomplishment is that Dr. Lapidus didn't walk out of the guidelines meeting. Which he was fully entitled to do, since we've made no progress whatsoever in the past month."

Toni clapped a hand over her mouth to keep from smiling. In the bathroom before the meeting she'd told me that pharmacy was going to start reporting to Therese. Was it too much to expect to have had a heads-up on that at home? Suzanne sighed. "I see that you've segued straight to issues, Brin. Is there anything positive you'd like to report?"

I thought for a minute. "I didn't yell at anybody all last week. How's that for teamwork?"

*   *   *

I walked into my one-on-one meeting with Suzanne fuming, "Suzanne," I said. "I just saw the new org chart. And I didn't get the promotion you and I discussed. I thought for the most part my customers have been happy with my work."

"Brin, the docs love working with you. They respect your intelligence and your commitment to clinical excellence."

"The formulary project went well and came in on time. The problems with the Coumadin project weren't my fault. Why am I being held responsible for those?"

"Brin, I sense that you're becoming defensive."

I groaned internally. I tried to dust off my vocabulary of I language, wondering when I'd last talked to Marlys and if Marlys were still using it. My sense is. I feel that. From my perspective. Whenever I entered the realm of I language at work, I was in trouble.

"OK, I don't feel that the problems with the Coumadin project were my fault. Is that how you want me to say it?"

Suzanne sighed. "Brin, we've talked about this before. You've got a lot of strengths, but you've got to make progress on your teamwork before I can promote you. You handled the formulary project very well, that's why I had you fill in for me at the FIT. But the feedback from IT staff on two of your other projects in the last year is that you order them around, you try to control the decision-making and that you don't respect their contributions. That you get emotional and storm out of meetings. That they're afraid to confront you."

My voice trembled. "No one is going to let me forget an incident that happened over a year ago. And I didn't storm out. I was upset, I left, and when I came back, we went on with the meeting."

"Brin, it's happened more than once. When you blow up, you have to go back to the person after you've calmed down. You have to talk to them about what happened. You need to acknowledge that you lost your temper and give them assurances that you're going to be able to handle that kind of situation better in the future. Otherwise, they can't forget because they didn't see you acknowledge that there was a problem."

I stood up. "It's not my fault if some people can't live up to my standards. These clinical projects need to be perfect, otherwise physicians won't have the confidence to use the software."

"Brin, I want you to distinguish between the clinical credibility of the end product and the human reality that each step of the project will not be perfect. Think about it, ok?" Suzanne stood up.

I grabbed my coat and left the building. I got in my car and drove around for a while, then parked by the river. Sitting in the car, I watched the little ice floes move downstream. It had snowed last night, a wet, heavy snow before the temperature dropped, and the blue spruces were coated with glistening silver. The small aspens and maples along the bank were bent forward with the weight of the ice. Numerous small branches had already cracked off, leaving a trail of gray limbs sprawled across the snow.

The sun came out. I took deep breaths as the interior of the car filled with warmth. I turned off the engine, leaned back against the headrest and drowsed. The warmth was fleeting. The winter sun moved in and out of its swirling cloud cover. I sat motionless until I began to shiver from the cold. I turned on the car engine and started to cry.

When Therese got to the house that night, I could tell she'd heard that I hadn't been promoted. She brought Chinese food in and set it on the table. She kissed me and gave me a single red rose. I put my arms around her and began to cry all over again.

"Maybe I need to look for another job," I said. Therese poured won ton soup into bowls.

"Because you're feeling under-appreciated?"

"It's more than that."

"What else?"

"I feel like I have something to prove. I'm a good project manager. It's Suzanne's problem if she can't see it."

Therese sighed. "Brin, you're bound to be disappointed sometimes in the people you work with. Give yourself a week or two to cool down before you make any decisions." She spooned kung pao chicken onto our plates.

"I'm going to put my resume together."

"It's up to you, Brin."

"You're damn right it's up to me." I hesitated. "What did Alan say about it?"

"Alan didn't say anything. You know he likes you."

"I also know he has to be loyal to his staff."

"Alan said that it must have been a difficult decision for you to hear. Period."

"So he's the one you heard it from."

"Yes. Suzanne doesn't know about us, so she wouldn't know it was news that I'd be interested in."

"But pharmacy reports through you now."

"Yes, as of last week. But that's so new that I haven't started meeting with pharmacy yet. I heard about this from Alan."

People in IT knew that Therese and Alan were friends. They also knew that Therese and I were friends, though I didn't think they knew the nature of the relationship. Probably IT management was just being cautious in making sure that the CIO knew why they didn't want someone in Therese's division to be promoted.

'Is this going to cause problems for you?"

"What?"

"That there are people in IT who don't like me."

"No. Brin, you know it wouldn't make sense for me to get involved in this."

"Because it would be a conflict of interest."

"Yes, first and foremost. And also because I'm not close enough to the situation to make informed judgments."

"And because you're a team player."

"What's that supposed to mean?"

"Just that you wouldn't want to interfere with another team member's decisions."

"Not if I can't add value to the decision." Therese reached across the table and took my hand. "Brin, I don't think any less of you because you didn't get promoted."

I sighed. "It's not easy watching you move up when I'm not going anywhere."

Therese sighed and looked at her soup bowl, as if the dregs contained some kind of answer. "It must be really hard."

I managed a wan smile. "At least you didn't say you understood. And by the way, it would have been really nice to have heard from you that you were taking over my division."

Therese sighed. "You're right. I should have told you." She came over and stood behind me. She put her arms around me and kissed the top of my head.

I felt her struggle with what to say. "You have the right to remain silent."

Therese laughed. "Thanks for Miranda-izing me." She put water on for tea, cleared the table and loaded the dishes into the dishwasher. She brought me a fortune cookie with tea. It read "A pleasant surprise is in store for you."

"Let's go to Italy," I said.

Therese sighed. "We just have to figure out when."

"What about this spring?"

"Why don't you come up with a plan? Then we can talk about it."

I groaned. Therese opened her fortune cookie. It read "A family member will make you proud." She managed to refrain from saying she was proud of me.

I was asked to give a presentation at a national formulary conference and threw my energies into that. Suzanne made sure I knew that she had recommended me for it. Like that made up for the fact that she thought I wasn't management material. But I decided that it wasn't a good time to make a change with Therese being gone so much.

David began to sprout hair on his upper lip and act surly on the rare nights Therese was around. He interrupted her, refused to make eye contact, swore under his breath and on Thanksgiving, slammed the front door in her face. He refused to feed or walk the dog. I yelled at him in private. I tried reasoning with him in a quiet voice. I yelled at him in front of Therese and grounded him for two weeks at a time. Nothing changed. Desperate, I was ready to try anything when a woman in the moms' group recommended family therapy. David and I went first. After a couple of months I asked Therese to join us.

*   *   *

Therese, Winter 1993

Snow lay in dirty hummocks around the parking lot and the trees dripped on me as I made my way into the clinic. The therapist was a man in his thirties named Charlie, with dark hair in tight ringlets and that slightly unshaven look that guaranteed interest from teenagers.

We sat in a circle, David and I across from each other, Brin between us. Charlie asked how I felt about joining them.

"Scared," I replied. "Like it's the biggest poker game of my life."

David snorted.

"What are you thinking, David?"

"She used to know what poker was, before she was a fucking vice-president."

"Do you miss your weekly card game?" Charlie asked me.

"Yes," I said. "I had a lot of fun with David then. He doesn't seem to want to play anymore."

David snorted again. "Got better things to do than to hang out at dyke heights on Friday nights."

Brin's lower lip trembled off and on during the session, but she didn't cry. David alternated between silent and hostile, and I between angry and guilty. Charlie refereed with the fluid grace of a soccer player, moving with whoever had the ball and periodically inviting Brin into the fray.

The three of us went to therapy for three months, until we established that David didn't have to like me but he had to respect his mother's and my relationship. I learned the importance of constancy to children, even teenagers, and reworked my schedule to have Thursday and Friday nights at Brin's house. Brin struggled the most, with guilt over the cards she'd dealt David, and with reshaping her expectations of who she was and the life she was supposed to lead. She and I went there once without David, where I admitted how frustrated I was that we weren't living together after being lovers for three years. Brin continued to see Charlie by herself for a while, which pleased and scared me at the same time. I thought it scared David, too, though neither of us admitted it.

CHAPTER 15

Brin, Spring, 1993

The national Carepath customer conference was in Cleveland this year. I went to cover the sales booth for three days. I'd been wondering aloud to Charlie about whether I was really a lesbian or if I were attracted to Therese because of the person Therese is.

After unpacking my garment bag, I logged onto e-mail, hoping for a note from David. It was too late to call him and I didn't want to talk to Teddy. I still got e-mail from Teddy sometimes, which I thought was pretty weird. David said he'd turned into a web crawler. Teddy put me on a distribution list with his brothers. The last time it was sick Waco jokes and a clip of biographical essays written by high school seniors. Beethoven wrote music. Because he was deaf he wrote really loud music. And so on. That time I sent him a joke back with no note. How many therapists does it take to change a light bulb? Only one, but the light bulb has to really want to change.

David used to send me e-mail while he did his homework. I'd find it that night if I logged on or see it first thing in the morning. I'd write back immediately and sign it Surfer Mom. He liked that. I scrolled through the list of 15 messages, scanning who they were from. Nothing from David, but one from Therese. My spirits started to lift. I opened the message, saw it was a memo to everyone in her division and closed e-mail without reading it. I'd forgotten that Therese had stopped sending e-mail love notes when some court ruled that employees had no right of privacy when they e-mailed from work. "So what," I'd challenged her. "So you're going to let corporate law control your every move?"

Therese laughed. "You're the paranoid one. I thought you'd agree."

I watched a cop show, the news and David Letterman. I was tired but didn't think I could sleep. I'd been through all of the relaxation tricks in the business travel book Therese gave me to make being away from home easier. I'd taken my pillowcase with me and slipped it onto the hotel pillow. I'd packed a swimsuit, a favorite candle and my gardenia bath oil. I'd put a framed picture of David next to the alarm clock. There was no way around it—travel sucked. I sighed and rang the desk for a wake-up call in case I overslept my alarm.

I worked the conference all day, running for brief bathroom breaks and asking a woman from a booth with two salespeople to bring me a hot dog at lunch. When I got back to my room, I ordered room service and took a shower. I tipped the bellhop and ate my hot turkey club with French fries. The sandwich was greasy and the fries mealy. Lonely and deprived is a bad combination. I decided I couldn't face another night in front of the TV.

I called the front desk and asked for a cab with a woman driver. I slipped into black jeans and a turtleneck and asked the cab driver to take me to a women's bar.

The bar was called The Women's Room. I ordered a scotch and water and talked to the bartender, until a woman came in and sat down at the bar, one empty seat between us. Her name was Ruth. She was tall and dark, with thick, graying black hair. She was dressed all in black. She said she was a potter and made her money as a massage therapist.

"I divorced my husband," I said. "It will be four years in June since we split. He cheated on me and I threw him out."

"Good for you," Ruth said.

"Yeah." I thought. "I guess I'm over him. I just worry that he'll make trouble for me with my son."

"You have to be careful," Ruth said. "The courts don't understand."

"You get it," I said. "I wish my girlfriend did."

Ruth told me about her break-up with a woman who'd since moved to Israel.

"I'm lucky," I said. "Therese is the sun on the pyramids. She is steady. She is sexy. She is kind to my son."

"She sounds ideal," Ruth said.

We had another drink. Ruth asked me to dance. She was lithe and gripped my hands with strong fingers. I followed her lead, moving through a country rock song. I ordered another round, scotch for myself, Merlot for Ruth.

Stirring my drink, I said, "The problem is, Therese is letting work run her life. I used to wrap myself up in work but I learned the hard way."

Ruth nodded. "If you don't follow their script, you don't go anywhere."

"I work hard when I'm there but I don't stay late any more and I don't bring it home."

Ruth went up to the bar and brought back a basket of popcorn. She looked me in the eye. "It seems like something else is bothering you about Therese."

I froze, then nodded.

"Are you afraid of her in some way?"

I started to cry. Ruth led me back out to the square of parquet floor. She cradled me in her arms during a ballad.

It was raw and windy outside when we left the club. Ruth took me home and into the room where she gave massages. Ruth left while I stripped, lay face down on the table and pulled a sheet over myself. She started with my shoulders, kneading the muscles down my back, knitting a column of air along my spine. She warmed the avocado oil in her hands and pressed the circle of her thumb and fingers into my buttocks. She wrapped one hand around my Achilles tendon and drew long, quivering arrows out of my arches.

I thought I could leave until Ruth touched my feet. When Ruth signaled me to turn over, I pulled her down on top of me. I pressed Ruth's hands onto my breasts and kissed her. Ruth led me into the bedroom and lifted the quilt from the bed.

I wrapped myself in the sheet, and after Ruth undressed, I drew it around the two of us. As we fell in slow motion onto Ruth's bed, I pulled the sheet around us tight as a mummy.

*   *   *

I moped for days afterward. Therese had taken a board member to a conference in Orlando but she noticed it on the phone. "What's wrong, Brin?"

"I'm depressed."

"Why?"

"Do I have to have a reason? I'm overwhelmed."

Therese changed the subject, proposing again that I come with her to a sales meeting in New Orleans the following month. "I'll have to see if Teddy will take David. It's not his week."

"Will you check with him?"

"If you want me to."

"Goddamn it, Brin, if I didn't want you to, why would I keep bringing it up?"

"You don't have to yell at me!" I started to cry.

"Brin, you're impossible."

"I'm sorry."

"Send me an e-mail when you feel more like yourself. Please?"

"OK." I didn't tell Therese I loved her before she hung up. I felt evil and gleeful and scared.

The next day I told Charlie about my encounter with Ruth. He asked what it meant to me.

"I enjoyed having sex with her. It was very disconcerting." I had fled Ruth's house in a panic when I awoke. I'd walked with a splitting headache to an all-night gas station and took a cab back to the hotel.

"Did it change the way you think about yourself?"

"Yes. I'd been thinking I was bisexual. Now I think I'm really a lesbian." I smiled at Charlie. Lately I'd been very glad that I had a male therapist and felt on the verge of flirting with him. One of the books I was reading said that it wasn't unusual for a woman experimenting with a woman to need to demonstrate that she could still attract men. The book was silent on the subject of needing to demonstrate one's attractiveness to another woman.

"What does being a lesbian mean to you?"

"It means I can't go back to the life I used to have. It means my life and David's life will both be harder."

"Do you want to go back?"

"I don't know."

"What's good about the life you have now?"

"That Therese loves me. Until she finds out what I've done." I began to cry.

"Do you feel bad because you slept with Ruth or because you enjoyed it?

"Both."

"What would it have meant if you hadn't enjoyed your sexual experience with her?"

"I shouldn't have enjoyed it if I really loved Therese."

"Do you want to push Therese away from you?"

"Maybe."

"Why?"

I gave Charlie credit, he didn't let me get by with much. "Because I can't decide whether to stay with her. Whether to go to the next level."

On the drive home along the freeway, orange road markers narrowed traffic to one lane, bumper to bumper. Above me on the overpass were sun-bronzed men in dirty jeans, white t-shirts and yellow hard hats. Two of them operated jackhammers, their bodies shaking with the force of the tool they tried to control. The mint green siding of the bridge had been removed. I saw the skeleton of the bridge, the slats nailed together with spaces in between, the gaps underneath the structure I took for granted every day. Suddenly I was falling through the spaces in the bridge. Dropping fast through overwhelming vertigo and nausea. The car behind me started honking. I tried to lift my foot from the brake. I crawled three feet forward to brake again behind the next car. The world was so flimsy.

I told Therese that I couldn't go to New Orleans because of a pharmacy formulary deadline. I knew that Therese wanted to romance me. I couldn't face it. It was more than sex with Therese. She was my soulmate. Therese stopped and started the music that played in my head. I felt absurdly proud, watching Therese give a presentation at work or playing David at some software battle game. I liked the way Therese grew quiet when I flared up, worried and entranced by the sudden gusts of my feelings. I was still overcome when Therese looked at me from across a conference room. When Therese touched me.

"Are you frightened?" Charlie asked.

"Yes," I replied. "What happens when she no longer needs me?"

*   *   *

Therese was whining about a company named Chronicom. What could they really bring in terms of earnings? Would there truly be synergy between their product line and ours?

"Oh, for Christ's sake, Therese," I snarled. "Do you think anybody cares? Carepath is a growing, stumbling mid-sized collection of mental midgets. Chronicom is a slightly larger, fumbling, inept assortment of middle-class robots. So what!"

"What was that old Bogart line?" Therese asked. "Our troubles don't amount to a hill of beans in this crazy world."

"Exactly!" I said. "The plot sickens. One life to live, one more company to buy. The young and the restless meet the old and the calcified."

Therese smiled. "So, should we clean the pantry? Haul the cans over to the food shelf to restore our perspective?"

"Who's this we, white woman?" I retorted. "Go to the food shelf. Take Christie for a walk. Go through the pile of bills I keep asking you to look at. Sit down with me and look for a Tuscan farmhouse for this trip we're allegedly going to take."

Therese rolled her eyes. "But whatever I do, I should just shut up about it."

"Thank God you're brighter than you look!"

CHAPTER 16

Therese, Summer, 1993

En route to Kansas City, I observed nightfall from the plane: a band of white gold at the horizon, the shore which night approached. The blue sky streaked with navy, the land black beneath it.

The light was fading, the border between sky and land obliterating, melting into a black pool. Above the clouds, a block of sky blue; above the plane, a planet winking in the dark sky.

I lay in bed in my hotel room, the ruins of dinner on a tray waiting to be carted to the door. I worried whether Brin and I were going to last. She went from abstracted and gloomy to snapping at David and me, from screaming fits to not wanting to let me out of her sight. She talked continually about coming out at work and finally came out to Suzanne, which was a big step.

"I'm proud of you, Brin," I said. "Did you say anything about me?"

"Yes," she said. "I told her I was in love with you and that you were the best thing that ever happened to me."

I felt pain begin to wrap itself around the back of my skull. "Brin, I thought we were going to have a discussion in advance about anyone at Carepath we wanted to tell about our relationship."

"We talked about it a few months ago. I told you someday I wanted to come out to Suzanne. That it would be an important step for me."

"Coming out is one thing. Telling her about me when I'm her boss is totally different. We had that conversation before your division started reporting to me."

"Coming out suggests that there's a relationship, and any sensitive person would ask about the person you're involved with. I can't do anything right as far as you're concerned. I thought you wanted me to be more out. Now you're mad at me."

"It's not fair to have Suzanne supervising you and reporting to me."

"Suzanne's been reporting to you for, I don't know, eight or nine months? And all of a sudden it's not fair?"

I grimaced. It was on my list of difficult things I hadn't gotten around to yet. Somehow I'd rationalized it that if she didn't know about Brin it would be OK that I was her boss. "Did you ask her to keep it to herself?"

"No," Brin replied. "I think you should tell all the senior management about us."

"Goddamn it, it's up to me who to tell and who not to tell," I said. Alan and Nate knew, but I had not wanted to disclose this information to Sandy. I hadn't wanted to tell Paul either but now I was going to have to. "I want you to call Suzanne tonight and ask her not to say anything." Suzanne was discreet and would realize that this information fed to the rumor mill could be a bombshell. It was probably not all over the office, and the necessity to keep news of our relationship confidential had to be reinforced. I kept after Brin until three days later she left Suzanne a voicemail about it.

The next week I called Suzanne into my office. "I understand Brin talked to you about our relationship."

Suzanne smiled. "It's nice to see her so excited."

"About something positive, you mean," I said.

Suzanne laughed.

"I want to acknowledge that you could feel like you were in an awkward situation," I said. "Reporting to me and having Brin report to you."

"I thought about it," Suzanne said. "But Brin said that the two of you have been involved for four years. I thought back to all of the ups and downs she and I have had just since you've been my boss. I couldn't think of one where you interfered in any way. The times I sought your advice about her you seemed very fair."

"That's good to hear," I said. "I've decided that I need to let Paul know that there's a potential conflict of interest here."

"Therese, I like reporting to you," Suzanne said. "You're the most supportive boss I've ever had. I don't want Paul to change my reporting relationship." She looked around and lowered her voice. "I don't want to wind up reporting to Sandy, for instance."

I stood up and deposited my dinner tray outside my door. I called Paul's secretary, Dorothy, and left her a voicemail to put me on his schedule when I got back to town.

*   *   *

Sitting outside Paul's office I felt as if I were about to go to confession. Forgive me, father, for I have sinned. I made copies of David's school papers on the company copying machine. I carried company pens home in my pocket and forgot to bring them back. I'm sleeping with one of my co-workers.

Dorothy looked up from her ringing phone. "It will be about five minutes, Therese. He has to take two phone calls."

I nodded. "Thanks."

Nate came out of Paul's office and stopped to chat. "So, are you bringing him good news or bad news?" he asked.

"Are you telling me he's in a bad mood?" I replied.

"When have I ever brought him bad news? Of course he's on top of the world when I walk out of his office."

"Or you'd be crawling out of his office," I smiled. "So, have you and Sherry set a date yet?" Nate and Sherry had announced their engagement in the spring.

"September," he said. "My wild days of bachelorhood are slipping away."

I groaned. "I don't even want to imagine your stag party. Cigar city!"

"Gotta go, Terry," Nate said. "There's outdated software inventory to be moved."

"Go and Godspeed."

Ten minutes later Paul came out to get me himself. "Go on in, Therese. My next stop is the men's room."

I walked into his conference room, the outer sanctuary, the chairs neatly pushed in around the long table. The white board wore the red marker remains of yesterday's three-hour strategic planning meeting, words scrawled in a four-column matrix: Strengths, Weaknesses, Opportunities and Threats. Dorothy would be in soon with her laptop to type up the notes if she hadn't already.

Deep cleansing breath, I said to myself. It was Stephanie's line before she tried to sink a 25-foot putt. Except it didn't really matter if she made it or not. I tried to think of an analogy for what I was about to tell Paul. The closest I could come was calling your parents a month after you got your license to tell them that you'd been arrested for drunk driving and you totaled the car. But Paul wasn't my father and I hadn't done anything wrong. I was annoyed by my fear. And I was afraid to think about what Paul was going to say.

I continued into Paul's inner office, which held his rolling leather chair and cherrywood desk, a matching credenza behind it stacked with neat piles. A framed picture of his wife and their two kids sat atop a bank of files to the left of Paul's desk, next to two softball trophies Carepath won before we went public, when there was time to field a co-ed company softball team.

I stopped briefly at his bookshelf to see what he was reading: a book entitled *Selling the Intangible*, Peter Drucker's last three management books, books on quality improvement and finance and a biography of Jack Welch, chairman of General Electric. To the right of Paul's desk was a sofa and chair arranged in an L-shape with a coffee table in front of the sofa. A lucite-encased clock, all of its workings visible, sat on the coffee table, next to the latest issues of *Fortune* and *Wired* magazines. I decided we'd be in here rather than in the conference room.

"Read any good books lately?" Paul asked, entering his office through the door behind his desk, the back entrance that every corporate CEO required should they need to make an unseen escape from the media, angry shareholders or a lunatic with a gun.

"Andrew Young's *An Easy Burden*. War stories from the civil rights days, all the jockeying of King's lieutenants trying to get his attention. I can't believe how young they were to have the eyes of the whole country on them. King was only 34 years old when he gave the "I Have A Dream" speech."

"Andrew Young is a smart guy," Paul said. "He made Atlanta the business capital of the South."

I gestured toward the shelf. "You have all the current stuff, except no *Internet for Dummies*."

We had a running joke about the "Dummies" books. We wished we'd been smart enough to have come up with the concept in a world where so many of us felt stupid because we couldn't keep up, despite our long hours, our dayrunners and car phones.

Paul waved me toward a chair. "What's up? This meeting had no title on my schedule."

"Let me see if I can find the sound bite," I said. "How about VP of Strategic Contracts Tells CEO She's Fallen In Love With Employee?"

"What?" he said. "When you say it like that I see that movie with Michael Douglas where his supervisor is rubbing up against him. Demi Moore? I get it mixed up with the one where Glenn Close is trying to kill him."

"Full Disclosure," I said. "I never saw it. Or "Fatal Attraction." They haven't made the one about the lesbians in the workplace yet."

"Don't tell me she works for you," Paul said.

"There's a layer in between," I responded.

"Aw Jesus, Therese," Paul said. "Didn't we just go through this with that crazy woman you fired?" He looked at me and stopped. He tried for a smile. "You're my good girl," he said. "I just wasn't expecting anything like this from you."

I felt my face getting red. "Anything like what, Paul? You're jumping to conclusions. There is no lawsuit, no put-upon supervisor in between." I took a deep breath and reported my conversation with Suzanne as close to verbatim as I could, leaving out the part about her not wanting to report to Sandy. "I'm trying to be responsible and proactive and all that good stuff. You know, does Nick need to put a letter in my file or something documenting my conversation with Suzanne. And I am not your good girl. You could at least ask me if I'm happy, damn it." My voice cracked and I turned my head to fight back tears.

"That was a really stupid thing for me to say. I didn't mean it the way it came out. I meant you're my model employee: smart, always thinking ahead, giving a hundred and fifty percent."

"Always thinking ahead," I repeated. "Except this time."

He reached for a box of Kleenex on his desk and set it on the coffee table in front of me. "Who is she, Therese?"

"Her name is Brinnae Anderson. You've met her." I blew my nose.

"She's blonde, right? Pretty. I thought she was married."

"She was. Her husband took up with another woman and she threw him out."

"And she was lucky enough to find you."

I forced a smile. "Flattery may get you somewhere. This is not a casual affair. We've been together for almost four years."

"I'm glad you're happy."

"So what am I supposed to do? As a model vice president with feet of clay?"

"Damned if I know. I guess it's good you told me. I'll have to talk to Nick."

"I figured that."

Paul sighed and slumped back against the sofa pillows. "So, who all knows about your relationship?" The CEO managing another crisis, sizing up the extent of the damage.

"Besides you, there's Alan, Nate, Suzanne and June. As far as I know, that's it."

"I don't think she can stay in your division, Therese."

"Isn't that part of what you're asking Nick?"

"Yes. But even if he says it's legal, how's it going to look if word gets out? People will accuse you of playing favorites. Your credibility will be shot."

"So, you're saying she transfers out of pharmacy or pharmacy reports somewhere else. Or"—I take a deep breath. "One of us leaves Carepath."

"Not you," Paul said.

"She's a great analyst, Paul. She shouldn't have to go anywhere."

"She's not you, Therese. I'm not saying it's fair. And I'm not saying she has to leave." He sat up straight and looked me in the eye. "I'd like to take your hand or put my hand on your shoulder or all the gestures that used to be allowed between people like us to show that we care about each other. But I can't do that in today's world. And neither can you, with the people that work for you."

"Arm pats," I said. "A light tap on the upper arm is allowed. You must have missed that seminar."

Paul reached over and gently flicked his thumb against the arm of my suit jacket. "I don't know how anybody's supposed to fall in love anymore," he said. "All we do is work. So that kind of narrows it down to co-workers and clients."

"Hell, if we can't hire people away from clients I don't suppose we ought to be falling in love with them," I said. "Excluding Nate, of course."

"Good point," he said. And then he was the CEO again. "Let me talk to Nick and see what he says. I'm just trying to give it to you straight. Prepare you for the worst if it comes to that."

I nodded, spent. "I know."

"You're the best, Therese. Don't think about going anywhere else."

"Thanks," I said and left his office quickly, heading for the nearest bathroom.

CHAPTER 17

Therese, July, 1993

Back in Kansas City again, I fell asleep with the tray still sitting on the other half of the bed. I sat bolt upright at 3:13 AM, wide awake, my brain churning with thoughts of Brin intermixed with T1 lines and the right number of levels to have in your voicemail system. I got up and put on my swimsuit. When I was on the road and couldn't sleep, I'd taken to swimming in the hotel pool. Technically the pool was closed but usually my room card key let me into the fitness club.

Nick had had me do two memos to file, documenting my conversations with Suzanne and with Paul. He agreed with Paul's assessment of the situation: Brin had to leave or transfer to another division. I'd objected to the idea of her transferring.

"For God's sake, Nick, she's a pharmacist. That's where she can add the most value."

"Well, she could work in Sales. I bet Nate would hire her."

"Well, she does sales support now. But it's not what she really likes."

"Paul wants you to have a chance to straighten pharmacy out. That group needs to be more productive and meet its deadlines. You're the one to turn it around, Therese."

And while Nick had first stated that Brin had to leave or transfer, every remark after that said she had to leave. "Look at Bill Agee and Mary Cunningham," Nick said at dinner yesterday, referring to the first well-publicized case of a CEO falling in love with an employee in the

1980's. "They got married and she left Bendix. He was the CEO, it was a heterosexual relationship and she still had to leave if Agee was going to have a shred of credibility left. Eventually someone who doesn't like a decision you make will go public with it. Imagine the outcry with a lesbian relationship. Therese, you could be written up in every newspaper in the country and savaged on every talk radio and crybaby daytime TV interview show there is. I don't think you want to go there."

"Nick, you have made your point. Quit trying to scare me with media bullshit. You are a walking department of redundancy department. Do not bring this subject up with me again unless I ask you to."

He shrugged and put his credit card on the table. We sat in silence while the waiter returned with his receipt. We did not say goodnight.

I stuck my card key in the lock, pushed the door open and flipped on the lights in the pool. The light gleamed off the surfaces of the chrome and black stair climbers and treadmills. The surrounding mirrors reflected the room's vast emptiness. I tossed my towel on a chaise lounge and slipped into the shallow end. I adjusted my tiny goggles and, without a bathing cap, felt my hair wave in the water on the first plunge below.

I told myself that having the courage to do the right thing and talk to Paul was a milestone in my own coming-out process. That I had acted ethically despite the near-certainty that either Brin or I would have to leave Carepath. But I couldn't shake the dread of having to talk to Brin. I kept picturing her outraged face, tears welling up in her eyes as yet another layer of innocence was shredded, another fear about the unfairness of lesbian life was confirmed. Another case of corporate rules taking precedence over human feelings. What happened if I defied Paul and Nick and did nothing? Would they fire me?

I glided through the green water, doing two laps of crawl for every one of breaststroke, the rhythmic splash of the water echoing off the tile. I tried to imagine starting the conversation with Brin. I couldn't get past the first sentence. After thirty laps I floated on my back, aimless as a lily pad, until my eyes glazed over and sleep was moments away. I climbed out, toweled briefly and propped my dripping self against the side of the elevator until it stopped at my floor.

Brin, July 1993

I went to Cleveland again, this time volunteering to train the pharmacy staff at a new hospital client. Ruth and I were out on her screened-in porch, eating pita bread and hummus with fresh vegetables and drinking wine. I edged the chaise lounge closer to Ruth and took her hand. It was twilight and the katydids were singing. A warm breeze blew through the windows. A small fountain trickled water over rocks in the midst of a large circular planter: a Norfolk pine, a blooming hibiscus, an asparagus fern and two palms. I felt safe in some tropical world, a vacation from life.

"You're quiet tonight," Ruth observed.

"I'm enjoying the tranquility," I said. I loved the humidity. I hadn't had to use my inhalers at all.

"How did you come to discover that you were interested in women after all those years of being married?"

"At first I thought it was just that I was lonely and that Therese was so kind to me, so insightful. I thought I was experimenting. I didn't expect to fall in love with her. I didn't want to fall in love with her."

"Why not?"

"I never conceived of myself as a lesbian. Teddy and I had a passionate sexual relationship. For a while."

"Passion has a short half-life," Ruth observed.

"And I've been so afraid of losing David."

"Even though you know that this happens to women all the time and that in most cases, they hang on to their kids. For the same reasons mothers always hang on to their kids."

"Maybe I've been focusing too much on the stories where they don't." I picked up Ruth's hand and examined it, traced the life line in the center of her palm. "Are you saying I should stay with Therese?"

"I'm not making any judgments about that."

"You're kind to me, Ruth."

"I'm drawn to you, Brinnae. I'm going to enjoy your company whenever you're here."

"Can we make love right here?" I said.

"Wherever you like."

I took the padding from the lounges and placed them next to each other, close to the fountain. I undressed Ruth slowly, caressing her melon-shaped breasts, moving over her body, letting passion engulf us both.

Afterward, Ruth held me in the dark. "I have a theory about women who come out after some heterosexual experiences. They need to re-enact their sexual adolescence and experiment, confirm their new choice."

Ruth had given me another kindness. "That makes sense," I said. I should be able to sleep with other women, to learn what I like, what I need to know. My feelings for Ruth were deepening. Why limit myself to Therese? We went upstairs to Ruth's bed and made love again.

CHAPTER 18

Therese, August, 1993

Flying home from Kansas City on Friday, approaching from the south, along the river. The glare of the sun on the river produced vapor. The river was a path of smoking ice.

Below was farmland, in neat rectangles, acres and hectares. Inlets of trees like patches of dark green mold. The valleys were filled with fog escaping from the sun. The hills were boulders emerging from the sea of fog. The plane was following the Mississippi, its gray eminence coursing around the swell of Lake Pepin.

A layer of gauzy clouds floated by, temporary perforations, a moving bandage. Why did I feel freer in the air?

Looking down at the freeways, as clogged from the air as they were from the ground, I decided that I couldn't put things off any longer. I'd talk to Brin this weekend about my conversations with Paul and Nick. I picked up the paper and read an analysis piece in *USA Today* stating that Colorado's Proposition 2, explicitly banning equal rights in housing and employment for gays and lesbians, was expected to become a national movement. I groaned and shoved the newspaper into the seatback pocket in front of me. The woman sitting next to me gave me a look that said she didn't want to be that close to anyone who couldn't read the newspaper calmly on a plane.

Brin had read the same article and was still apoplectic 48 hours later, after we'd spent the afternoon working out and going to a movie.

"We ought to move to Scandinavia or somewhere else civilized. The Republicans won't rest until they put you and David and me in a concentration camp!"

"Minnesota state law prohibits discrimination on the basis of sexual orientation, so we're not at legal risk. It's upsetting, but you're making more of it than it is."

Brin stood at the stove, pouring a bottle of spaghetti sauce into a pan to heat, and regarded me with a condescending look. "You're a wimp, Therese."

"I'm a wimp?"

'You're willing to accept whatever crumbs you're thrown when you should be demanding higher standards."

I started to laugh. "Brin Anderson, the great defender of gay and lesbian rights. You can't even decide whether to live with me or not!"

"You think you're the goddamned authority on everything, whether it's Internet commerce, gay and lesbian rights or the best way to cook a turkey. Maybe I don't want to live with somebody who will never acknowledge that I can win an argument."

I listened to David's door slam upstairs. He'd been doing that a lot lately. "You're worse than David. At least he can blame his mood swings on hormones. What's your excuse?"

"I'd rather have the passion of adolescence than pretend like I have the answers to everything."

I got up from the chair where I'd been slicing mushrooms for salad.

"Go ahead and leave. It's what you do every time you can't get your own way."

Christie, who'd been lying peacefully under my chair, began to whimper.

I sat back down. "Just what the hell is that supposed to mean?"

"Exactly what I said."

"And just what am I supposed to stick around for? A woman I've loved for four years in almost total secrecy, who when I beg her to live with me, brings up the fact that her loutish ex-husband left her for another woman. Five years ago. And then calls me a wimp because I'm not marching in the streets for gay marriage."

Brin was crying now. Christie began to howl along with her. "It's more complicated than that and you know it. I have David to think about. And I don't want to be a wife again."

"What's wrong with being a wife if you're married to the right person?" I shouted.

"Being a wife means being subservient. You have the high-powered career. I have the child. I want to have something that's mine and know what it is." She stopped stirring the spaghetti sauce. "Just leave me alone," she said. She went upstairs.

I put a kettle of water on the stove to boil for the pasta and peeled and sliced an avocado. Cradling Christie in my lap, I sat in the big chair in the family room and stroked her. I reflected on the saying, the personal is the political. I decided that what it really meant was that the political was a big stick to be used in personal relationships. What I couldn't figure out was which way Brin was trying to go. Her behavior suggested that she couldn't decide either. So why was I the one always raising the flag for our relationship, to expand it and make our commitment more real?

I'd been trying to work myself up all weekend to reporting the conversations with Paul and Nick. I alternately snuggled Christie and massaged my temples, the back of my head and my neck. Brin complained that I spent more time with Nick than anyone else. I told her he was an empire builder, but that he was very good. More than once she'd said she was glad that Paul didn't hire a woman attorney.

Beyond my tension headache and my fear of relating my news, I felt out of touch and uneasy. I couldn't get to the bottom of whatever was troubling her. Did she somehow know already what I had to tell her? Was she reacting viscerally to my discomfort before even knowing what it was? Brin often knew that I was upset about something before I knew it myself, which was disconcerting and inevitably put me on the defensive.

I fed Christie, put dinner on the table and called upstairs. David came down, Brin didn't. I asked David what he'd done today.

"Nothing," he said. We ate for a few moments in silence. "How was the movie?" he asked.

"Fine."

"So good you and Mom had to fight. Again."

I shook my head. "I'm sorry, David. I wish I knew why we weren't getting along."

He laughed. "You mean, besides the fact that you're never here?"

"Maybe it's better that I'm not around much. I don't seem to be very welcome when I am."

"Mom's getting ready to go to Cleveland tomorrow. She gets uptight when she goes to Cleveland."

"Why is that?"

"I don't know. When I told her that, she said I was imagining things."

He helped me clear the dishes, then said he was going to hang at the coffee place at the strip mall. I stored the leftovers, cleaned the kitchen and picked up the downstairs. I walked Christie up and down the cul-de-sacs, trying to appreciate the beauty of late summer. The zinnias stood tall, their pinks and reds slightly sun-bleached like t-shirts washed too many times. Bumblebees buzzed in and around the sunflowers that grew in the border between the sidewalk and the pond. I left Christie in the kitchen, and recycled the newspapers from the last week and watered the plants while watching the last half of "60 Minutes."

When I went upstairs and knocked on Brin's door, she was hanging clothes in her garment bag. "Where are you headed?" I asked.

"Cleveland. I've got an early flight."

"There's something I need to talk to you about."

She regarded me warily. "What?"

"After you told Suzanne about us, I decided I needed to talk to Paul. I felt it was a conflict of interest to have Suzanne report to me and supervise you."

"So? It's good that you told him."

I sighed and sat down heavily on the bed. "I can't have you in the same division as me. It's a conflict of interest."

Brin's eyes got very large. "What are you saying, Therese?"

"Either you or I are going to have to leave Carepath. Or at the very least, you'd have to transfer out of pharmacy."

Her tone got icy. "Let's see if I understand this. My boss's boss, who also happens to be my lover, is firing me."

"Brin, that's not what I said!"

"Well, I don't see you nobly offering to resign your post. Do I?"
I remained silent.

"Well that tells me everything I need to know."

"What's that supposed to mean?"

"You're putting your job above our relationship. I don't know why
I didn't see this before. Your job has always been more important than
our relationship."

I looked at her, incredulous. "How long are you gone?"

"All week." She hung a pair of black pants next to her dresses.
"Where are you going to be?"

"Here."

She put shoes into their individual compartments. "It figures."

"Will David be home? Do you want me to stay here with him?"

"I never know where you'll be, so he'll be with Teddy."

I sighed. "What's in Cleveland?"

"The regional show."

"I thought the regional shows didn't start until Wednesday."

"I have to set up. And, if you must know, I'm taking a day of vacation."

I sat on the edge of the bed, uncomprehending. "Vacation? In
Cleveland?"

"I have a friend there."

I sat very still, the fear gathering in my stomach. "Brin, are you
seeing someone else?"

"I guess you could call it that."

"And what would you call it?"

"Trying to figure out if I'm really a lesbian."

I wrapped my arms around myself, trying to ward off the next blow.
"So you're sleeping with her. Whoever she is."

"Her name is Ruth."

I didn't want her to have a name. It was more than I could bear.
"How long has this been going on?"

"Five months. But I've only been there three times."

"Five months. And when were you thinking of telling me?"

"I just did." She zipped the garment bag and for the first time
looked at me. "I didn't know what to tell you. I didn't know what to tell
myself. I've been trying to figure out what it means."

"And what does it mean? Besides the fact that you've been lying to me for five months."

"You don't own me, Therese."

"No," I agreed. "I'm just the one who loves you. Who thought you loved me."

"I do love you."

"It's a funny way you have of showing it."

"Well, firing me has got to be the ultimate way to prove your love."

I tried to stand up. Instead, I sat back down heavily and began to cry. Then I went into the bathroom and locked the door. It's odd what will make you revert to kid behavior. I hadn't locked the door to the bathroom since I was fourteen and had to get away from my brother.

I closed the lid of the toilet and sat there in shock. I'd had no inkling that there was someone else. I didn't know which was more frightening, the existence of Ruth or how clueless I'd been. I'd been so focused on my own problems that God knew what else I should have known and didn't.

I held my head in my hands. I saw a car in slow motion headed for a concrete wall. I replayed the scene again and again but still the car exploded and burst into flames. I ran to open the driver's side door, but I couldn't get close to it. I couldn't get my breath. The twilight seeping in the window was too bright to bear. I drew the blinds and sat down slowly. I felt like I was a hundred years old. How could I live without Brin? How could she leave me for someone else?

I cried for what felt like a long time. I stood up slowly and washed my face in ice cold water. I unlocked the door and stepped into the hall. Brin was picking out clothes to wear on the plane. She looked at me with a cool hostility. "I guess we're at an impasse, Therese. But look at it this way."

"What are you talking about?"

"If we break up, neither one of us will have to leave."

I looked at her blankly.

I grabbed my purse. Crying, feeling the bottom drop out of the floor. "I guess we should split up, Brinnae. Because how can I ever trust you again?"

CHAPTER 19

Brin, September 1993

On the flight to Cleveland, I felt as cold as I did after I left Teddy. I'd tried to imagine Therese's reaction to my seeing someone else. I'd visualized her angry, verbal, in a magnificent rage of fierce, hurled words followed by cold silences. Eventually, I'd grovel and Therese would forgive me. What I hadn't foreseen was Therese's arrogance about our jobs. Her assumption that because I was more junior, that I'd sacrifice my career. Therese had shown her true colors. Better to find out now.

Ruth and I went hiking in a state park. Ruth showed me how to read a topo map, how to read a compass. I was hot and sweaty when we finished and sore by the time we got home. We showered together and Ruth gave me a massage. I tried to give Ruth a massage but it turned into sex almost immediately.

I made dinner for Ruth, who was grateful that she didn't have to cook. Our expectations of each other were just right. We delighted each other. I could be my true sensual self in the unhurried space that was Ruth.

Each night that week I came home to Ruth from working the show. I called David and we talked about school, about people I met in the booth. Ruth had a glass of wine waiting and gave me a foot massage. We ate dinner and made love. Sometimes we made love before we finished dinner.

I held the image of Therese at bay, behind the wall of her arrogance. In the plane on the way home, I brushed away a tear. Why did Ruth have to live so far away?

*   *   *

Therese, September, 1993

I got up in the morning with difficulty. I put on a George Winston CD, solo piano, which played my anguish back to me. I was relieved to get to the office. There I could forget about Brin for as much as a half-hour at a time. Sitting in a meeting I'd feel a stab of pain which I tried to push away. Sometimes I had to leave and cry in the far bathroom stall. Once I left the building and went home, but it was worse there.

On the weekend I was at a complete loss. I sat and played bridge against the computer for hours. I pictured Brin in bed with another woman and cleaned the entire house. I went out to breakfast with Stephanie.

"Maybe it could be worse," she suggested.

"How?"

"Maybe the good news is that this is as bad as it gets. You've hit bottom. There's only one way to go."

"I'm on the bottom of the pool, Steph. And I'm not coming up for air."

She told me stories of her failed relationships. The prison guard she met at the Y whose idea of a first date was a monster truck rally. I almost smiled at that. I imagined Brin laughing at 5'1" Stephanie standing next to the wheel of the truck. I started to cry.

"It's my own fault, Steph. I tried to make the job thing totally her problem."

"You both screwed up," Steph said. "There's plenty of blame to go around."

I thought back to my break-up with Deb. Deb said she left me because I was a workaholic. I protested, but knew beneath my stubbornness, in some non-verbal cranny of my brain, that she was right. I said she left me because she had problems with intimacy and couldn't commit to only one person. We'd each been to just enough therapy to be dangerous: a combination of smug about our sophistication and sorrowful about our inability to find the complementary puzzle piece.

The miracle was that anyone was willing to put up with anyone else. I pictured the heart as surrounded by imperfect armor, something resembling a tomato cage. Another human wormed its way in by being cute or vulnerable or challenging enough to bend the wires apart. Once they connected sexually, they wrapped around you like a morning glory, hogging your light and water and nutrient supply. After they'd strangled you sufficiently to stunt your fruit growth, they'd move on to a healthier-looking plant, leaving you yearning and subject to blight or end rot, vulnerable to further penetration.

*　　*　　*

Brin

On Saturday morning, when I got up, I noticed that Therese's clothes were gone from my closet. I went into the bathroom and found only my toothbrush. When David got up, hours later, I asked when Therese came over.

"I don't know, OK? I wasn't here, I was at Dad's, remember?"

"You don't have to take that tone with me, David."

He finished his toast and stood up from the table. "I don't know which of you is a bigger baby. You or Therese."

I watched him stomp up the stairs. What had Charlie called it? The importance of constancy to teenagers.

I went to see Charlie on Monday. "I'm outraged that Therese assumed that I'd be the one to leave Carepath."

"It's arrogant," Charlie agreed. "But it's not surprising. No doubt she's getting a lot of praise from the CEO, reinforcement about how important she is to the company."

"She is important to Carepath," I conceded. "But I am, too."

"Absolutely," Charlie said. "The situation really isn't fair. Unfortunately it happens a lot."

"To gay people."

"To everyone," Charlie said. "Gay or straight."

After therapy I went to work. I was grateful that Therese and I no longer had offices on the same floor.

I ran into Alan in the lunchroom. We sat down at a table in the corner. "What's going on?" Alan said.

"What do you mean?" I said.

"You don't show up at Nate's wedding on Saturday. Therese seems to be going through the motions. I ask her what's the matter and she says she can't talk about it yet."

"We seem to have broken up," I said. I told him the whole story.

Alan sighed. "This is really not good."

To my surprise, I started to cry. "I've been so mad at her about the job. I can't imagine how hurt she must be about Ruth. Has she said anything at all to you?"

"That she is not meant for happiness. This was right after Nate gave Sherry the ring."

I stared at my plate. It sounded more like something I'd say, a fortune cookie on the edge of melodrama. Therese must have said it like she was giving a weather forecast.

I remembered Therese's words while she was packing. I can't have you in the same division as me. The words I steeled myself with whenever my resolve started to waver. "It's too bad," I said. "I guess we're going to have to learn to live with it."

*   *   *

Therese

In a window seat instead of my usual aisle, ascending, I watched the thin band of orange glowing above the horizon, underneath the darkening sky. The lights of Louisville blinked in long strings, ciphers, a code reminiscent of warmth and home. A thin mass of clouds lay above the orange band, a dark mountain range above bright water. Rowing to the other side. The light faded as the plane climbed. Clouds obscured the view.

Anger was a garage for hurt, a breakfront for fear. For the thousandth time, how could Brin. I sighed, set aside my work and read a novel, Robert Stone's *Damascus Gate*, a pilgrimage made by characters of different faiths. The plane dropped out of the clouds to gleaming grids of light. Runway lights, bright cul de sacs, street lamps, porch lights. For once, I arrived home early.

CHAPTER 20

*A*nother day, another flight. On the ground, Therese drove through Indiana. Fields of brown cornstalks, sunflowers, weathered barns falling slowly into the earth. A field awash in pumpkins. A sign for eggs, honey and herbs. A roadside memorial of colored glass stones and flowers. Throughout the day, she imagined life at home.

The house sat silent in the middle of the block. Dawn glowed pink against the blue-black sky. The sun edged above the horizon, a halo of its blazing self.

Inside the house a clock ticked quietly on the mantle. Motes of dust in the air became visible against half-closed blinds. First light filtered onto the dieffenbachia and ficus growing towards the window.

Yellow leaves slipped from the elm on the boulevard, one of the city's survivors. The leaves coated the sidewalk in front of the house. A child scuffled through the drifts on her way to the school bus stop.

A cat slipped into her backyard and stalked a starling. The cat wore no bell on its collar, despite entreaties from the neighborhood. The cat left the bird near the feeder hanging from the silver maple. A century's worth of bluebirds, jays, robins, finches, sparrows and cardinals had sheltered in its branches. The leaves falling from the maple reflected the full palate of sunset: orange pale as creamsicle in the center of the spine. Veins blazing scarlet at leaf tip. Leaves with yellow centers melting into apricot tendrils. The blue-black bird was bathed in peach-colored light.

Ten miles southeast, the river meandered in its bed of reeds, a ribbon of wetland snaking through city and suburb. An egret stood fishing, its slender white geometry arched against the grass. A second egret flapped overhead, slowed to a glide above the reeds, hovered at the edge of the bank and untucked its stalky legs. The air was damp and cool, awash in the odor of marsh, alive with the sound of crickets, planes buzzing overhead, the cries of birds.

The paths leading from the road into the wetland were festooned in chains, marked with signs prohibiting human entry and featuring images of cranes flying. A deer drank at water's edge, grazed on alder seedlings. A misshapen frog hung on a lily pad.

By noon the sun was encircled in passing clouds, lush, fleecy Botticellis sailing at an altitude of fifteen thousand feet. The wind blew the clouds across the sun, creating cool gusts which announced the coming of October to pedestrians in parking lots.

School buses deposited children into the day's accumulation of leaves, their slow passage home announced by barking dogs. Coreopsis and coneflowers, descendants of the prairie, shriveled into seedpods. Squirrels buried corn kernels and acorns. Cars herky-jerked through rush hour. Forthcoming dinners waited in humming freezers.

After dinner the light of autumn was hazy. Dark ripples swelled upon the lake and ebbed on the sandy shore. Twilight descended, the color of a tangerine. Her house stood silent save for the clock, the refrigerator, the furnace. Dust gathered on the computer screen. The petals fell from a vase of roses going dark at the edges. The bags of unplanted crocus, tulip, iris bulbs sat in a corner of the front porch. The house, bereft, awaited its mistress.

CHAPTER 21

Brin, October, 1993

"What was it like, to have feelings for a woman?" Ruth asked. We were lying in bed on Saturday morning. I had used a frequent flyer coupon on a long weekend David was spending with Teddy.

"Terrifying," I said. "Like walking on the ceiling, upside down."

Ruth smiled. "Tightrope walking without a net."

"I didn't expect it. I'd never had a doubt that I was straight, was only vaguely aware that gay people existed.

"Never really thought about it," Ruth said.

"When did you know?" I asked. I watched yellow leaves drift by the window. I was not quite ready for autumn.

"It was different for me," Ruth admitted. "I had no interest in boys. I lived for sleepovers with my girlfriends in junior high. I had a crush on my best friend in high school though I didn't dare talk about it."

"What was your first experience?"

"I went to the feminist bookstore on campus a lot. A woman named Nancy worked there. She had olive skin, a mole on her cheek. She wore tank tops without a bra and didn't shave under her arms."

I smiled. I'd forgotten that Ruth was older than I was.

"She invited me over for dinner," Ruth recalled. "Some kind of bulgur-mushroom-tofu thing. She was a terrible cook, but it didn't matter."

"Did it last?" I asked.

Ruth shrugged. "A few months. I'd thought I might be lesbian. But after Nancy I knew. It was good to know. I was so curious about women, who they were, their stories. I went to the bars a lot. I volunteered at Take Back the Night and gay pride."

"You must know a lot of women," I said. I wondered how many women Ruth had slept with. The thought was disconcerting. I didn't know what the rules were.

"I do," Ruth said. "I have a whole community. So when I don't have a girlfriend, or," she smiled, "she lives far away, I feel connected."

I mused. My connections were to David, to my mother and sister. To Therese, though I'd been hacking away at it in my mind every day. I told Ruth about the moms' group.

Ruth nodded. "Exactly. You need to spend time with other women in your situation so you can see what's possible. Not feel so alone."

"I guess I am," I said.

Ruth looked at her quizzically.

"A lesbian, I mean. I haven't wanted to admit it. But you're the proof." I put my hand on Ruth's belly.

"You make it sound like geometry," Ruth smiled.

I laughed and climbed atop her.

CHAPTER 22

Therese, Fall 1993

En route to the airport I called Paul and told him I needed to take a vacation. When he asked about Brin, I told him it looked like we were breaking up so he could stop worrying about making her leave. He didn't press me further. We agreed I could have two weeks. I carried the thought with me on the road where one minute it felt like a balloon that lifted my head from the page and the next like an albatross. I hadn't taken two consecutive weeks off in the nine years I'd been at Carepath.

Coming home from Pittsburgh, I flew with a head cold. I screwed air plugs into my ears in an attempt to keep most of my hearing, after a shot of nasal spray twenty minutes before boarding. Through the fog in my head, I realized that I could go up north and see my brother, Danny.

Danny made a precarious living by serving as a caretaker for absentee landlords of cabins and for several wealthy families who had summer estates on the north shore of Lake Superior. In his spare time he painted watercolors and, I suspected, drank too much. We made plans without ever speaking to each other in person. The last message I left him said that I'd drive up the second to last Sunday of October.

After I packed the car, I detoured to visit the house I grew up in. Every few years, when I was feeling particularly depressed or nostalgic, I drove by the old place to see what color the trim had been painted and how the big maple and elm in the front yard were holding up. The little bungalow looked pretty good: the trim was an olive green, the front porch had been screened in, and yellow leaves crowded the gutter above it. I drove down the alley in back and looked into the window of the room Carolyn and I shared, on the other side of the downstairs bathroom from Danny. My father put in a bath with a shower for he and my mother upstairs and finished the basement with car-side paneling, track lighting and a pool table. The basement had probably been turned into somebody's home office by now.

I drove around to the front and parked across from the house. I fumbled in my pocket for the letter, touched the flap of the envelope, not wanting to tear it. I unfolded the letter and leaned back against the headrest. I read it four times in a row, as if it were written in cuneiform and I could decipher the code by repeated study. I'd confessed my mistakes. Should I mail it?

Last night at dinner Stephanie told me the story of a Jewish sage. She took me to our favorite neighborhood place in Minneapolis, a small owner-operated French bistro, dark and quiet. She ordered a bottle of Merlot, two walleye filets encrusted in pecans and pulled a pack of Kleenex out of her purse.

She listened to me talk and cry, held my hand, and made me eat. "I can't remember exactly how this story goes so bear with me," she said. "A woman goes to the rabbi to discuss her troubles. She says, 'Rabbi, why does the Old Testament say that God's love rests on the heart, not in the heart?'

"The rabbi sighs and pats her hand. 'Dear woman,' the rabbi says, 'God's love lies on the heart so that when the heart breaks, it falls in through the cracks.'" I started to cry again. Steph held my hand. "It's such a beautiful image," she said. "Love falling on the broken glass of the heart."

Steph didn't give me advice, though she continued to catalogue her failures. "Remember the married woman I dated while we lived in Ann Arbor?"

"The one who ultimately went back to her husband?"

"Yeah."

"I definitely needed to be reminded of that."

She shrugged. "So, at least Teddy's remarried."

I looked at the side window to the living room, the room that held the piano where Carolyn played, where we held family meetings and argued about chores. I set my glasses on the seat beside me, rested my head on the steering wheel and wept.

It was drizzling when I left Minneapolis. I put the car on cruise control. Two and a half hours later I saw the hills of Duluth spilling toward the lake and the aerial lift bridge arching towards Wisconsin. I remembered that Brin went to UM-Duluth. I began to cry again. A gusty rain followed me along the shore, blowing the few remaining yellow leaves off the birch trees and whipping up whitecaps on Superior.

My uneasiness started north of Duluth, driving the famed Highway 61 which ran along the shore of the lake, past still-sputtering taconite processing plants and an increasing number of large resorts. What if Danny viewed a visit from his sister as an occasion to enter one of his raving extrovert phases? The queen of what ifs, Brin called me. When she was angry with me, the last sentence of her rebuke was, almost inevitably, "Stop anticipating life and start living it." It had been six weeks since I had the conversation with her that brought my world crashing down around my ears. I didn't know what I needed, except that I needed to be somewhere else.

The concrete-colored sky and the wet film on the windshield corresponded well enough to my mood that I began to relax. If my expectations were low enough, there was only one way to go. Danny's directions, which relied on measuring the miles from a liquor store landmark and paying attention to mail boxes of various Swensons and Olafsons, were good. I pulled into the three-cabin resort past the "closed for the season" sign and found an envelope on the door of the third cabin with my name on it.

My spirits lifted as soon as I entered, because it was clear that I'd be the only one staying here. The cabin was one room, paneled in knotty pine, with a large picture window facing the lake. The double bed was to the right of the window and a glass-enclosed wood stove sat to its left. Beyond lay a tiny kitchen with two chairs pulled up to the bar that served as table and counter space. A love seat faced the wood stove and a framed photo of surf crashing against large granite boulders. Across from the bed, tucked into an alcove, was a small bathroom with a stall shower.

I'd stopped in Two Harbors for groceries which I now unloaded: a bag of split peas and a double ham hock, spaghetti sauce and pasta, a box of tissues, cereal and milk, bananas and strawberries, a bag of cough drops, a whole chicken with a lemon for the cavity, onions and garlic, cheese and crackers, two bags of salad, a loaf of rye bread, two bottles of wine.

Danny's note said that he'd gone north of Grand Marais to clean cabins and would see me the next day. I sat on the love seat with a bowl of cereal and a glass of wine, too tired to build a fire. No TV, no phone, no computer, no dishwasher, no microwave. No World Series or ads for the November elections. The only sounds were the whoosh of the gas heater when it kicked on and the hum of the little refrigerator.

I pictured Brin, a familiar thought that curled my arms around my knees to prop up my chin. The letter I'd written sat in the inside pocket of my jacket. I hadn't told her where I was going, though she could find out if she were to call Alan. In my latest formulation of what went wrong, it was my fault that Brin strayed because I was on the road so much. The grief that I'd deferred, packing it in small suitcases and sending it on planes around the country, rolled over me again like a wave. I cried for a long time. I lay down on the bed with a cold washcloth over my eyes and fell asleep.

When I awoke, my watch said I'd slept for nine hours, a decent deposit against my chronic sleep deficit. I sat in sweats and slippers with a cup of tea and looked out at the slate gray lake. The rain pelted the window and the waves crashed against the granite outcroppings below. I blew my nose and sucked on a cough drop. I thought about quitting my job and traveling around the country with Brin in a motor home. I watched the rain ease up, the sky lighten to the color of pearl.

I lit a fire in the wood stove, stacking kindling over birch bark and paper, and watched the flames accelerate. The smoke streamed out the chimney into the trees, like great gusts of fog. The expanding metal of the stove pinged and clicked like a gas furnace as the fire licked the kindling trapped between two logs. The rain sounded like rifleshots against the gutters as the storm picked up again.

I ate toast and jam. I pondered taking a month off to travel with Brin and David to Nepal and New Zealand. My reveries were interrupted by the battered half-ton pick-up that pulled up in front of my window, honked and considerately moved further along the gravel drive so as not to spoil my view.

"Hey, T," Danny said when I opened the door. He wore blue jeans, boots and a fluorescent red rain jacket. His curly reddish-brown hair was damp and his glasses spattered with raindrops. He enveloped me in a massive hug and lifted me off the ground. His beard felt scratchy against my face and he smelled like wood smoke. I pulled back to look at his craggy reddish eyebrows, his lightly freckled skin, the grin in his eyes that had always meant Danny.

"Daniel," I said. "Daniel and his amazing north shore rest cure."

"No rest for the wicked," he said, "so you must be cleaning up your act."

I made him a cup of coffee. We sat on the loveseat and talked about his cabin empire. "These cabins I only have for a month," he said. "The owners took their money from the fall color trade and went to Florida to see their parents. Then there's the three estates between Tofte and Lutsen and the motel and cabins I just came from. The owner's getting too old to clean every day, so she just stays in the office."

"Where are you living?"

"In a remodeled garage on one of the estates. It's about this size but the view's not quite as nice."

"By yourself?"

"Yeah, most nights."

"Got a new girlfriend?"

"I've gone back to Cathy. We're trying the two night a week routine." Cathy was a school bus driver and potter with two girls who must be nearly done with elementary school by now.

"How long were you two broken up?"

"About two years. She was involved with another guy and finally decided he wasn't marriage material." He laughed. "Course she doesn't think I'm marriage material either."

"Are you?"

"More than I was the last time. It's not much fun being thirty-six and single up here." He grinned. "Except during ski season." He looked over and caught me frowning. "Seriously, T, I'm trying to do it right this time. I'm hoping Cathy wants to take a chance on me."

When the rain stopped we put on down vests and went for a walk along a gravel road that ran parallel to the shore. We talked about my parents' health and speculated on why I bought so heavily into my father's work ethic while he and Carolyn had avoided it. We talked about Danny's scramble for money and my search for time and our old fantasy of a job-share that would allow us to have the right mix of both.

"I could have held up my end when you were doing technical writing," Danny said. "But you're way beyond me now, T. I don't understand what you people even make."

"Software, Danny. Mostly."

"I guess I'm more of a hardware kind of guy. I like to see what it is I've done, even if it's only a pile of clean sheets and towels."

"It's gotten to be too much work, Danny. I don't have enough time at home. I had to give up my golf league. I feel like I know the CNN anchors better than I know my friends."

"Yeah, I've gotten to know those CNN people pretty well myself. I've got my own satellite dish now, it's made me newly attractive to those two little girls. The kids are the only ones can keep up with what's on all those channels."

We went out for a late lunch and ate hamburgers at a place where Danny was a regular. He introduced me to the waitresses and half the people in the bar. We visited his place and sat in the living room of the estate for a while, playing with the CD changer, the home theater and the rest of the gadgets. He didn't ask me about Brin until we were back at the cabin, after I'd put the chicken and a couple of baking potatoes in the oven. Danny liked Brin.

"I miss her," I said.

"She called," he said.

I stared at him. "She called you?"

"Uh huh. About a week ago."

"Did you tell her I was coming up here?"

"I told her we were talking about it. She said she hoped you would. She was worried you didn't have anyone you were talking to."

"Did she tell you what she did?"

"Yep. She owned up to it. She knows it was wrong."

"Huh," I said. I'd been too angry and too crushed to consider that Brin might be learning something.

"She also told me what you did."

"Talk about stupid."

He nodded. "You don't screw up much but boy when you do, it's a doozy."

I smiled. "You got that right." It was a relief to own it.

"I can see how she might have got herself into it," Danny said.

I looked at him. "Oh, are you going to take up for her?"

He gave me a look of disgust. "Of course not. I'm your brother. I'm just saying that I can see how she could have been scared and done something stupid."

"She's pretty impulsive."

"Yes, she is. And you're the furthest thing from it. You don't do anything you haven't thought through six ways from Sunday."

"That's true."

"It seems to me you're in a relationship of opposites attract. She counts on you to be steady and you count on her to be impulsive."

"I didn't count on her for this."

"I'm sure not."

We sat down to dinner. The chicken was wonderful, moist and perfumed from the lemon, onion and garlic I'd stuck in the cavity. We finished a bottle of wine and ate caramel apples Danny brought for dessert.

We'd said our goodnights and hugged when Danny lingered a moment at the door. "You haven't asked me for advice and you aren't likely to, being as older sisters never do," he said, "so I'm only going to give you one piece."

"I'm listening," I said.

"Your problem is that you haven't screwed up enough in your life," Danny said. "You don't know how to forgive yourself or when you should forgive other people."

"How do I know when to forgive and when to give up?"

"You don't," he said. "It's a guess. You can think about it from all the angles and it's still going to come down to a gut feeling."

"Which angles are the most important?" I asked.

"It's pretty basic. Do you love her? Does she love you? Can you both learn something and go on? Do you love her enough to take a risk? That's what it comes down to."

He gave me another hug.

"You better figure out how important that job really is," he said. "You don't get too many chances at the brass ring."

"Thanks, little bro," I said. "Little big bro."

"Tomorrow I'm in Tofte and at Cathy's. I'll see you on Wednesday," he said and got in his truck.

I slept ten hours and woke up hungry. I ate cereal and toast. I lay on the loveseat and stared out the window. The sky and water were a fierce, brilliant blue. The wind lashed the waves across the rocks, sending a frothy meringue toward shore. In the afternoon I went for an hour's hike along the Temperance River. I climbed the narrow and winding path that ran along the river as it made its rocky way down to the lake. I sat on a log and stared into the depths of the root beer-colored water. I wondered what it would be like to live up north and have life and work driven by the seasons and the weather. I put the thought under the category of retirement fantasies, went back to the cabin and reread my letter.

At six o'clock I stood outside and watched the sun fall below the ridge across the highway. The sky across the lake was pink edged with long, thin blue clouds, like a nursery painted for both genders. The curling fronds of the Norway pines were green-black and spidery in the fading light. The bare branches of the white birch trees were etched dark against the water. I ate salad and leftover chicken warmed in the oven, then went back out again.

CHAPTER 23

Brin, October, 1993

Dawn came too soon. Splashing cold water on my puffy eyelids, wondering if I could navigate the stairs toward coffee without falling. I surveyed the wreckage of the bed, the down quilt strewn across the mattress, its flannel cover of tiny flowers printed on cream half unbuttoned. My down pillows, crushed by the weight of my head, crumpled in the fury of sleep. Therese's cold pillows, askew, with a stray dark hair glued to the case.

I gathered her pillows to me, hugging them, breathing in her aroma. I sat on the bed, crying. Then I ripped her pillowcases off, scented them one more time and hurled them down the stairs.

I lifted the Van Gogh calendar from my night table, blurry riots of color, humble still-lifes, field hands collapsed in the shade of a haystack. Vincent's self-portrait, red beard and stolid, hunted eyes staring back at me. I pulled on my flannel bathrobe and made the slow trek down the stairs.

*   *   *

After dinner, thumbing through a book of Grecian photographs. A plain wood table and three cane-bottomed chairs stared out at an azure sea. A stark white church, rounded cupola, blue door, sat astride a hillside of purple and yellow flowers, above a twisting strand of highway descending toward the water. A sheer granite cliff rose from a beach, a handful of boats anchored offshore. I didn't need Therese to go to Europe. Maybe David would come with me, though we were barely speaking. I looked out the window, bleary with rain, into the wind-whipped night. I picked up the book. An ancient ruin, a door frame standing amid sun-bleached bricks beside the sea. I crawled into the picture, the warmth of the sun on the bricks, the rolling blue.

Quiet classical guitar on the CD player. The comfort of a flannel nightgown and a cup of green tea. A pitcher of slightly wilted sunflowers. Numbness the most I could hope for, a temporary ice pack on my bleeding heart.

*   *   *

Christie started to bark as soon as the truck pulled into the driveway. I saw the mailman put a stack of catalogues and envelopes in the mailbox but I didn't get up.

I yelled "no bark" at Christie and began to cry. I was a waterworks most of the time. I was working from home as much as I could, having asked to set up the data for the next formulary release myself. It was the kind of work I'd normally do anything to avoid, but the words in the drug dictionaries seemed to calm me. When I was at my wit's end, I scrolled through the lists of generic names and brand names. Percodan. Warfarin. Cardizem. Lidocaine. Demerol. A kind of soothing repetition, a child playing the same video game over and over. Prayer and supplication, an attempt to master the incomprehensible nightmare. Diltiazem. Furosemide. These moments of fragile tranquility were shattered by crying jags and dreams that sent me bolt upright in bed, visions of falling through a well or a tunnel or the open bridge slats on the freeway.

I wondered about the drug names my father would have said to himself in the fifties. All I could think of was Thalidomide. I shuddered.

The wind howled outside. The skeleton David hung in the front window rattled. It was almost Halloween and then my least favorite month of the year, November. Shrinking daylight and the holidays without Therese.

David was distant, still angry. Probably mad at both of us. The last time I cried in front of him, he laughed. "Go ahead and cry. It's a break from watching you wander around in the fog." He'd decided to go out for flag football. Running through the feelings sounded good. Tackling would sound even better.

I called Ruth on the weekends but we didn't have much to say. I began to realize that Ruth was a vacation, not daily life. A part of me didn't find this surprising. My newfound adolescence must be over. What a pity. Adult life was so grim.

I stopped for lunch, heating a can of soup, toasting a piece of bread, slicing an orange. I decided to look at the pile of catalogues. Maybe it would give me ideas of what to buy Marlys and my mother for Christmas.

The letter was stuck between the gas bill and a plea for money from public radio. I saw the handwriting and my fingers trembled. I licked the butter knife and sliced the envelope open.

The letter was dated October 2 and postmarked Lutsen October 23. Therese had debated for quite a while before mailing it. I wondered if Danny had mentioned that I talked to him.

"Dear Brin," I read. "I hardly know where to begin. I am stumbling through my life, trying to stay on automatic pilot, and not succeeding.

"I think of you while I'm driving to work, while I'm in the building, when I'm on a plane and when I'm in a meeting. Being at home is even worse."

I cried, reading slowly. "Maybe I needed my life to explode in order to learn what's important. I am stunned at my stupidity when we talked about who would have to leave Carepath. You're right, I assumed it should be you. I realize now that Carepath is more than a job to me but it is definitely less important than my relationship with you.

"I am also stunned that you are involved with someone

else. I know that I've been gone too much but I still don't understand it.

"I think that what we have is too important to ignore just because we've each been wounded. If you agree, I'd like to talk.

Love,
Therese"

Tears became sobs. My steady, reasonable girl had reappeared. I hadn't let myself hope for reconciliation. Now I was on fire. I realized that I didn't know how to reach Therese. I called and left a message on her voicemail at home. "I got your letter. I think you're up north. Please call me, I want to talk to you. I love you" and hung up. I called Danny's number and got his answering machine. I asked him to convey the same message.

*   *   *

When the phone rang two days later, I assumed it was for David. He'd eaten dinner and gone off to play roller blade hockey with his friends. I'd awoken at 3AM feeling as if I were inside a pinball game, neurons randomly firing, my mind and heart caroming from one obstacle to the next. I'd been exhausted when I got up. I trudged through the day hauling a sack of wet sand.

Since school started, a girl had called twice for David. I didn't answer and listened instead for a voice to start talking to the answering machine. When I heard the beep and a moment's hesitation, then "uh," I picked up the phone.

"Hello?"

"Brin?"

"Yes. Therese?"

"Yeah."

"I'm glad you called." The tears started immediately. I struggled to keep my voice level. "Where are you?"

"Up north."

"With Danny?"

"In one of the cabins he's looking after. He's not staying here."

I let the silence accumulate for a while. "How's the weather?"

"Rainy. But that's OK."

"It's been raining down here, too." I waited a moment. I heard my father's voice, telling me to breathe. "It's good to hear your voice, Therese."

"It's good to hear yours, too."

I put my hand over the receiver to muffle the sobs.

"Are you crying?"

"Yes."

"Yeah. Me too."

"Two girls with tears in their ears," I said.

Therese laughed her rueful laugh. "Yeah. Did you get my letter?"

"Yes. It made me cry."

"That's good. Is David there?"

"He's out with his friends. I can talk."

"OK."

I felt slightly irked that Therese was being so passive, but my relief overwhelmed the irritation. "How's Danny?"

"He seems good. He's scrambling for money but he looks good. I think he's cut back on the booze."

"What have the two of you been doing?"

"I got here on Sunday, so I've only seen him twice. He showed me where he's living and one of his estates. Then we had dinner here. He worked today and he's with his girlfriend tonight."

"He told me he was back with Cathy."

"Yeah."

I sighed. "I miss you, Therese."

"I miss you, too. Now that I'm up here and slowed down, the feelings are catching up with me."

"What are you feeling?"

"Sad. Angry. Baffled."

"What are you baffled about?"

"How we got to where we are. What I should do next."

I started to cry again. I could hear Therese listening. Therese had a particular kind of attentiveness when I cried. But she didn't say anything. "I'd like to see you, Therese."

"Why, Brin? I'm not being mean, I just don't want to assume anything."

"Because I miss you. And because I want us to be back together." I paused. "I haven't stopped loving you, Therese. Not for an instant."

Therese started to cry. One thing different about loving a woman was that there were so many more tears, so much more unshuttered emotion. It was exhausting.

"Why are you crying, Therese?"

"I suppose it's because I still love you."

"Do you?"

"I haven't stopped."

"Good." We snuffled together for a while and compared notes on Kleenex supplies.

"You'll let me know if you want me to come up there?" I asked.

Therese thought about it. "I don't know if that's a good idea or not."

"Tell me the pros and cons," I said, stifling a sigh.

"Well, maybe it would be good to see you some place that wasn't either of ours. As long as it was private. On the other hand, I need a lot of time by myself right now. I'm feeling pretty fragile."

You don't have a franchise on fragile, sweetheart, I thought. "If you decide you want to see me, I could rent a cabin up there. That way you could always go back to the place you're staying now."

"That's true." I could hear the gears and the wheels turning in Therese's brain as she thought about it. My girlfriend, the world's best analyst.

"Do you want to think it over and call me back?" I asked.

"Why don't you come up Friday?" Therese said.

Thank you, God. "I'll have to figure out what to do with David. I think Teddy's out of town."

"Is this Teddy's infamous annual hunting trip?"

"I guess. It's that time of year. Maybe David could stay with Tami and Brad. He won't be too excited about it. I'll owe him big time."

"Do you think he wants us to get back together?"

"I think so. But he doesn't want to get his hopes up."

Therese laughed the rueful laugh again.

"I'll call around and see if I can get a cabin," I said. "Any ideas?"

"Just a minute," she said. She came back with a list of resorts that Danny had marked up with his ratings. We made arrangements for Therese to call again on Thursday night. I said I didn't want to do this through voicemail.

After I hung up, I went upstairs to my bedroom. I knelt on the floor and prayed to a God I hadn't been sure I still believed in. Then I got on the phone and called all the places Danny had given four stars to. When they were all full, I called the three star places. I prevailed upon a woman to call the one person who hadn't sent their deposit in. When she hadn't called within a half-hour, I called her back and talked her into letting me have the cabin.

When David came home, I told him he had to help me out.

"You were right about Cleveland," I said. "You've got a sharp eye, maybe too sharp."

David grinned. I told him about Ruth. "This is the worst I've ever screwed up. I need you to stay at your dad's and to not argue with me."

He nodded. I wondered whether he was more shocked by the fact that his mother had a sex life or that I'd admitted the equivalent of adultery to him. Then I made a list of all the things I needed to take up north, including groceries, and sent e-mails to cancel out of my meetings on Friday. I decided that even if Therese called back on Thursday and changed her mind, I was going up anyway. It would be up to Therese what she wanted to do, but I'd be available just in case.

There was one more thing I had to do. I hesitated, then picked up the phone. After we exchanged greetings and chatted, I said, "Ruth, I've been thinking."

"About?"

"About what I need to do. I need to go back to Therese."

"You're sure?"

"As sure as I am about anything."

Ruth sighed. "I knew I couldn't keep you. That's not what this was about."

"I needed to learn what you taught me."

"What did you learn?"

"That passion has a short half-life."

"I hate it when my words come back to haunt me. But remember one thing, Brinnae."

"What?"

"Don't come running back if it doesn't work out. I can't be your safety net."

I sighed and my voice broke. "I know."

"Au revoir, Brin."

CHAPTER 24

Therese

The townhouse Brin rented was a half-hour south of the place I was staying. It was brand new, one of a handful of units built below a ski lodge. She told me that she was driving up Friday morning and that I could come anytime after one o'clock. When I got there at two, she had a vase of red roses on the kitchen table, a bottle of Chardonnay in the refrigerator and a fire in the glassed-in fireplace. She walked me through the cabin, took my coat and then put her arms around me.

"You've lost weight," she said.

"Probably."

"I'm so glad you didn't change your mind." She hesitated. "Can I kiss you?"

I raised my face to hers and felt the softness of her lips on mine, her fingers in my hair. We kissed carefully, like people afraid of catching a cold from each other. We sat on the sofa near the fireplace, each with a glass of mineral water.

"How've you been spending your time?" she said.

"Reading. Sleeping. I saw Danny on Wednesday. We went for a hike and out to dinner."

Last night I'd called Stephanie. "What do you think I should do?"

There was silence while she thought about it. "Talk to her. Listen. You've got a lot tied up with Brin and it isn't easy starting over. Try to figure out if you want the same things."

I watched Brin look out the window. She exclaimed over a rose-colored bird. She turned toward me. "What did you do this morning?"

"Went for a walk. Stared at the lake. Fretted."

She smiled at me, one of her small smiles, like a child on her best behavior. "How's Stephanie?"

"She's fine. I've had dinner with her a couple of times. She's been a good friend."

"Has she been giving you advice?"

"She listens to me."

"It's good you have someone you can talk to," Brin said. This was a surprise. Brin and Stephanie were polite in their interactions, but didn't like each other. I thought Brin had some kind of weird jealousy about Stephanie because she'd known me for so long. Brin denied it.

Steph thought Brin was a princess and that I catered too much to her. "Takes one to know one," I responded. Steph stuck out her tongue at me.

I handed Brin a lump wrapped in tissue paper. "I got you something."

She unwrapped it, exclaiming over the beauty of the pink stone jutting out of the gray granite. "It's Thomsonite. It's mined up here."

"Thank you, Therese." She took my hand and placed the rock in it. She guided my index finger to the smooth part of the stone. "You could rub it and make a wish."

I held the stone in both hands and closed my eyes. Then I gave it back to her. She held the stone for a few moments, then put it on the coffee table in front of us.

"Are you still fretting?" she asked.

"I'm too tired."

The sofa was long and deep. "See if you can relax around her," Stephanie'd said. "If you can fall asleep."

Brin stretched out behind me, then beckoned me toward her. I backed up against her and put my head in the crook of her arm. She pulled me in and put my head on a pillow next to hers. She stroked my hair and held me. I felt her softness, her size, her warmth and let myself be enveloped by her. I nodded off.

When I awoke and rolled over on my back, she was propped on one elbow, staring into the fire. "What are you thinking about?" I asked.

"I'm trying not to," she said. "I'm just enjoying being with you."

"Did you bring the paper?"

"Mmm hmm."

"We could do the crossword."

"Sure. If you want."

I got the paper from the kitchen and a stubby pencil from the pocket of my jean jacket. I put my left arm around Brin, propped the puzzle on a book she'd brought and filled in our collective guesses.

"We can still fill in the blanks," I said.

She smiled at me.

"What's this book?" I turned it over. It was a cookbook. "Are you going to make me dinner?"

"If you'll let me," she said.

"What are we having?"

"Cornish game hens with an apricot sauce. New potatoes. Pea pods. And creme brulee I bought in town for dessert."

"Sounds great. Do you need me to do something?"

"You can help me later. I'm not ready to have you go anywhere yet."

I stretched out on the sofa and put my head in her lap. She rubbed my head and massaged little circles around my temples. I felt something wet land on my face. "You're crying," I said.

"Yes."

I opened my eyes and looked up at her.

"What's making you cry, Brinnae?"

"Please say that you're giving me another chance. A chance to redeem myself and make it up to you."

"Danny said I should go with my gut."

"And what does your gut say?"

"That we should try again. I'm wary, Brin. But I do want to try."

She burst into tears. I took her in my arms. I cradled her as she sobbed and I cried as well. I felt the tension drain from my back and shoulders. I was as limp as one of Brin's dolls.

"I never dreamed I'd miss anyone as much as I've missed you," she said. "Even when I thought about what a jerk you've been."

"I know." I sighed. "Do you want to talk about that?"

"Not yet. Do you remember years ago you once told me you were afraid that you loved me too much?"

"Mmm hmm. I remember."

"You said one always loves more than the other. Now I know what you mean. Now the shoe is on the other foot."

I took her feet in my hands, pulled off her fuzzy slippers and began to massage her arches. "I don't see the shoe on either foot, Brin."

"I've always loved how funny you are," she said. Full Brinnae smile, two hundred and fifty watts. She lay on her back and beckoned me. I ran my hands up the curve of her ankles, over her calves and thighs clad in blue jeans. She put my hands on the zipper. I unzipped her jeans and pulled them off. She put my hands on her stomach under her sweater. I caressed her belly and she moaned. I unhooked her bra, gathered her beautiful, full breasts into my hands and kissed her nipples.

"Please make love to me, Therese," she said. "I'll do anything."

"Anything?"

"Anything you say. Anything you want."

I looked at the beautiful blonde woman before me on the sofa, who wore only white cotton underpants. I decided to believe that the lust and innocence I saw were meant for only me. I went to the closet for extra linens and slipped a sheet underneath her. I stretched out on top of her and began to kiss and caress her. She rocked against my hand, moaning. "Say it," I said.

"I want you. Only you." She repeated it until I put my mouth gently over hers.

After she rested in my arms, she removed my clothes and made love to me slowly. I concentrated on her touch, the authority of it, her certainty about what I liked, how much I'd missed it. Every time I envisioned Ruth, I dragged my mind back. I pulled a second sheet over us before we drifted off to sleep. I tried not to be afraid of all the good and all the difficult times which would come next, if we were lucky.

CHAPTER 25

Brin

Therese stayed with me the entire weekend. We didn't talk much at first. It was as if talk might crack the thin film of ice we walked on and send us crashing into the frigid water beneath. We slept in on Saturday and went for a hike in one of the state parks. I made a picnic of cheese, crackers, apples and sugar smoked trout I'd bought on the scenic shoreline route between Two Harbors and Duluth. I broiled fish for dinner and we watched Atlanta beat the Yankees in the World Series. We took Danny and his girlfriend out for Sunday brunch.

We went back to her place afterward. Therese said, "Brin, there's something I need to tell you."

I felt dread mixed with curiosity.

"I need to apologize for assuming you should be the one to leave Carepath."

"Your letter said that our relationship is more important than your staying there. Is that really true?"

"I'm not going to lie and say I haven't struggled. Carepath is more than a job to me, it's a crusade. But I will leave if that's what's best. I'm absolutely clear that being with you is more important."

"Tell me what Paul said." I scowled when Therese recounted the conversation. "I'm not surprised he'd decide that. What an asshole to talk to you that way. You've been his right hand since the place started."

"Somehow I thought that I was special and that the hard and cold rules of business as usual couldn't apply to me," Therese said. "I was wrong."

"You're not even defending him this time," I said.

"I don't have the energy to spin anything," Therese said. "We just need to decide what happens next. It's more important for you and I to be together than where either of us works."

"You can't say that often enough for my ears."

"I was completely consumed by worry about what I should do about work until our relationship was in question."

"He doesn't want you to leave, Therese."

"No. He doesn't. And I don't think it's fair that you should have to. You do a great job. You've had your ups and downs with Suzanne but mostly you seem to like it."

"Mostly I do," I said. "But I've been thinking about leaving since Suzanne passed me over. I hate to admit it but she's right. I'm not the right person for that job."

"Why not?"

"I'm not corporate enough. I don't know when to shut up even when I'm right about something. I don't want to do the political calculus in my head on how to balance pleasing one faction with another. I want to be able to say what I think when I think it and let the chips fall where they may. And you can't do that when you're in management."

Therese smiled. "You seem to know what you don't want, Brin. But it sounds to me like you've rationalized why you should stay, not why you should leave."

I shrugged. "I'm really torn. I like the people. I'm good at what I do." I remembered telling my mother, my sister about the feeling of family on my teams. It felt like a long time ago.

I sighed. "Jeff's gone. You're too big a mucky-muck to stand at the board with me and draw. I've been asking myself what am I staying for."

Therese sighed. "It's not what it was. That's true."

"I'm trying to look at it this way. One of us has to leave. You're good at your job, you want to stay and the CEO wants you to stay. I'm good at my current job but I get in trouble with my boss and have no prospects for promotion. Analytically, it's pretty obvious who should stay and who should go."

"I would be lying if I said I wanted to leave," Therese said. "I don't. I'm not done with the place yet."

"You do need to be careful, Therese. Corporate power and software construction can seduce, can make you think it's a world on its own terms and it's not." I was surprised to hear my mother's voice echoing. Would these people think of you a week after you're gone?

"It is seductive, Brin. I can't deny it."

"I do miss patient care. I've been thinking I should go back to working in a drugstore or maybe try a clinic this time. I like counseling patients on their meds, even cranky old patients complaining about how much they have to pay for them."

"I thought you liked the systems work, Brin. Wouldn't you miss it? And it pays better."

"I do like the systems work. Maybe I could do both if I worked for a big place." I stood up and stretched. "We're not going to figure this all out today. I need to go home so I can spend some time with David before I go back to work tomorrow. But I'm not ready to leave you."

Therese put her arms around me. "I also don't want you to think you have to leave Carepath to somehow make up for Cleveland."

"I don't think that at all." I hesitated. "What I did was wrong. But it didn't come completely out of the blue. There was something out of balance with us."

Therese looked at me, quiet for a long time. "How can we do better?"

I shrugged. "It's not rocket science. We both need to practice empathy. Take time to listen. Admit what's hard."

Therese smiled a little sadly. "No silver bullets."

I nodded. "Enough talk. Just lie here with me."

When it came time for me to go, I clung to Therese and cried. "I'm afraid if I let you out of my sight, you'll change your mind."

Therese pulled her into a long kiss. "Things will feel a little tentative for a while. That's normal."

"I'm not feeling tentative. Except about the job." I sighed. "I'll try to understand if you are."

Therese smiled. "You're a steamroller, Brin." She helped me pack the car, and promised to call as soon as she got back to town.

Therese drove back on Wednesday and came for dinner. She and David chatted as though nothing had happened, about school, the Vikings, the Internet. They took Christie for a walk while I did the dishes. I asked her to stay and she did. She seemed sober, a bit distracted. I didn't press her.

Therese spent the next couple of days at her house, supervising a parade of painters, window washers, carpet and upholstery cleaners and a chimney sweep. She took her oriental rugs and her summer clothes to the cleaners. She raked and bagged leaves. She caulked around doors and windows outside while her house was transformed. She had David and me over for dinner on Saturday. After dinner, one of David's friends came by and picked him up. She sat with me on the couch in the living room.

"The place looks great. What inspired you?" I asked.

"I felt like I needed to get things in order. Get ready for winter before I go back to work." Therese fell silent.

We sat in silence. A simmering silence where I didn't want to ask what she was thinking. I remembered Ruth's porch, the palm trees, the shimmer of light off the Norfolk pine. I asked Therese if she wanted to watch a movie on cable. Halfway through it she got up and went to the kitchen. I found her cleaning her pantry and putting canned goods in a bag for the food shelf. When I said I was going home, she didn't ask me to stay. She kissed me good night, but seemed relieved that I was leaving.

Therese went back to work and immediately left town for three days. She called every night from the hotel and talked a lot about the negotiations. It seemed easier to talk when we were apart.

The following Friday David went to Teddy's. I asked Therese to spend the weekend and she accepted. On Saturday night, when I started to unbutton her pajama top, Therese told me she wasn't in the mood. I was hurt but didn't say anything. I lay awake and thought while Therese slept. In the past either of us could and did initiate sex. The frequency had fallen off over the past couple of years. It seemed to start when Therese was working all those weekends on the company going public, but I couldn't be sure. We'd gotten out of synch with our menstrual periods, which basically ruled out half the month. I hadn't reached out to Therese sexually during the time I was seeing Ruth. I decided I'd better take my cues from her.

The next shock came when I invited Therese for Thanksgiving. Therese hesitated and said that she was going to her brother's but that she'd like to spend the rest of the weekend with me if that was OK. "So I shouldn't automatically expect to have holidays with you?" I challenged.

"I should have talked to you first," Therese said. And silence descended again.

I decided that I couldn't face having Augustina over. Marlys would be with Jessie and granddaughter Meg, now two and a half years old. No doubt Marlys would include our mother. I bought a small turkey and got up early to oil the bird and rub the skin with a molasses paste. While I made the stuffing, I wondered what Ruth was doing for the holiday. I thought about what I wanted from the day. I watched the Macy's parade, basted the turkey, wrote in my journal. I asked David to peel potatoes with me and tried to recall my blessings as we ate. Therese surprised me by showing up for dessert and coffee.

The next day David went to Teddy's for the rest of the weekend. Therese and I did a little shopping and went to a movie. That night, I asked Therese if she would take a bath with me. She agreed, without much enthusiasm.

We sat in the soaking tub, across from each other, obscured by bubble bath. I reached for her hand. "Therese, I need to talk to you. I'm not trying to put you on the defensive. But you've barely touched me or talked to me since we were up north. I feel like you're somewhere else."

"I'm still feeling kind of sad, Brin. I need you to give me time."

"I need some kind of a sign from you. I feel like the lights are on but there's nobody home."

"I don't know what kind of a sign I can give you. I'm here. That's about the best I can do."

"You're not here. For the last month you've been in some kind of fog, like you're afraid to really look at me."

She moved away. "Did you practice safe sex?"

"What?"

"Did you use—what do they call those things? Dental dams?

"Jesus Christ, Therese!"

"It's a fair question. You don't know who she's slept with, do you?"

I said nothing. Ruth could have been sleeping with half of Cleveland for all I knew.

Therese moved further away and propped her elbows on her knees. "You want to know what I'm thinking?"

"Yes."

"OK. When I see you without your clothes on, I'm wondering about how you touched her. About how she touched you. About how much you liked it. What you were thinking about when you gave yourself to someone else." She began to cry. "Another woman making love to you. I can't get it out of my mind."

I remembered Ruth embracing me from behind, cupping my breasts, nuzzling my ear. I stayed silent. I watched Therese cry for a few moments, then slid behind her to put my arms around her. She didn't push me away.

"I felt so powerless and so confused. You were the one who knew everything about being a lesbian. You'd had other lovers. You were the shining star at work. Everything was going your way. And I was totally lost. David was acting out. I couldn't even bring myself to say the word lesbian. And you wanted me to commit everything to you."

"And why did you think I was pressing you for a commitment? So we could have a life together!"

"What I should have done was insist on more room for myself. I needed some way to keep you at bay, to protect myself. I picked the worst way possible."

"Were you in love with Ruth?"

"No."

"Do you miss her?"

Like the sunlight. Like curling up in a quilt on a rainy day and never leaving the house. "Therese, I was only with her three times."

"Do you pretend that I'm her when I touch you?"

"For God's sake, no." Because I bring up a blank screen. "What is the point of tormenting yourself and me like this?"

The tub water was cooling off. I let some of it out, then added hot water. Therese stayed slumped in my arms.

"Are you going to hold this over me for the rest of our lives?"

"No. You wanted to know why I'm distant. I'm telling you."

"I love you, Therese. You're going to have to decide for yourself if you trust that. I can't dig you out of your hole." I willed myself to count through the breaths. Not to explode. "Is there something I *can* do?"

"I don't know, Brin. I really don't."

I sighed. "OK, I'm going to be more specific. When I want to make love with you, what should I do?"

Therese shrugged. "I don't know. You usually think of something."

"Can I touch you in a certain way? Should I say something rather than touch you?"

"Touch me. Then tell me you want me."

"OK. Can we get out of the tub?"

"OK."

We toweled off. I led her into the bedroom. I sat next to her on the bed. I put a hand on her belly. "I'd like to touch you. Is there something I can do?"

Therese pulled back the quilt. "You can hold me and stroke my head."

"OK."

I held Therese until she fell asleep in my arms. I reminded myself to keep my expectations low. The image of Ruth's lips upon me rolled through me. This time I didn't banish the fantasy.

The next morning I awakened to Therese spooning me, touching me. I sank back into the pillows, gathered her into me. It took two weeks of following Therese's careful instructions before she allowed me to make her come. I thought of getting to first base, second base, third base and Ann Landers' instructions to keep three feet on the floor. I held my tongue. I had a fleeting wish that someday we could laugh about this, though I knew it was impossible.

CHAPTER 26

Where we started. The anatomy of passion began with the skin: the magnetic pull of mouths, the electrifying sensation of fingertips approaching the groin, the feel of every pore opening to the body of the beloved. The world began and ended with her. Plundering each other's bodies like they were buried treasure. Waxing bold and shy within minutes. You didn't know each other well. All obstacles could be overcome. You could barely get out of bed long enough to buy bagels on Sunday morning. Life had a meaning and significance you'd never guessed possible.

Passion transformed over time into comfort and knowledge. Its residue sank below the surface into the rhythm of quiet breathing, bodies spooned together in sleep, hugging and hand-holding. You were no longer enchanted by the way she sneezed. Fighting over whose turn it was to walk the dog. Yelling at each other, then having long, serious conversations about what set you off and the need to share power in the relationship. Identifying the differences which led to fights. Deciding to pick your battles.

What was the magic that transformed intense attraction into lasting love or left the lovers to founder and drift through the vortex like disembodied spirits?

Where we were now. Surreptitiously reading the column in the Sunday paper titled can this relationship be saved. Trying to remember when you decided that a chronic irritant wasn't worth arguing about. When you quit talking. When her mind wandered elsewhere. Wondering how the unthinkable happened. Which of you first lost faith. Reaching for a familiar hand and falling into the abyss.

*　　*　　*

Passion was the tidal wave that carried you from one life to another. A hunger that drove you to leave an existence that no longer fit, for something wild and uncertain. That sustained you long enough to give up everything you knew and loved before. Passion was the molten rock that must cool enough to build something on top of it, but not so much that it could no longer absorb heat and light.

*   *   *

Passion, a roaring Pan, a lustful Venus, a lazy god only when sated. Sharp hooves of passion bruised the heart and the heart filled full again. The catalyst, the match that struck tinder, the cycle of blaze, warmth, smoke and ash. Wending one's way through the forest of passion. The small flame of hope, barely alive. The raging conflagration, headlong, heedless pursuit. Fire contained in the hearth, warmth and order. The rubble and ash of the burnt dwelling, lifeless and abandoned.

*   *   *

Passion was a spinning planet, intense and momentary. Surviving it took the patience of trees. And a faith that could overcome gravity in every vortex and black hole.

CHAPTER 27

Therese, December 1993

In December, a deal I'd been working on for months to buy SureHelp, a company that provided computer help desk services to other companies, fell through when their board voted it down. Paul, Alan, Nick and I dissected the carcass in Paul's office the week before Christmas.

"We seemed to have a good fit strategically. Their staff turnover was low for that type of business. Their board felt that the stock price we offered was fair. I don't know what happened," I said. "I'm sorry, Paul." I looked out the window. A pale winter sun bobbed in and out of the clouds. The sky was the color of eggshells. A snow sky.

"You don't need to apologize, Therese," Paul said. He sighed. I sat back and looked at him. His hair was receding from both sides of his forehead and was flecked with gray. There were dark bags beneath his eyes. The buttons of his white shirt strained across his middle. Frankly, he looked like shit. I wondered if I looked as old and tired as he did.

"We're here to figure out what happened and what we want to do about it. Nick, what do you think made the deal go south?"

"I agree with everything Therese said. I think though, that their investment banker has always had another fish on the line. They used us as bait to raise the asking price. I predict that after the first of the year they'll be bought for big bucks."

"Why couldn't we hire people and provide a competing service?" Alan asked. "Building a help desk is not exactly rocket science."

"Looking to build that empire, Alan?" Paul chided.

"Hell, I don't need it in my shop," Alan said. "I'm just being practical."

"Help desks are management intensive," I responded. "That was our whole reason for looking to buy. Or maybe I've been away so much that we've acquired some management talent with time on their hands that I don't know about?"

Paul sat back in his chair and stretched his arms wide. "This conversation is getting a little tense. Maybe we should pick it up after the holidays. I assume you're all taking next week off. If you weren't planning on it, I suggest you strongly consider it." He smiled to take the sting out of his words and stood up.

"Going skiing?" I asked, as he walked us to the door. Paul had a condo in Sun Valley.

"Yep," he said. "Leaving the day after Christmas. Kerri and Billy already have their skis packed."

I wished Nick a Merry Christmas and headed down the hall to my office. Alan followed me in and closed the door. "What was that all about?"

"I feel badly that this acquisition, which I've been working on since June, is dead. And I feel blindsided by Nick—he never told me that we were being outbid."

"You know how lawyers are, they have to justify their existence. He probably heard something at the bar association or playing racquetball. So you express your frustration by making a crack about the lack of management available in my shop?"

"You didn't have to take it that way, Alan. You'd just finished saying you didn't want to run a help desk."

"But that's how you meant it, isn't it?"

I sighed. "Alan, you know your shop has management problems. And you also know that you're not the only one. We've grown so fast that we haven't been able to bring people along. And with a few exceptions, we haven't been willing to spend the money to bring the talent in from outside. We're in over our heads."

"I can't argue with that."

I looked out the window. Snow fell softly on the trees along the river. The ice near shore was firm and white. In the middle of the river the snow slipped into a wet gray hole.

Brin was to start her new job the week of New Year's. She'd work for a health plan that owned a medical group, half time in a clinic pharmacy and half time helping the health plan automate its prescription refill system. She seemed excited about it. I watched the snow drift down and imagined her cube empty, then full of the items of someone I didn't know. Suzanne was having a going-away party for her the Friday before New Year's.

I turned from the window to look at Alan. "What are you and Jill doing for the holidays?"

"Jill is going with Madame and her beau to the Caribbean." Alan often referred to Marina as Madame or Her Highness. "Jill has, however, deigned to spend New Year's Eve with her boring father."

"Why don't you come for Christmas dinner?" I asked. "David will be with Teddy. Brin would be happy to have you, I'm sure."

"How are you and Brin getting along?"

"Better."

"That's encouraging," Alan said. "Since, if you were going to stay together, there was only one way to go."

"As you've said to me before, Alan, the ones we really love are the ones who know how to gut us . . ."

"And leave us hanging outside the boat for the whole world to see," he finished. "It's still a better analogy than the tomato cage of love."

I started to laugh. "Says you. So, are you coming for dinner?"

"I'm going to call Brin first. Maybe she was thinking of covering herself with whipped cream and tying herself up with a silver ribbon. I wouldn't want to interrupt anything."

"If she is, you can bring your camera and take pictures," I said. "Isn't getting between two women what you straight guys fantasize about?"

"This straight guy fantasizes about a dinner that's not from a box and a good night's sleep."

I walked him back to his office. My corner office was diagonally across the floor from Paul's. Paul was fond of saying that he put Nate and Alan in the corners closer to him because they were more likely to spend money than I was. My stock response was that was only true before I went into acquisitions. Of course, since Sandy came on board, no one spent more than $50,000 without her signature.

"Alan, what happened to Shana? She wasn't on the org chart I got yesterday."

"You missed that one, didn't you? The axe fell two weeks ago. Can't say I was sorry after what she did to Jim." Alan had to take one of Jim's departments away from him because of the brouhaha over the Chronicom project.

"You told me that Jim did it to himself."

"That's true, he did." What we both knew but didn't talk about was that the diabetes database still didn't work right at high volumes. Since the two largest customers for it had not renewed their contracts, this fact was no longer in the public eye.

"So, all the Chronicom managers are gone now," I mused.

"The sign of a truly successful merger," Alan said.

"Alan, you are the most wickedly bitchy man I've ever met. Are you sure you're not gay?"

"Positive. Or should I say, negative?"

"Good night, Alan."

"Good night."

*   *   *

Brin

I cleaned out my office, grateful that so many people were on vacation the week after Christmas. I found the picture of Therese from the annual report of so many years ago. I stared at it, tears forming in the corners of my eyes. Remembering how the light glinting off her hair had made me reckless, ready to leap off the ship into the roiling sea. I put the picture in a box, along with my photo of David, the painting called Abalone, the green Gumby and Bigfoot eraser. I threw out the Carepath project tschotzkes, the Dilbert cartoons from Jeff and several reams of e-mails.

This box would go with me to my new office. Carolyn had given me a silver picture frame for Christmas. I'd use it to display Therese's picture on my desk. During the final interview I came out to my new boss, a younger woman named Jenny. "I don't want to make a big deal out of it," I said, "but I also didn't want to work here if it were going to be a problem."

"That's cool," Jenny said. "I think there's a diversity group here if you want to connect up with other lesbians."

I smiled. "Thanks. The fact that you can say the word without choking is all I need to know."

Jenny smiled. "No problem." We went on to talk about our children and ex-husbands.

I went through my files, leaving a history of the diabetes, Coumadin, pediatric and adult asthma, cardiology, cholesterol and formulary projects. I kept business requirements, design specifications, test plans, training materials, marketing brochures and post-implementation reviews for each and threw out everything else. Why was it that you got to feel good about the condition of a project only when you were leaving it?

I put duplicates of the formulary requirements and test plans and software methodologies in the box. The list of generic and brand name drugs surfaced and I flipped through it. Lasix. Lanoxin. Cardizem. Zoloft. Medications for the heart, to regulate its beats, to flush its by-products, to calm its anxiety. I took a puff of beclavent. I wiped the tears from my eyes, put the list in the box and sealed it up.

CHAPTER 28

Therese, January, 1994

Paul came back from the holidays all revved up for change. He introduced the consultant at his executive staff meeting, the people who reported directly to him. The consultant's name was Don Baker. He'd been with one of the big six accounting firms until he left to start his own business a year ago. He was forty-something and a big man, about 6'4" and 220 pounds. Probably a linebacker in college. He wore a navy blue suit with a white shirt and red paisley tie, giving him a flag-like aura. His head was long and narrow, an effect accentuated by the short, wavy cut of his black hair. Max Headroom on steroids.

"Don's going to help me evaluate our management structure and compensation policies," Paul said.

Sandy said something politically correct and friendly and Nate made a joke. Alan stared grimly and I asked whether our management structure was typical of other firms our age and size.

"In our industry, typical is still emerging," he said with a little smile. "For companies primarily in Web products, the key is how quickly they can move and change direction." He went on with a speech that mentioned continuous quality improvement, self-directed work teams, enlightened leadership, workforce diversity and managing change. The only things he left out were building a bridge to the 21st century and solving the year 2000 computer problem. But after all, it was only our first meeting.

Paul promised that Don would interview each of us individually, then Don shook hands all around and left.

My appointment with Don was a week later. I fretted about what to say about Carepath's problems, our growth opportunities, my own frustrations, potential deals we should go after. I made notes in the middle of the night by flashlight on those nights I woke up at three and couldn't go back to sleep. Brin advised me to say what I really felt. I smiled and said big six consulting firms didn't believe in feelings.

Don declined coffee. We sat at the one end of my conference table that wasn't piled high with files and magazines. He asked about my background and I began to talk about my undergraduate degree from the University of Wisconsin at Madison in economics and psychology, and my MPH from the University of Michigan.

"What about your childhood," he interrupted.

"What about it?" I replied.

"Where were you in the birth order?"

"First," I said.

"I might have guessed," he said.

"Why?"

"Paul says that you take initiative and that you're very responsible."

I smiled warily. "Paul could say the same about himself."

"Were you athletic growing up?" Don asked.

"Mmm hmm. Basketball. Tennis. Track. I ran the 440."

"A balanced runner," Don said. "Capable of speed and capable of distance."

"What about you? What was your sport?"

"I had several," he said. "Football. Basketball. In college I added squash."

"Ivy League," I guessed.

"Yale," he said.

He asked about the positions I'd held at Carepath and skillfully steered the conversation toward how the company had changed and my views on that.

"I was the third employee," I said. "Now we have a thousand. For the most part we've done a good job of managing growth. Change is hard, but the old saw is true. Grow or die."

I gave him a brief history of our technical innovations, bragging about Alan because he wouldn't do it himself. "Alan was one of the first CIOs in the industry to create a Microsoft-focused group, develop Windows experts and be a beta tester for Windows for Workgroups and Windows NT. He knew early that the Web would be big and steered us through the initial dominance of Netscape, the emergence of Microsoft Explorer, Sun's Java product and applet strategy. Our software runs on appliances for net browsing, the Internet toasters, as well as full-service workstations."

Don ignored my paid political advertisement and cut to the chase. "Has the company become overly driven by the financials?"

I hesitated. "I think we're at a point where we need to rearticulate our purpose. The stock price drives so much of our day-to-day activity. We've had a reputation for reliability in our products, for helping our customers cope with change in technology. I view that as our core mission. I'd hate to see it change."

I went to lunch with Alan, who was nervous about his interview the next day.

"You should be nervous," I said. "Because you can be such a hothead. I don't know what his real agenda is. I think he's trying to get a read on whether we're disillusioned with the new order."

"Did Sandy put Paul up to this?"

I considered the question as I picked at my Cobb salad. "I hadn't thought of that. Maybe."

"When was the last time you talked to Nate?" Alan asked.

"I don't know. I've been traveling so much I've lost track of him."

Alan shook his shaggy brown head at me. "Wake up, Therese. CEOs don't bring management consultants in unless they're getting ready to shake things up. Aren't you curious about whose head is on the block?"

I reached for the French fries on his plate. "Maybe a change would be good. If the severance was right."

"You're just trying on the words. You don't believe that."

"You're right. I'm not looking to leave. Especially with Brin just having changed jobs." I ordered coffee and watched him eat a piece of tiramisu. "You're worried about yourself, aren't you? You'd probably have an easier time than any of us finding a job. Mr. techno whiz."

Alan looked gloomy. "I'm not looking for more change, Therese. I'm still in shock from Marina leaving."

"Alan, dearest. It's been almost three years. Isn't it time to come out of that particular cave?"

"Jill says I'm a curmudgeon. I guess she's right."

"Jill's got a great vocabulary. I'm going to say it again to you. Go. To. Therapy. Get yourself unstuck."

"What's a therapist going to do for someone who believes Camus was right? Every day we push the rock up the hill and every night it rolls down and we start over. If we're lucky the rock doesn't totally crush us on the way back down."

"And Camus said our job was to exult in the absurdity of it, not crawl into a hole and wait to die. You're depressed. They have medication for that these days—it's biochemical."

"My ultimate goal in life is to get an endlessly-refillable supply of Prozac," he said, writing a check for his half of lunch.

"You're impossible," I said.

"Yes," he agreed. "It's why you love me."

CHAPTER 29

Brin, February 1994

I came home at six o'clock on Valentine's Day, endured Christie's fervent nightly greeting and began making dinner. At my suggestion, David had invited his first real girlfriend over for dinner. Maris had been named Marianne when I first met her Christmas afternoon. She'd since renamed herself after the invisible woman on the TV show "Frasier."

"Not every 16 year-old has a taste for "Frasier," Therese said, after David explained why the voice of the girl on the telephone with the strange name sounded familiar. "As long as she doesn't start calling David 'Niles'."

I sighed. "I'm not ready for David to have a girlfriend. He's not even 17 yet."

"How old were you when you started dating?"

"Fifteen," I admitted. "But why is she renaming herself after someone who never appears on the show? Is she depressed?"

Therese started to laugh. "Whoa, Dr. Freud. Maybe it gives her the freedom to re-invent herself. It's my job to ponder the great imponderables and make something out of nothing. Move over."

I took a filet of salmon out of the refrigerator, set it in a baking dish, dotted it with butter and sprigs of fresh dill, covered it with foil and put it in the oven. Christie sat in front of the stove gravely, regarding the salmon. I gave her a biscuit. I'd followed Therese's advice and planned a simple meal. Still, I was exhausted. The pharmacy was overrun by women picking up last-minute Friday night prescriptions and we hadn't been staffed for it. I was supposed to have left at 4:30 and had plenty of time to make dinner. I called David from the car phone to tell him to clean the bathroom and not to have Maris come over until 6:30. I called Therese and told her to find dessert at the bakery where she was to go for bread. I'd wanted to bake a cake from a mix and decorate it with the pastel candy hearts we'd eaten as children, the ones with the two-word slogans. Be mine. You're sweet. Kiss me. Another would-be ritual forsaken for lack of time.

"It's going to be completely picked over," Therese complained.

"I don't care what you get, just deal with it," I said and hung up.

David had complained, too, when I'd asked him to vacuum. The dog hair and dust seemed to be bothering me more lately. Probably because the house in winter had been closed up for so long.

Therese came in and shoved her briefcase into the coat closet. "Happy Love Day, Brinnae," she said, presenting a vase of red roses.

"They're very pretty," I said. "Thank you." I turned from slicing potatoes and we kissed. "What did you find at the bakery?"

Therese pulled items out of her shopping bag with a flourish. "Herb baguettes. And chocolate cupcakes with red cinnamon hearts."

"Good," I said. "I need help with the salad."

"Just let me hang up my coat," Therese said.

I slid the potatoes into the oven beside the salmon. I took a deep breath, coughed and exhaled. Picked up my inhalers. "Pace yourself," I muttered, the same mantra I'd been using behind the counter at work. I had been away from retail sales a long time. Customers had become more demanding.

Parts of my clinic day were good. Mid-morning a wizened woman with white hair and half of her dentures missing had approached carrying a bag of medications that she poured out onto the counter. "Dr. Peterson told me to come see you about these," she announced. I instructed my clerk to take the register, led the woman slowly into my office and spent half an hour sorting through the bottles, tossing some and having her put the contents of others into her four seven-day pill dispensers.

"My son and his wife are taking me out to dinner tonight," the woman proclaimed.

"How lovely," I said. I listened to the woman recite her children's names and accomplishments, admired pictures of her grandchildren and pulled David's school picture out of my wallet. My son gazed steadily into the camera, the hint of a smile on his lips, his hair cropped close.

I heard Christie start to bark, my early warning system for passing dogs or visitors. At the sound of David's key in the lock, I put on my hostess face.

"Maris, how are you?" I murmured.

"Fine, Mrs. Anderson," Maris said, shaking hands with a soft touch. She had long, straight hair the same wheat blond as David's was in the winter, and an oval face set off by plum lipstick and silver eyeshadow. She handed me a bouquet of yellow freesia wrapped in a bag with the name of a supermarket on it.

"They're lovely, Maris," I said. "Thank you."

"Notice anything different about me, Mom?" David asked. I looked him up and down slowly. The same blue jeans and Nike cross-trainers he had on this morning. His hair the same length. A Wallflowers t-shirt under his open ski jacket, Jakob Dylan's brooding face staring out at me. Please God, not a tattoo.

Therese walked up, greeted Maris and punched David on the shoulder. "Nice earring," she said.

"Yeah," David said, looking at me.

"Turn your head," I said. There was a diamond stud in his left ear.

"Maris gave it to me," David said. "For Valentine's Day."

"It's striking," I said. "You'll have to give me time to get used to it, David."

"One of my friend's boyfriends fainted," Maris said. "David didn't even wince."

"Not worried about being called a fag anymore, big guy?" Therese challenged.

Maris and I winced simultaneously.

"Hell no," David said. "Cause I know you'll protect me." He and Therese whooped like this was the funniest thing anyone had ever said.

"Can I do anything to help?" Maris asked. I noted that Maris had enough poise to remember her manners in the face of gay jokes.

"Do you like cheese?" I asked.

"As long as it's not, like, Roquefort," Maris said.

"You're in luck," I said, handing her a plate of crackers, slices of cheddar and a hunk of Brie. I wished I had some kind of blue cheese, my favorite. "You can take these into the living room."

I took a swig of wine from the glass on the counter and decided to make the salad myself. Therese and David were jousting over what music to put on the CD player. Maris picked Smashing Pumpkins over David's suggestion of Marilyn Manson and Therese's preference for Enya. I wondered if I would have over-ruled my boyfriend at that age about music. Maybe not. No, definitely not. I tossed green leaf lettuce, sliced mushrooms, toasted almonds and sunflower seeds in my crystal salad bowl, a wedding present. The salad was David's favorite.

I ran my fingers around the rim of the bowl, looking for other relics of life with Teddy. The copper-bottomed Revereware pans in the cupboard. The Orrefors crystal vase which held Therese's roses. The china in the dining room hutch. Teddy's image loomed, standing over me with roses, asking why I didn't greet him at the door wearing only Saran wrap. David tugging at my leg, five years old. "Mom, what's Saran wrap?" I grimaced. Teddy had never been at his best on Valentine's Day. Whatever his best had been. Shaking my head slowly, smiling at the thought of David as a relic. A relic with an earring. What we're left with. What we embrace and what lives unseen for years. I cut open a pomegranate and scraped the gleaming red-black seeds into a cereal bowl. In a moment I'd go out and ask the kids whether they'd ever had pomegranate before. It would liven up the salad.

I sliced a loaf of bread, spread garlic butter on it. I wondered if Ruth were alone tonight. I hadn't thought about Ruth for a while. Therese and I were getting along. The sense of living on a fault line, of suspense about the future had faded. I was a lesbian. Therese and I were together. David had a girlfriend.

I slid the loaf of foil-wrapped garlic bread into the oven. In the second month of my job, there was still no one to go to lunch with. I reminded myself that I'd usually read e-mail at my desk over lunch at Carepath, but it didn't seem to help. The clinic staff was waiting to see whether they should invest any energy in a part-timer. It was too cold to go for walks, so I ate at my desk in the back corner of the pharmacy, furthest from the window where I greeted patients. I walked into the waiting room when there was a lull and stared outside. Bird tracks in the snow, nature's cuneiform.

Therese returned. "I was coming to do the salad this instant."

"It's OK," I said. "You're doing a fine job of entertaining. Keep it up."

"Hard day?" Therese asked, putting her hand on Brin's shoulder.

"Really hectic," I said.

Therese looked concerned. I knew she was feeling guilty. It irritated me. "Go taste the salmon," I said. "It should be done by now."

Therese obediently took the foil cover off the pan and scraped a piece from the underbelly. "Superb. Nice and moist."

"Put the foil back on and set the pan on top of the stove," I instructed. "Turn the oven up to 400 so the potatoes can brown."

Therese executed a smart salute. "Yes sir, general sir."

I smiled wearily. "Thank you. You can go back to the kids. You sound like you're having fun."

"David seems happy," Therese said, wrapping her arms around Brin. "She seems like a nice young woman. Let's not make any more of it than that."

"OK," I said, kissing Therese, sending her back to the living room.

I heard Therese head up the stairs, the door to our bedroom close, the sound of water running and remembered the pomegranate. I walked into the dining room and stopped. Maris was sitting on David's lap. Her head pulled down to his. His hand snaking up under her blouse.

I backed away in shock, retreated to the edge of the kitchen. "David!"

"What, Mom?" Annoyed.

"Never mind. I'm going to put it in the salad."

I stood at the counter holding the bottle of raspberry vinaigrette. Holding a baby bottle and the breast pump. The physical sensation of giving milk, him suckling. Sustaining a creature helpless as a sea anemone on land. Bathing him, gurgling, in the sink. Patting him dry, powdering him, his legs waving in the air. The passion you had for your child. The way he called for you, cried for you. Only you could soothe him. Then one day he loomed over you and called another woman's name. Christie rubbed against my leg, whining, looking concerned. I sat on the kitchen step, pulled Christie into my arms and buried my chin in fur.

When Therese returned, I had her toss the salad with the pomegranate seeds and raspberry vinaigrette and take it to the dining room. I put the salmon on a platter, emptied the browned potatoes into a glazed pottery dish, unwrapped the steaming garlic bread. I admired my work, and called David out to help me carry the dishes to the table.

"Looks great, Ma," he said. "I'm starving."

"Put the dishes down for a minute," I said.

He set the salmon on the counter. "What?'

"Give your mother a hug," I murmured, putting my arms around him.

"Aw, Mom, don't go mushy on me," he muttered, but complied.

"Just don't forget the first woman who loved you," I said. "And still does." My voice trembled a little. "And wipe that lipstick off your face."

David looked momentarily abashed. "You're way over the top now, Mom. That calls for noogies," he said, rubbing the top of my head fiercely.

"Knock it off," I said, reaching for his belly to tickle him. "Pick on somebody your own size."

He successfully evaded my tickling fingers, picked up the salmon and potatoes and ran for the dining room. "Last one to the table does the dishes," he called.

I brought out the salad. I poured wine into Therese's and my glasses and sparkling grape juice for David and Maris. I lifted my glass in a toast. "Happy Valentine's Day, David. And Marianne."

I saw the look Maris gave David, the look that said was it early Alzheimer's or did she do it on purpose. The first of a lifetime of looks I would see some woman give my son whenever I said anything other than banal pleasantries. "I mean Maris." Maris. Give me a break. And covered my hand with my mouth to keep from laughing.

"To romance," Therese said.

"Hear, hear," David said. They clicked their glasses lightly.

CHAPTER 30

Therese, April, 1994

Brin picked out a three-bedroom townhouse in a new development in Minnetonka. The townhouses were nice without being luxurious. They were connected to two adjoining developments by several miles of asphalt paths that could be used for walking, biking or my old favorite, roller-blading. We'd have a view of a pond frequented by Canadian geese.

Brin and I would have the master bedroom with a huge bath complete with whirlpool tub. David's room could become a guest room after he went to college. The third bedroom could double as a place for Brin to paint and an office for me. The unfinished walkout basement would provide private space for David to hang out with his friends around the pool table, room for exercise equipment and plenty of storage.

David and Maris tromped around the unit, discussing the placement of the CD player, his computer and other key appliances. I stood at the back of the big, sunny kitchen and took Brin's hand. "What do you think?"

"I can see myself standing here, making fresh pasta, stirring a homemade tomato sauce, baking bread."

I grinned. "I think I like your Italian fantasies best of all."

"What do you think, Therese?"

"It's beautiful. But it's a big change. Let me stand in each room and get used to it before we go."

She fixed me with her steely eye. "Just remember that change can be good."

*   *   *

Brin

Therese rolled in about seven o'clock, coat half-buttoned, blowing her nose.

I looked up from the remains of lasagna and refolded the front page of the paper. "Dinner is served at 6:30 sharp unless prior arrangements are made."

"It's nice to see you, too," she said, throwing her coat on the sofa.

"Did we have a cellular outage which struck the Midwest into a collective silence?" I asked.

"My entire day was a four-alarm fire."

"Your every day is a four-alarm fire. It's not even worth mentioning unless the building burns down."

"We've missed our quarterly target by half a million, which means the stock will tank by Friday, the second help desk deal in a row is toast and Suzanne quit." Therese walked into the kitchen and put her plate into the microwave.

"Why did Suzanne quit?"

"She's tired of Sandy kicking her ass. To quote the Harvard Business Review, your relationship with your supervisor is the most accurate predictor of employee satisfaction."

"The supervisor as the corporate mother," I said. "Much maligned, always at fault."

"Thank you, Dr. Freud. Where's David?"

"Out with Maris."

Therese sat down at the table and began to eat. She picked up the sports page, scanned it and put it down. "Baseball season hasn't even started and already Carepath is in last place."

"You really don't get it, do you?" I said.

"What?"

"It's not baseball season at Carepath or at any other behemoth, publicly-traded corporation. Paul will not pitch twenty winning games this season. There is no World Series. The metaphor is purely Darwin. There are a half dozen fat, ugly sumo wrestlers clawing it out on the mat. A couple of them will emerge, bruised, bloody and half-blind. The others will die. Wall Street will cheer the winners and 90 days later it will happen all over again."

"I'm so glad I came home to relax and renew my energy."

"If you choose the wrong metaphor, you will not dig yourself out of this particular cesspool."

"I think I prefer sumo wrestling to plumbing."

"This is your only life, Therese. If you're going to devote it to serving a corporation, be aware that you won't get much back, at least in terms of meaning."

*   *   *

Walking around the house late at night, looking into the linen closet, Teddy's closet where I kept my off-season clothes, wondering if Therese and I should buy a new bed, new bedroom furniture. Should we stay with white walls, white ceilings and get some bright, modern rugs?

Therese and I were almost living together now, except for nights when she got home late from the airport and camped at her house. Still, we'd both have to get rid of stuff. Therese's basement was full of old softball uniforms, bikes, skis, cooking magazines, textbooks from graduate school and other stuff there was no point in saving. Most of David's old toys should be tossed, except the bunny he slept with until he was six and maybe a favorite sled. I could get rid of Christie's original crate which she'd outgrown. An extra ironing board in the basement. So many skins we'd shed along the way.

I checked my watch. Twelve thirty. David was still out with Maris. I yawned and rubbed my eyes. It was time, past time to move in with Therese. We had somehow made a life together, despite my fears and worries about David, Therese's workaholism, the affair with Ruth.

What would change when Therese and I moved in with each other? Would we sit slumped in our chairs in the living room like

Tweedledum and Tweedledee, with Christie curled up on the rug beside us? Would we ever go out? Would I fall over in the bathroom from a cerebral hemorrhage some future day after David was married and Therese was still running around the country?

A glint of fear, then a calm certainty. We would grow old together. Despite our mistakes and the ways in which we irritated each other. We'd keep each other company as my hips grew arthritic and Therese's eyesight failed. I caught a glimpse of Augustina sitting alone by the fire. If we were lucky.

*　　*　　*

CHAPTER 31

Therese, April, 1994

When a meeting canceled at the last minute, I took a rare break and went down to the cappucino stand on the ground floor for a double latte. Getting off the elevator on the way back, I walked through the north end of our suite to stop and say hi to Nate, but he wasn't in.

"Toledo," his secretary said.

"Lucky man," I said.

She grimaced. "No Godiva chocolates for me this trip."

Coming back, I saw a man I'd never seen before standing outside Alan's office. The door to the office was closed. He wore a navy blue suit, a white shirt and a rep tie. I grinned. Must be an IBM veteran who couldn't change with the dress code. I made a mental note to ask Alan if he gave the sales rep grief.

I logged onto the home page and read the Carepath on-line newsletter, the press releases on new products, and the summary of changes to the most recent version of the cardiology package, which I still kept up with for old times' sake. I wrote a couple of e-mails, called two of my directors and left voicemails and looked for June who wasn't there. Probably at the copy machine. I was restless but I didn't know why. Not used to having an unscheduled minute, I chided myself. I took the elevator to the vending machines and bought a can of mineral water. When I re-entered my office, I noticed that the little red light on my phone was blinking, meaning voicemail.

I entered my password and listened to Phyllis Phonemail's voice telling me I had one new message. June had dubbed the mechanized voice Phyllis. I'd said more than once that it was the voice I heard the most often. It was a wonder I didn't hear her in my dreams. Phyllis said, "Message one, from Alan Dockman, was received at 12:08 PM."

The first thing I noticed was that Alan hesitated before speaking, which was unusual. I had to replay the message three times before I could absorb what he said. "Therese, it's Alan. It was my head on the block. Call me at home." Then there was the click, the sound of the line going dead. After the third time, I deleted the message. Phyllis droned on. "You have one old message. You may listen to your old messages or continue. To listen to your old messages, press listen or three. To continue, press enter or pound."

My fingers seemed to be operating in slow motion. They didn't respond to Phyllis' choices. I hung up the phone and stared out the door. I stood up with a sick feeling in the pit of my stomach. I walked out of my office and headed for Alan's. The man in the blue suit was gone. Alan's office door was open. The familiar stacks of manila file folders still sat on his conference table and on top of his credenza. His computer with the flashing rectangle screensaver and Bach background music hummed on his desk. The cactus garden near the south window looked healthy.

I looked around the office more slowly. The picture of Jill on the desk and the Egyptian mummy were gone. The framed prints of Edvard Munch's "The Scream" and of a Navaho woman completely wrapped in white except for her face no longer hung on the walls.

I leaned against the doorframe of Alan's office feeling like someone had died. I wondered if I'd misunderstood. Then a surge of energy overtook me, a feeling of pure rage. The man in the blue suit had been hired to stand guard while Alan cleaned out his office, door closed, no doubt in the presence of another blue-suited man. Alan allowed to take only what Nick would call his personal effects. His one phone call to me before he was marched off. Alan escorted from the building with a carton that used to hold paper for the copy machine. A man released from prison with a small suitcase into a jail of another kind. His access card with his photo taken from him. His company cell phone removed from his car. And a copy of Carepath's proposed severance agreement in the breast pocket of the gray tweed jacket he wore today.

I strode down the hall toward Paul's office. Dorothy was at lunch. His door was open. I walked in and looked at the calendar on his desk. A neat line was drawn through the schedule from eight to five and the word Phoenix written at the top. The son of a bitch didn't have the nerve to do it himself. He wasn't even in town when the axe fell.

So who had the pleasure of telling Alan he was fired? Or let go or downsized or whatever the current euphemism was? I headed for Nick's office. His secretary was out, but Nick sat at his desk, dictating into his telephone. He saw me and hit the pause button on the console.

"Did you do it, Nick? Did you fire Alan?"

Nick sighed and looked out his window. "What did Alan say?"

"He didn't say anything. I haven't talked to him, he left me the world's shortest voicemail. Why, what isn't he supposed to say?"

Nick sighed again. "He's supposed to say that he has resigned from Carepath."

"That's what he's supposed to say if he signs the severance letter. Tell me you at least offered him a severance package."

"Yes. Paul was more than generous."

"Paul was too much of a chickenshit to tell Alan himself. So you did it for him."

"I don't like this part of my job any better than you do, Therese. You've had to let people go."

"Yes, I have. After there's been a process of coaching or warning. Not completely out of the blue. Not to someone who was as much the soul of this company as Paul. Not in a power play organized by an outside consultant." I stopped for breath and tried to decide if I was shouting. I felt like my face was on fire. "Who's next, Nick? Who else's head is on the block?"

"I don't know any more than you do, Therese." He looked me squarely in the eye, then he took off his bi-focals and rubbed his eyelids. He put his glasses back on. "Go call Alan, Therese. Call him or drive over to his house. You don't want to hang around here this afternoon."

"OK," I said.

"But don't push him on the terms of his agreement. He's not supposed to talk about it."

"I almost thought you were human there for a minute, Nick. Thank God you're a lawyer again." I turned on my heel and marched out of his office.

I went to my office and sank into my chair. I tried to remember if Brin was at the health plan or the clinic today. I jumped back up again. I left her a message at each place saying that Alan had been fired, that it wasn't public yet and that I was going to his house. I got my purse and my coat and went to the elevator. When the doors opened, June stepped out.

"I have to go out, June. I probably won't be back."

"What's up, buttercup?"

"I'll call you later, OK?" I didn't wait for an answer and got into the elevator. She searched my face for a clue as the doors closed.

I got into my car and drove out into a day of blinding sunshine, blue sky and late melting snow. Instead of heading west on the beltway towards Alan's, I turned east and immediately got off at Fort Snelling State Park. I drove the wet roads around the park, past the park office and toward Pike Island cross-country ski trail where Alan and I had taken our first ski of the year three months earlier. Pike Island, named after the explorer Zebulon Pike, was one of three islands which sat in the confluence of the Mississippi and Minnesota Rivers. The river flowed steadily here, carrying little ice floes south until they melted. In January the trail had been pristine white and deep, marked only by ski, squirrel and dog tracks. The April snow was sketchy and dirty, and the path icy in the shaded areas from trees dripping above the trail.

Mendota Bridge traffic careened by above the park. Planes thundered overhead, descending to the airport a mile away. Despite its proximity to loud urban noise, the trail was pretty and flat enough to jolt the cross-country ski quad and lat muscles into action without danger of falls. I pulled my car into the trailhead parking lot and began to cry.

I was stunned at Alan's firing. I was ashamed of my own naiveté about corporate politics. How could I go back to a place where my best friend had been treated so shabbily? But how could I turn my back on a company into which I'd poured my heart and soul for ten years?

I blew my nose, put the car in gear and stopped for a chicken sandwich from a drive-through. When I got to Alan's, Brin's car was parked out front. I felt a wave of relief wash over me that I wouldn't have to face him alone, followed by shame that I could feel that way.

Brin answered the door and took me into her arms. We hugged wordlessly for a few minutes. "How is he?" I whispered.

Brin shook her head and led me down the hall to the family room. Alan sat in his leather recliner, a fire in the gas fireplace, with a throw over his legs and his cat Turing in his lap.

"Turing is purring," I said. I could never resist saying it and immediately felt stupid.

"Hello, Therese. Are you still gainfully employed?" Alan said. He picked up a glass of red wine from the coffee table beside him. The half-empty bottle sat next to his glass.

I shrugged. "I haven't heard otherwise. I'm in a state of shock." I came around beside him and carefully put my arms around him without disturbing Turing. Alan didn't resist my hug. I held him for a few minutes.

"Nick did Paul's dirty work," Alan said.

I nodded and switched to holding his hand. "I know. I talked to him."

"What did he say?"

"He told me to come and see you. And not to ask you about your severance agreement."

Alan laughed. "The bastard." He sipped from his wine again and sprawled further back in the chair.

"Do you have a lawyer?" I asked.

"Only for divorce. Brin and I were just discussing that."

I let go of Alan and went to sit on the sofa next to Brin. "Teddy's brother has been through this. I'll call him and see who he used," Brin said.

I nodded. "My friend Chris from golf was let go last year. I'll call her."

"I've joined a new, invisible alumni club," Alan said. "Just imagine the education I'm going to get now."

"Other than getting a lawyer and getting the severance agreement resolved, you shouldn't try to do anything," I said.

Alan laughed and looked at Brin. "Look at Therese. She's already writing a workplan."

"That's what Chris told me," I pressed ahead doggedly. "She said she just sat in her house for two weeks until she got over the initial shock."

Brin took my hand. "Therese, try to calm down. Try to just be and not do for a minute, OK?"

"OK," I said. I looked at Alan. I took a deep breath. I sat back on the sofa and began to tear up. I cried and Brin held my hand. "I should have quit on the spot," I said.

Alan looked me in the eye. "Don't you dare. You may need to become a bank."

"Whatever you need," I said, wondering what I meant. Wondering what he meant. Alan looked at his cat.

"Alan, have you eaten?" Brin said.

He shook his head.

"Can I fix you a sandwich? Some soup? Scrambled eggs?"

"Grilled cheese," Alan said. "Thank you, Brin."

With Brin gone, Alan and I sat and looked at each other in silence. "I feel guilty," I said.

He sighed and leaned his head back on the headrest. "It's not your fault."

"I know," I said. "I'm just so outraged. And so sad. And bewildered." I blew my nose. "What did Nick say to you?"

"It was mercifully short," Alan said. "Here's the play by play. He came into my office and sat in the chair in front of my desk. He said 'Alan, I have some difficult news for you.'

'Yes?' I said.

'You're being let go,' he said.

'Let go?' I said. I felt stupid, like a parrot. 'Why?'

'It's a layoff due to restructuring. Paul wants to do something different with the CIO position.'

'What does he want to do?'

He sighed. 'I don't really know. I'm authorized to offer you a severance package.' Jesus, he actually said that. I'm authorized to offer you a severance package. Then he handed me an envelope, told me to call him if I had questions after I read it and opened the door. There were two guys in navy blue suits standing there."

I nodded. "I saw this guy outside your office. I thought he was an IBM sales rep who hadn't heard about the dress code changing. I was going to tease you about it. Duh."

"The one guy was nice," Alan said. "He told me he was sorry for my loss, like they do on the cop shows. He let me pack my copy of my personnel file and my performance reviews. He asked me if there was anyone I needed to call, so I called you. He carried my pictures downstairs to my car, took my badge and my cell phone and said they'd mail my check. I got in my car and came home."

"Handed you your hat and said goodbye," I said.

Alan shook his head. "I never expected Paul to be such a gutless wonder."

"Neither did I," I said.

Brin came back with a grilled cheese sandwich, potato chips and a sliced orange on a plate. She put a bottle of spring water on the table next to Alan's wineglass. She looked at me. "Do you want anything?"

I stood up. "A wine glass. I'll get it."

When I came back, Brin was telling Alan about a computer project that David was working on for school. I half-listened and let my eyes roam around the room. Alan had a full wall of bookshelves to my right and built-ins around the fireplace behind him. To my left, a sliding glass door led onto a deck. I watched a bright red cardinal skitter around the feeder, land briefly and fly back to a tree to be with his mate. I sipped my Merlot. A squirrel sat beneath the feeder greedily polishing off the leavings of the birds above him.

I put down my glass and propped my feet on the ottoman in front of me. I leaned back into the couch. The sound of a key turning in the lock jarred me. I sat up fast and looked at Alan.

"Jill," he said. "Coming home from school."

"Jill," I said. "Oh, Jesus."

The back door closed. "Jill, I'm in the family room," Alan shouted. I heard her footsteps come quickly down the hall. A blonde head with two braids, a ski jacket, a backpack slid over the door handle. She took off her boots and jacket and set them neatly on a throw rug.

"Daddy, what are you doing home? Hi Therese and Brin."

"Come here, honey," Alan said.

She came over to his chair slowly, glancing at Brin and me, trying to read our faces. She knew it wasn't a party.

Alan hoisted her onto the arm of his chair and she pushed the cat aside. Turing hissed with great dignity and climbed out of Alan's lap. "I got fired today, Jill."

"Daddy, why?"

"Well, honey, I don't know the real reason. What they said was they're going to reorganize the company."

Jill looked at me. "Do you still work there?"

I shrugged. Brin says, "As far as we know, Jill. We don't know any more than your dad does."

"But why Daddy? And not you?"

I sighed. "We don't know, Jill. It doesn't seem fair, does it?"

"No. Daddy's good." She slid her arms around Alan's neck and buried her face in his shoulder.

"Your daddy's the best," I said.

Jill sat straight up. "I could get a paper route, Daddy."

Alan smiled. "Don't worry, I've got some money in the bank. We're not to that point yet."

"I could get one. But you'd have to drive me until the snow melts."

"That sounds like fun," Alan said. "Getting up at 4:30. Driving you around the empty streets, watching you practice your fastball."

"Are you going to tell Mom?" Jill asked.

Alan sighed. "Telling Marina will certainly be fun. Not today, honey. Today I'm going to sit here with you and my best friends and get used to the idea that my earth no longer revolves around their sun."

"That's a good way of putting it," Brin said. She stood up. "Come with me, Jill."

I heard them walk into the kitchen and the sounds of cupboard doors opening and closing. "So, pardner," I addressed Alan. "Should we start our own business? Form a solar system where the natives are more to our liking?"

"We'd be a little shy on capital," Alan said. "Brin was telling me about those townhouses you're looking at. And my discretionary income is better known as child support."

"Maybe we could get a bank loan. We'd be good risks. We have track records."

The sound of a mixer came from the kitchen. I hoped that Brin was teaching Jill to make chocolate chip cookies.

"I've watched Marina's sister's husband start his own business," Alan said. "He had fifteen years of public relations and marketing experience, but he couldn't get a loan." His voice had the detached quality of someone who was watching himself from the ceiling. I remembered our lunch conversation about Prozac. I thought of all of the benefits I took for granted from my employer. Health insurance. Disability. A 401 (K) retirement plan. Vacation and sick leave. Stock options. Alan could sell his stock if he had to.

"He's been in business for five years," Alan said. "He started out writing brochures, annual reports, training manuals, any kind of freelance writing. The first year he earned enough to pay for one of his kids' daycare. Unfortunately he had expenses that were twice that—setting up a home office, incorporation, having an accountant set up his books, doing a marketing brochure.

"Now he specializes in frequent flyer programs for restaurants. Last year he broke even for the first time. This year he thinks he might clear five thousand dollars. This is all without paying himself a salary. Marina's sister pays all of their expenses. He's there when the kids come home from school, takes them for doctor's appointments, waits for the plumber." He shook his head. "Being dependent on someone else for money to rent a video or buy a book. I'd hate that."

"Are they happy?"

Alan shrugged. "They worry about money. He either has too little work so he worries and has to make cold calls, or too much so he works nights and weekends. On the other hand he doesn't have anyone telling him what to do. He slops around the house in sweat pants unless he has to see a client. He's been to all of his kids' school plays."

I picked up a photo album off of Alan's bookshelf. I flipped through a few pages of pictures of Jill as a baby, Jill learning to walk, riding her first bicycle. Then I came to a 5 x 7 picture that had its own plastic sleeve. I sat in the middle, my hair cut in a modified shag, my arms around my companions' shoulders. Paul, grinning and full bearded, his hair flopping over his glasses, on my left. Alan, with a bushier beard, his hair curling over his collar, on my right. Paul and Alan each had fingers curled around a plastic wine glass, the three glasses pushed together on the table for a toast.

"Our first sale," Alan said.

"Yep," I said. Ten years ago. It was a late night in our little office in the funky old brick building in the warehouse district. I smiled at the janitor and talked him into taking our picture. We gave him a glass of wine. "What happened to us?"

"We got big," Alan said.

"Grow or die," I said.

"Grow and die," he replied.

Jill bounced in with a plate of chocolate chip cookies still warm from the oven. We played a few games of Sorry with Jill. We ate cookies and watched Dan Rather on the evening news, which we were never home early enough to see. Brin heated two cans of split pea soup and baked garlic bread in a bag. I slipped away and left June a voicemail, saying that I was not feeling well and that I didn't know if I'd come in tomorrow or not.

I hesitated, then dialed Phyllis Phonemail. I had two messages from clients, which I forwarded for staff to return. The third message was from Paul proposing breakfast. I hit the reply key and left a message that I couldn't make breakfast. I suggested lunch instead at a Chinese place near the building.

CHAPTER 32

Therese

I got up an hour after my normal time, and left a message for June to cancel my morning meetings.

I headed down to the basement and ran on the treadmill for twenty minutes with Michael Jackson's "Off the Wall" CD fueling me. I kissed Brin before she left for work. I sat at the table eating toast and watched David leave for school. I felt delinquent, like I was playing hooky. I drew a hot bath and took a long soak. I read the newspaper from cover to cover.

I called Stephanie and caught her between patients. "That really sucks," she said. "Sounds like a macho move for the analysts,"

"What do you mean?"

"Paul showing Wall Street that he's so serious about cutting costs that he'll fire an old friend."

I sighed. "The three of us started the company. So how can that not matter to Paul anymore?"

"You are not in the same world you were, Therese," she said.

I logged on, read my e-mail and checked the stock price. I put on a navy suit, drove my car through the carwash and filled the gas tank, then headed for the restaurant.

Paul was late. I drank tea and made notes for a trip I was scheduled to take the next week. He arrived fifteen minutes later, breathless. "Sorry, Therese. I was on a conference call to California and we ran over." He brushed his hair back from his forehead. It was a gesture I'd seen thousands of times over the years. I felt pain and willed it to recede into numbness.

"What did you want to see me about, Paul?"

He searched my face, looking for clues. "I assume you're upset about Alan. I wanted to tell you why I made the decision I did."

"I'm listening," I said.

"Alan has always kept up with technology," he said. "But we need a CIO who's a good manager and someone who can recognize when to strike deals with others and when to build it in-house. Alan is not that person."

"Alan is brilliant," I replied. "He has kept us from major investment errors in technology many times."

"Yes," Paul said. "But he's not a good manager. He can't fire people who should have been fired long ago. Like Jim Heywood. Like a half dozen other people either of us could name. In fact, I don't think he's ever fired anyone."

The waiter came and asked, "The usual?" We both nodded.

"Is that the chief criteria for being a senior officer at Carepath now? The ability to fire someone? Because if it is, Paul, you just failed the test yourself." I stopped when I felt my voice beginning to shake.

"Therese, I know you're angry. I know Alan's your best friend. I want you to know this isn't easy for me either. I believe it's the best answer for the business, but I don't feel good about it."

"Paul, the three of us started this company. Carepath wouldn't be where it is today without you or me or Alan. Doesn't that count for anything?"

Paul shook his head, sadly, like I'd missed a key question on the exam. "Carepath doesn't belong to us anymore, Therese. It belongs to the shareholders. That's who we answer to."

"It's a balancing act, Paul. We also have a responsibility to the customers. And to the staff. There's more to life than quarterly returns."

"There's more to life, yes, but quarterly returns are the first hurdle. If they're not good enough, we're gone. It's that simple."

"I thought the quarterly returns had been good. Am I missing something?"

The waiter put two steaming bowls of soup in front of us. Paul's was won ton, mine sizzling rice. He left a curried beef and a curried pork puff for me, and returned with Paul's order of sesame noodles with chicken. I looked at Paul while I sipped my soup and thought about the conversation we had after I fired Karen Fisher, the times he promoted me, how my sexual orientation didn't matter to him, the battle over Brin, the promptness with which he returned my phone calls, how he'd fit me in if I really needed to talk to him about a deal, the fact that he listened to Sandy more than me. He's been right about a lot of things, I thought. Could he be right about this?

Paul sighed. "I was in New York last week. I go there with Sandy every six weeks to meet with the investment analysts, trying to persuade them to keep our ratings high, convince them that our strategies are sound. Our returns have been good, but expectations keep rising. The Dow's over 7000 now. We're at the top of the technology curve. A fifteen percent return isn't good enough anymore. They want twenty to twenty five, minimum. We can't do it all on growth anymore. We've got to figure out how to bring our costs down."

I envisioned Paul and myself and the others on a tiny, enclosed treadmill, running faster and faster to the exhortations of people gathered around our cage, waving the stock pages from the newspaper. "Why didn't you tell Alan yourself, Paul?"

Paul looked at his soup. "I knew he wouldn't understand. I knew he'd be hurt. I couldn't face him." He sipped from his spoon, then looked up at me. "How's he doing?"

"I don't know why you're asking. You don't really want to know."

"I'm sure he's in shock. But he won't have trouble finding a good job. Once he's up to going to outplacement, he'll have all kinds of interviews."

"He didn't want to leave, Paul. When it happens like this, with no warnings, no mentions on performance reviews, it shakes your confidence."

"What about you, Therese? I want you to stay. I hope you're not doubting that."

"I'm not going to make any snap decisions, Paul. Part of it will depend on what you're going to do. How you're going to fill Alan's spot. How you're going to restructure."

"I'm going to outsource the CIO job for now, Therese. I'm going to have Don fill it while we go through an executive search. We'll have the top candidates interview with you, Sandy and Nate."

I shook my head and felt anger boil up again. "You knew you were going to do this before you brought Don in. Doesn't it strike you as a conflict of interest to have someone pass judgment on Alan and then give that same person his job?"

Paul stiffened. "Maybe this is as much as we can discuss today, Therese. I've decided that this is what the business needs. Give yourself some time to think about it."

I watched him pull out a credit card and lay it on top of the bill. "I hope you were generous to Alan."

"Very generous," he replied. "You don't need to worry about that."

"What's the official word to the staff?" I asked.

"There's a memo going out this morning. Alan has decided by mutual agreement to look for other opportunities." He hesitated. "I'd like you to go with Don to Alan's staff meeting this afternoon."

I shook my head, feeling what the bull sees when the red flag waves. "I'm not up to an Oscar-winning performance this afternoon, Paul. Don's a big boy. He can handle it."

We walked out to our cars. He gave me a little wave. I turned the key in the ignition and sat there. This was the company I'd been so loyal to. I flashed on Brin's face. Thank God I hadn't screwed things up completely.

I drove to the building and told June to come into my office.

"Have you seen the memo?" I asked.

"What memo?" she said. "What gives?"

I told her the official reason and that it wasn't Alan's choice. I watched the shock register on her face, the shock that said that Carepath wasn't the kind of place she thought it was, that it was like all the other companies in the '90's who down-sized and right-sized and restructured and moved jobs without regard to the human cost. I felt old and complicit, like my crisp white blouse was spattered with blood. I was furious that Paul thought I would lend my credibility to Don, standing in front of people who'd worked for Alan for ten years. And there was an ache in my heart for the three of us, irrevocably split. For the Carepath I'd known and loved, irretrievably lost.

CHAPTER 33

Brin, Summer 1994

Therese slipped into a depression. She did it quietly, like she did most things, but the signs began to accumulate. She had trouble getting out of bed to go to work in the morning. She stopped talking in the middle of a sentence and stared into space. One day I came home at 5:30 and found her sitting in the living room listening to one of her record albums from college, America's "A Horse with No Name." She took a pile of albums over to Alan's when Jill spent the weekend with Marina and came home reeking of marijuana.

She began telling me stories from college, about the professor she worked for while she was a student at UW Madison. "He wrote the first on-line textbook for family practice residents. At the end of every chapter there was a quiz. It was one of those really ugly green and yellow video screens, where each field where you had to enter something was numbered and highlighted." She shook her head. "Of course, twenty years from now, people are going to look at what we've done and laugh at it, too."

"Therese, do you think you should look for another job?"

"I don't know what I should do. I feel like the company is being taken over by people without souls, like Don and Sandy, and the people who should know better, like Paul, have lost theirs. I don't know whether to stay and fight or give up and run."

"Maybe you should talk to Nate."

"Maybe I should."

So she scheduled and rescheduled lunch with Nate three times because one of them had to leave town at the last minute. She came home shaking her head. "Nate liked your sumo wrestling image. He says this is what it's like out there—it's no better anywhere else."

Then two months after Alan left, June quit. She called me at the health plan to tell me the day before she told Therese. "I'm tired of getting these weird looks because I don't wear these little suits like the rest of the secretaries do."

"Therese will be devastated. You're the bright color in her world of zebras."

June laughed. "I'm chartreuse, girl. I'll miss her. And I'll miss Nate. But that's it. And it's not reason enough to stay. I've got to find a smaller company where they still know how to have fun and don't take themselves so seriously."

"Just find one where they take meeting payroll seriously," I said.

"You've got a point, Brin."

We agonized over whether to buy the new townhouse. I tried to be the logical one. "Therese, it'll be ten percent less than we're collectively putting into our mortgages now."

"I just can't make a decision yet."

Meanwhile Alan spent his time sleeping, surfing the World Wide Web and studying the stock market. "We got it all wrong," he announced when he came over for dinner. "We should be paying more attention to our investments than to our jobs. America's not a country that does anything anymore more except watch TV, make violent movies and put money in mutual funds."

"Yet somehow millions of people go to work every day and run themselves ragged," Therese responded. She'd just returned from a trip to Denver where a freak snowstorm stranded her for an extra 24 hours.

"What do you hear from June?" Alan asked.

Therese grimaced. Her new secretary, Laurie, was competent and as innocently friendly as a cocker spaniel. Laurie called me Mrs. Anderson after I'd asked her to call me Brin. The last time I snapped at her that if she couldn't say Brin, maybe she could learn to say Ms. "June's temping and booking for her downstairs neighbor's rock band. They come over and practice in his garage. She brings them butterscotch brownies. I think she's sleeping with the drummer."

Alan laughed. "Hmm, maybe I could hire myself out as a temporary CIO. The average tenure is only 1.5 years anyway. Why not make that clear from the start?"

Therese looked glassy-eyed. She had that look on her face that said she only wanted to play bridge against the computer and forget that the rest of the world existed. One of my professors in pharmacy school had an acronym for it: MEGO. My eyes glaze over.

Therese complained about her vision and about waking up sweating in the middle of the night. When I suggested she might need bi-focals, she dismissed it. When I asked if her night sweats were hot flashes, she said it wasn't possible. I sat her down on the couch after dinner.

"Therese, you're 40 years old. You've been burning the candle at both ends for a long time. Do you think you can just skip menopause because it's not convenient for your travel schedule?"

Therese looked incredulous. "This is not how life was supposed to be."

"What were you expecting?"

"I don't know. That Carepath was going to stay fun. That aging wouldn't happen until I was seventy." She managed a small smile. "That you and I would grow old together."

"One out of three isn't bad," I said and put an arm around her. "Don't disappear on us because Carepath is turning out to be like any other company."

"I don't know how to unhook," she replied. "I feel like I should stay there and fight for the good things."

"You can't save a place that doesn't want to be saved," I said. "You have to change your ideas about what Carepath is."

Alan started going to outplacement. He made fun of the counselors, the sessions on how to build a resume, the tests that show you what your true interests are. Then one night he came over with an official-looking piece of paper, typed, signatures on the bottom, tied with a red ribbon.

"What is it?" Therese asked.

"My divorce decree," Alan said.

"I thought you got that a couple years ago. Don't you keep it in your safe deposit box?"

"We had a ceremony at outplacement today. It's my divorce papers from Carepath."

I started to laugh. "That's great. What a sick metaphor for our society."

Therese leaned back in her chair. "So Paul kicked you out of the house and took up with another CIO on the sly."

"Laugh if you want to, girls," Alan said. "But this is the first thing that's made sense to me. I felt as betrayed by Paul as I did by Marina and her tennis boy. Maybe more so—I'd known Paul longer."

"Maybe you're right," I said. I looked at Therese. "They say you have to move out of the house before you can admit it's over and get on with your life."

Therese groaned. "Yeah, well, I stopped having sex with Paul a long time ago. Before I met him."

"There's more to passion than sex," Alan said. "Otherwise there wouldn't be so many video games in the world."

After Alan left, I said, "Therese, our life's been on hold long enough. It doesn't seem to me that your job is in jeopardy. Paul's made it clear he wants you to stay."

Therese nodded.

"Now it's up to you to decide whether you'll stay or go. And that's going to take you a while."

"Also true," Therese agreed.

"And you've said for a long time that you want to live with me. That hasn't changed, has it?"

Therese smiled. "That hasn't changed."

"Then let's buy the townhouse."

Therese sighed. "I guess I'll need to find a realtor."

"I'll take that as a yes," I said.

Therese got up from her chair and put her arms around me. "Yes, Brinnae."

"If something happens and you decide you need to leave and we're down to my salary for a while, we can sell your stock," I whispered.

"OK," Therese said.

The next week we put down deposits, hired realtors and started painting our respective houses.

Standing in the living room of her house, the hardwood floor covered with newspapers, paint roller in hand, Therese talked as we worked. "I used to be ironic about institutions. In my twenties I scoffed at people who went to work at Bank of America or General Mills. I knew that one person couldn't change an empire. When did I start believing my own fuzzy hopes?"

"You thought a small company would be different. As a founder, you expected to stay in control."

Therese tugged at the bill of her baseball cap which was partially deflecting paint. "I believed the bullshit that comes when you've been a director and a vice president. That because I had all these people working under my direction, I was powerful."

"I think you let work be too important to you. Maybe it's because you haven't run into a wall yet. When I wasn't named pharmacy director, I had to change my idea about the importance of career. It's just one part of life."

"But for me it's the part where I used to live out my ideals, get my intellectual stimulation. Where I felt connected to others and part of something larger than my self."

"So when did it start to change?"

"After we went public. Damn it, I can't break myself of the habit of saying we."

"Therese, you haven't stopped caring yet. You'll know when that time comes."

*   *   *

Walking the dog on the first day of summer, the sunlight at five o'clock still as strong as fresh coffee. A brief storm during dinner on the porch, the sky darkening and then relit to twilight. Every aroma was intense after the rain, lingering on the grass, the trees, the water-laden air. Peonies, blood red next to creamy. The pine resin wafting off the needles and into the air. If a perfume maker could bottle it: Fir, a fragrance for men, a man in a flannel shirt with a cordura briefcase. Spruce, a crisp looking woman awaiting her commuter train.

Three days later, the linden trees shed their blossoms, all on the same day. A blanket of white petals on the sidewalk, crushed velvet on the footpaths around the lake. A subtle aroma, the inexpensive fragrance that you pour on, wanting more intensity. It faded as soon as it hit the skin, the air.

I curled around Therese when she turned off the TV news, and scented her the way a dog would. I sniffed the salty skin at the edge of her neck. I tasted the wash of lotion left on her elbow. Passion took its hold slowly. I kissed Therese deliberately, the curve of her spine, the underside of the pale white globe of her breast. She protested, she was too tired, but rolled over anyway. She absorbed slow kisses and wandering hands, my nose leading the discerning tongue. And after she was satisfied, Therese moved over me with the same dreamy deliberation, the first crack in the humid misery that had enveloped her for weeks. Brought me to a simmer that became a boil before I could even cry out. I scissored my legs around her to hold the moment, the fleeting sense of being sated, as we fell over the cliff of sleep.

CHAPTER 34

Therese, July, 1995

I was in a room full of boats. A woodcut with a sailboat and a rowboat, beached. An oil painting, blue and gray waves lapping against a harbor town, boats riding the swells. Nautical clocks and wheels, a cane fishing pole, four red flotation cushions. A shelf which held clear glass bottles filled with ships. A huge wooden oar festooned with fishing lures. A ship's bell, a grappling hook, a halyard. Fifteen different sizes of lanterns. A Bourdon steam gauge. A lamp with a steering wheel. A thermometer in the shape of an anchor. A bag made of yellow oilcloth. Devices I didn't know the names of, but knew that they were nautical. Shells, rocks and fragments from the bottom of Lake Superior. Floats and buoys. The presence of mariners.

"My father's basement was filled with this junk," Steph said. "It took me most of a week to sort through it. After my brother bought the place, I decorated and we brought Dad up here once before he died. He could barely speak by then, but he looked almost radiant."

Steph and I had driven up individually from Minneapolis. Brin was spending the weekend with David and would arrive the day after tomorrow. Steph gave me the cabin keys and introduced me to the joyful mysteries: the gray electricity boxes outside and in, the artesian well in the village where we'd stopped to fill six two-gallon jugs with clear, icy water. She plugged the telephone into its jack and unfolded the checklist for opening and closing the cabin. We carried the kayaks out of the cabin, as well as the big inner tubes, the wheelbarrow and the gas mower.

I took in the view from the gravel driveway. The birch trees towered between the cabin and the lake. Ten percent of the world's fresh water was 150 feet away. An old propeller sat in a grove of four young fir trees alongside a square hulled canoe. A stairway cut into the side of a cliff dropped toward the rocky beach.

Stephanie's anchorman brother owned the five acres, the two hundred fifty feet of lakeshore. She had prevailed upon him to leave the single-room cabin and outhouse exactly as it was while he drew up plans for a proper A-frame. "Enjoy it before he gets another wife," she advised.

Steph reviewed the elaborate rituals around the use of water. "It's been dry," she said. "We have to haul water up the steps from the lake to water the petunias in the whiskey barrels." I'd forgotten how heavy water was. Even in the cool breeze off the lake I was sweating after we'd fetched the second batch in large blue plastic jugs which looked like watering cans with caps.

"Here's the shower," Steph said as we continued the tour. Bathing occurred in the alcove alongside the outhouse, which held the rigging for a solar shower and two hooks for clothes and towels. During the day the water warmed in its plastic sleeve inside the wheelbarrow. Water for dishes was boiled on the stove and carefully apportioned between pans for washing and rinsing.

"Stay and have dinner," I said. Steph was on call starting Saturday afternoon. I fixed cheese and mushroom omelets and toast and served them with a handful of grapes.

"Have you ever thought about getting a second place?" I asked.

She shrugged. "I've considered it. I don't want to be tied down with cabin maintenance. I like being able to go anywhere if the mood seizes me."

"Yeah," I said. "Still, if I had a place on Superior, there'd be something to pull me away from the cities. To get in the way of going in on a Saturday just to get caught up."

"In your case, any anti-workaholic measure would count as success."

I stuck out my tongue at her.

After Steph left the next morning, I listened to the rustle of trees in the wind. I watched the slow movement of the sun among the clouds. Sitting in the sun with the wind blowing from the south brought luxuriant warmth, basking marred only by biting flies. Five minutes later, the shifting wind from the north held a hint of the Arctic and generated desire for a sweatshirt.

The cabin interior was light pine, a concrete slab for the floor. Open beams stretched the width of the cabin, holding oars, a toboggan bearing cross-country skis, poles and boots. Half the cabin was lofted, with two single mattresses nestled below the eaves. Sleeping in the loft, high above the rigging and the captain and his mate's marriage bed below, I woke in the crow's nest at four AM, worrying about a new customer. I watched the nearly full moon descend below the trees as dawn approached. I fell back to sleep.

After breakfast I covered myself with bug spray. I donned pants, a long-sleeved shirt and a hat, and took a poetry collection to the hammock. Reading Wordsworth, wandering lonely as a cloud, the sing-song rhythms of Emily Dickinson, I drifted back in time. I'd read Tillich and Merton in college. Agape, the word which combined knowledge and love. What was absolute and what was relative. I pictured a woman in hip waders, picking her way up a rocky river, flicking her pole at absolute trout, silvery and swift. Catching weeds, plastic bags, snagging her own hat. Eyes fixed on the gleaming nuggets of fool's gold in the river.

I woke up an hour later, the book sprawled in the pine needles beneath me. The sun sparkled on the water. Cottonwood spores drifted by like thoughts made visible. The south shore seemed much sunnier than the north end of Superior and an occasional sandy beach appeared among the rocks. Twenty miles to the east lay Bayfield, a proper town with restaurants, antique stores, a five-star inn and a harbor from which boats set sail for the Apostle Islands.

I stretched, feeling the sun's warmth radiate through my bones, into the cavity in my chest, along the sinews of my calves. I could worship nature, I thought, and then rolled out of the hammock to answer nature's call.

The outhouse was dark and cool. It contained rakes and shovels, a row of paintbrushes, a radio and a gas can. The toilet seat was up, above a square piece of wood with a brass handle. It covered the entrance to the pit below, which looked to be about six feet deep.

I read and dozed for another hour, strolled to the cabin and made lunch out of tortillas and cheese, avocado and tomato, strawberries and grapes. I sat out on the concrete slab and stared at the lake. I could watch the relative waves hit the absolute shore for hours. Watch the pounding of the water wear away the rock and the sand. Was I the shore or the waves?

The waves had shifted direction, revealing a sandy current running towards the lagoon. What Stephanie called the Jesus rock was now visible. When the water was deeper, you could stand on the rock and look as though you were walking on water.

I thought back to high school when I was involved in a small group of students who met with a seminarian weekly to discuss Catholic social activism and ideas. We visited nursing home residents, volunteered in various community activities and went to see "Bananas" and other funny movies with serious underpinnings. Brin said that David had joined a youth group at Maris' church. I was surprised that the youth group experience was still alive and that it spoke to David.

Restless, I walked the overgrown paths which led to the driveway, a shed, the descent to the beach. You're a fool, I thought, picking my way down the rocks. You spend all day reading when you're in beautiful country. You try to impart meaning into a company that's lost its soul. I put my foot in the water and gasped. The water temperature couldn't have been more than 45 degrees Fahrenheit. If you fell out of your kayak and couldn't right it quickly, you'd die of hypothermia in twenty minutes.

Brin had said, you're going to serve somebody, Therese. Try to figure out what would be a decent cause, with colleagues who read more than the stock page. Unlike a lot of people, you've got decent choices.

I heated some soup in the microwave for dinner. I sat at the kitchen table and let my eyes rove around the cabin. Above the window to the left of the bed was a stylized painting of a tsunami, a foaming white and navy cliff of water about to drown several orange longboats.

I tried all of the light switches and discovered that the lanterns were connected in series. Lanterns in each corner of the room glowed red and aqua, red and red, interspersed with small white globes and lamps in the shapes of large seashells, nautilus and conch. I started a mystery, read fifty pages and decided I didn't want to be scared right before I went to sleep. I thumbed through the newspaper, did the crossword puzzle and crawled into the master bed.

I woke up with a start, totally disoriented. The full moon, yellow as buttermilk, was rising. The moon spilled its light into the lake, which appeared to be alive, lantern-lit from below, awash in waves of light. I pulled on a pair of pants over my nightshirt and stumbled down to the lake. Transfixed by its beauty, aware that the moon was rising, that this moment would not last. I knelt on the flat rock closest to the shore and dipped my hand into the frigid water. I gestured toward the lake, a wordless homage to its beauty and majesty.

The next morning it was raining and the lake foamed with milk. I drove twenty-five miles to a putt-putt golf course and driving range. Inland the rain was lighter, the kind that somehow evoked the chill of April, yet hints of a bright and hazy day when the fog burned off, and the first thought of humid August ahead. There was a man at the other end hooking long drives into the fog, but otherwise the place was deserted. I hit a dozen balls each with my driver, my three wood, my five wood. I wore a sports bra under a light Gore-Tex shell which billowed over my shorts and a Sherlock Holmes-shaped rain hat which kept my glasses clear. My arms and torso were warm and loose despite the chill of the rain. I bent down to place the ball on the tee, picked up my three iron and hit a towering fly ball. I was in a groove of bending, teeing, driving and watching the ball sail forward. I moved with the club, with the ball. I entered a rhythm that was not driven by my brain. I flowed.

When the bucket was empty, I realized that I was famished. I watched a squirrel skid across the wet grass, the flash of red that signified a male cardinal streaking for the bare trees to my left. I went into the building with video games and bought a candy bar from a machine. Leaving, I saw two deer in the ditch alongside the highway and stopped in the middle of the road.

I watched the deer, unwrapped the candy bar. I don't have to do this anymore, I thought. Alan's gone. June's gone. Paul has become someone unrecognizable. I can leave.

I drove slowly back to the cabin, transfixed by the grass momentarily green as spring. Repeating the words I can let go now silently, like a mantra. Brin arrived in the afternoon.

*   *   *

Brin

Therese teased that I had turned into a total earth mother on her country estate. I took my paints down to the shore and created vast seascapes. Weeding the herb garden which was covered with chicken wire to keep the deer out, I marveled at the parsley, oregano, thyme and rosemary which were perennials here and annuals four hours away in Minneapolis. "As cold as the lake gets," Therese said, 'it's a moderating influence."

"That's good," I retorted. "You need a moderating influence."

"I'm going to leave Carepath," she said.

"I've heard that before," I said. Firing up the lawnmower, I cut elaborate paths through the grass between the cabin and the road, down towards the lake and around the perennial garden of lupine, iris, phlox and a lone peony bush. David and Maris came up for the weekend and accompanied me to buy pottery in Port Wing and browse the used bookstore in Bayfield. Up in the crow's nest, Therese exclaimed over the aroma of the pasta sauce I made from scratch and let simmer on the stove all afternoon. I steamed fresh asparagus and marinated it in lemon juice, butter, salt and pepper. Constructing my own recipe scrapbook from the basket of recipes I brought along, I talked of the fresh sea bass and Malaysian curries I'd make when we got back into range of a Byerly's or Lund's.

"You make me tired just watching you," Therese said. I scoffed and kissed her, then hurried off to encircle another young fruit tree with wire.

At the cabin, Therese fell into complete lassitude. Once, on a day where the lake was as clear and silent as glass, she kayaked into the village for groceries from the general store: fresh local raspberries, milk, pasta and frozen meats. Another day she drove in with me to visit the four tiny shops huddled by the marina and eat fresh whitefish at the local tavern. Otherwise she sunbathed with a magazine, curled up in the loft with a book, slept or listened to cassette tapes of Enya or Hawaiian slack key guitar. Her skin browned and her step grew lighter.

I prevailed upon her to go for walks with me in the evening before the mosquitoes got too thick, along the road which identified properties by their fire numbers. In pitch darkness we stood on the concrete patio and looked up at the stars drifting like milkweed across the night sky.

"I'm planning our trip to Italy," I said. "I need to know if you're coming with me."

"Where are we going?"

"We're flying into Rome. We'll spend three days there, see the Coliseum, the Pantheon, the Vatican. Then we'll stay at a villa in Tuscany for a week. We'll go to the markets and cook fresh pasta with eggplant and broccoli rabe."

"I thought you wanted to spend time in Florence."

"We'll go into Florence for day trips. We'll go and see the statue of David and spend half a day at the Uffizi Gallery. Then we'll go to Venice, sit in St. Mark's Square, ride a gondola, buy blown glass."

"How are we getting from one place to the next?"

"We're renting a car. We can't get around Tuscany well enough by train. After three days in Venice, we'll drive to Milan and fly home from there."

"Sounds lovely."

"When we get back, you pick two weeks when you can get away."

"OK."

"I mean it, Therese. I'm serious."

CHAPTER 35

Brin, August-September, 1995

August arrived with its sensibility of transition: shrinking days and cooling nights, school ahead, summer behind. Gardens became unkempt. White alyssum sprawled onto the sidewalk. Color leached out of the red yarrow which toppled toward the bright flags of petunias. Tall, arching sunflowers succumbed to squirrel attacks and keeled over. Morning glories thrived, wrapping their tendrils around fence posts and the stems of tomatoes, their swirling blues and pinks and purples disappearing by noon. Purple coneflowers shriveled in the heat and acquired brown edges. Sweltering humidity dropped at twilight and clouds of mosquitoes emerged.

David was admitted to Carleton, a private school about an hour's drive south. I took a day off and we drove to Northfield to visit his dorm. He had his own room with a sink, more like a cell, on a floor where group bathrooms, TV lounge and kitchen with microwave were available. I measured the dimensions of the walls and made a list of things to buy: sheets, towels, book shelves and standards, hooks for the backs of doors, brackets for his stereo speakers, a hanging rack for CDs.

I went to Target and filled a shopping cart: the items on the list, a retractable keyboard shelf for his computer, a hat rack for his collection of baseball caps, a plastic cabinet for microwave popcorn, cereal and other essentials. I added a couple of bags of red licorice twists and toilet paper. Standing in the checkout line, I pictured David's room taking shape, the tiny refrigerator I'd buy next. Flashing to his room at home, all of the items about to go missing. Seeing myself going into his closet to stand among his winter clothes, to find his scent. I cried, a middle-aged woman snuffling into a Kleenex, trying to smile reassuringly at the woman with the scanner.

Therese bought David a travel bag on rollers and a huge duffel. Teddy got him a 13" TV. I took him to buy new jeans, a couple of sweaters, a blazer and extra underwear. Therese stopped at a garden center and got an umbrella plant.

He gave her a funny look when she handed it to him. "I had one when I was in college. It's a way of assuring you get oxygen in your room. As long as you remember to water it."

"OK," he said. "Thanks."

The three of us were quiet on the drive to Northfield, the Saturday before school started. We hauled his treasures to his third floor room and went out for an early dinner.

"I'm going to run the car through the car wash," Therese said. "I'll be back in half an hour."

David and I sat on the single bed. I took $50 in phone cards out of my purse.

David smiled and took my hand. "Did you think I'd forget to call you?"

My eyes welled with tears. "I've tried and tried to prepare myself for this moment. How did it come so soon?"

"Aw, Mom. You're going soggy on me."

"If you're lucky, someday you'll have a fine young man or woman to go soggy over."

David put his arms around me.

"I love you, David. On the days when you're lonely or scared, remember that. Remember that I believe in you."

"I love you, too, Mom."

I cried and clung to him. Therese told him to come home for a weekend in October and she'd get Vikings tickets.

He smiled. "OK, Dad."

Therese gave him the finger and they both cracked up. Even I smiled.

*   *   *

The house was a museum without David, a collection of artifacts from a past life. I kept thinking he was at Teddy's, looking at the calendar on the kitchen door to see when it was my turn to have him. Therese was respectful of my silences, my wanderings around the townhouse. Usually I was grateful to have Therese home. I grimaced at the notion that I could be living by myself.

When the phone rang, I ran for it. Usually it was a voice selling storm windows or mutual funds or a young person asking for contributions to Planned Parenthood or various gay rights causes. I was patient with the charity requests and often promised donations. I wondered what David would care about so much that he would donate his free time to talk to strangers.

Occasionally it was David on the other end of the line. "How are your classes?"

He talked about the history professor he liked, his computer science lab where he was learning about Unix and Windows, Java and Linux. A biology class with lots of Internet research about cloning and gene replication.

"How is Maris?" Fine. They missed each other but she had a car and often went to see him on weekends. He talked about intramural soccer and midnight pizza and poker with his dormmates. I remembered my own college days, late night gabfests around the TV, discovering cheap wine and marijuana, starting to date Teddy and the thrill of sleeping with him.

I ended these conversations with, "Be good. And if you can't be good, be careful."

David laughed. "I'm good enough, Mom."

Occasionally I caught myself sitting in front of the TV folding laundry or watching it while I ironed. I couldn't quite bring myself to turn it on if I wasn't doing something else, unless there was a movie on. I could lose myself in the right kind of movie. I scanned the listings of the cable channels, for classics I'd never seen or quirky movies that I missed five years ago, like "Gas, Food and Lodging" or

"Mermaids." Women's pictures, movies that I wouldn't have taken the time to see because I was taking David to hockey practice or stealing an evening with Therese.

Awaking to the sound of car wheels, and a loud radio, high-pitched teen laughter. The crashing guitars faded, and I felt the breeze through the open car window, the sense of possibility with your arm around someone in the dark. The feeling of being completely consumed in the moment, the sense that life was as vivid and as instantaneous as a falling star. Feeling the pull of sleep heavy as gravity itself, I hoped the driver wasn't drinking.

*   *   *

Therese took me out to dinner for our sixth anniversary. "Remember how we wrangled about who we should and shouldn't tell?" Therese asked.

"You were so mad when I gave you that look in front of Jeff," I recalled. "We don't fight as much now."

"No," Therese agreed. "When one of us is having trouble, we don't see each other as the reason."

I smiled. "Is that the definition of being old and married?"

Therese shook her head. "I can't imagine going through the nightmare of trying to leave Carepath and figuring out what comes next without you, Brin. Not that I'm doing a good job of keeping it in perspective, but every once in a while I come to my senses and realize how lucky I am."

I reached for her hand across the table. "We are lucky." She sat back in her chair. "I'm still waiting for you to give me dates for Italy."

"I know," Therese said. "I will."

Alan finally got a chief information officer job, for a company doing human genome research into cold viruses. He came for lunch and told us about it over pasta salad and leftover chicken drummies.

"They've got a great name for the company—Cold Fusion."

"Cold Fusion," Therese said. "A scientific concept that's supposed to be impossible. That's a confidence-building name."

Alan ignored her. "There's only three guys coding and I get to hire six more. They've got two women doing the network and tech support and one of them's an MIT grad. Plus, I get to play with two super computers."

"Alan, you're such a boy!" Therese groaned. "Could you jump up and down when you say that and rub your hands together?"

"What's their financing?" I asked.

"Venture capital, mostly local. The first offering they had investors coming out of the woodwork to sign up and it was oversubscribed. I interviewed with one of the VC guys. He kept asking questions designed to see how driven I was. What did I do in my spare time? Did I like to travel? I told him I was divorced and didn't have anything better to do than sit in front of a 21" monitor. I guess it was the right answer."

"Macho nerd plays well with the finance types," Therese agreed. "Congratulations, big guy." She seemed genuinely happy for him. I was relieved.

"All in all, I came out ahead on the deal," Alan bragged. "I put some of my severance in the stock market upfront and the gains carried me through the last few months. I'm making 15 grand more in base salary. If and when we go public, I get lots of stock, cheap."

"Don't count your chickens before they're fully cloned," Therese scolded, but she smiled.

"What I want to know is are the two women you mentioned married?" I said.

"Ooh," Therese teased.

"They're too young to look at a fossil like me."

"You look like you've lost a little weight," I persisted.

"I'm trying to shape up a little before I start work," he admitted.

"You, pizza boy?" Therese said. She looked at his gut. "Can I pat those washboard abs?"

"Jealousy of my superior physique does not become you, Therese."

"I'll challenge you in any sport you like," Therese said. "Come on, name it. Tennis. Golf. Racquetball. Rollerblading."

"Risk," Alan replied.

"Risk is not a sport," Therese said. "It is a fetish for maladjusted boys whose parents don't buy them computers."

"I have mine on computer."

"How about bowling?" I said. "I'll go with you." So we went bowling, then to a late matinee and out to dinner. Therese was animated and Alan sardonic. Laughing at them closed skin over the wound of missing David.

CHAPTER 36

Brin, Fall 1995

When Therese was out of town, I set projects for myself. I cleaned the kitchen cabinets, ordered the spices in the spice rack alphabetically. I fumbled through the linen closet and separated the winter flannels from the cotton sheets. It was not very satisfying. We hadn't lived here long enough for things to be in complete disarray. Sometimes I looked in the cupboard of pots and pans and tried to remember which had been Therese's and which had been mine.

I got out my easel and set it up in a room we hadn't used yet, put a clean piece of canvas on it. I covered the top of the desk with newspaper and arranged oils and watercolors. The next night painting seemed too big a leap. I bought a sketchbook and drawing pencils on the way home from work.

I sat in a chair and looked at the easel. I took a puff of albuterol. My allergies didn't seem as bad since I'd started a daily dose of Claritin during ragweed season. I put the sketchbook and pencils in my lap and looked at them. "OK, I'm ready. What comes next?" Christy came over to be petted and I rubbed her head, circled my fingers around her ears. She curled up at my feet and went to sleep.

I mused, sitting with the sketchpad, a jug of sunflowers and a glass of pear brandy, listening to an old CD, Joni Mitchell playing piano, alternating laments and romps. I had not been creating beauty. I'd neglected my impulsive displays of finger-length blue and hyacinth glass bottles, seashells, and favorite stones gathered from the Great

Lakes. Drying yellow roses upside down from a window clasp, their
red-tinged ends flaring above the baseboard of the sink. Placing
curling fronds of birchbark around a floor vase of cattails and reeds.
Making a batch of preserved lemons or spring rolls out of the greens
and carrots spied at the Farmers' Market. Arranging Bosc pears and
blood oranges in a black wire basket. Drawing a bath, mixing lavender
salts with a thick rose-scented liquid. Still, I needed an audience for
my improvisations, my bold designs. These were the times I missed
Ruth.

I made myself a pear, arugula, blue cheese and walnut salad. I
reheated lasagna in the microwave and ate at the kitchen table, putting
little pieces of ricotta in Christy's bowl and shaking the dry food over
the cheese. After dinner I sat down to watch TV. Flipping from channel
to channel, I finally settled on the Home and Garden station. Muting
the sound, I picked up the phone and called Marlys.

"How's Mom?" I said.

"Slowing down," Marlys said.

"How so?"

"She needs a hip replacement but she won't get one. She can't get
around with the cane anymore so I took her to get a walker."

I gasped.

"She's almost 80 years old, Brinnae. Time doesn't stand still."

Sighing. "I suppose I ought to call her."

"If you get stuck on ought, you won't do anything. Just go over
there. Neither one of you will be so defensive then."

*   *   *

I took a vacation day while Therese was gone and drove to Waseca.
Steady rain and the rhythm of the windshield wipers lulled me,
brought me into the world I could see, a world of color, light and
texture. Crossing the Minnesota River, I watched cornucopias of fog
swell and recede, obscuring the bridge. The maples stood bare against
the gray sky. My mother was a tree, wind-whipped and leafless.
Stationary, infinite. I laid a hand on my stomach, to quell the hum of
fear.

The cattails in the ditches were half-burst, their brown heads turning to wet fluff. I drove past field after field of tawny, dried cornstalks, glorying in the red sumac, low-lying, clinging to its leaves, and the rippling, golden grass. The brown oak leaves, waving, bereft of their acorns. The older I got, the more I appreciated the subtleties, the darker tones of fall. Embarked on a pilgrimage, en route to cold and ice, counting the hopeful signs along the route. I passed roadside stands featuring pumpkins, gourds, Indian corn. Maybe Therese would buy a pumpkin, carve it, hand out the Halloween candy. It sounded like a lot of work.

Pulling into my mother's driveway, I looked around. The lawn had been mowed and partially raked. The hoses had been put away. Everything looked OK from the outside. I opened my umbrella and walked up the front steps. I rang the doorbell. I waited, straining to hear any sound from inside. I counted to sixty twice and rang the doorbell again. Where could she be?

I headed for the car. Maybe a neighbor had taken her to a doctor's appointment. I realized I had no idea how my mother spent her mornings. As I got out my car keys, the front door opened.

"Brinnae?" my mother said.

"Hi, Mother," I said, hurrying up the steps.

I watched my mother make her way painstakingly through the living room, the dining room, the kitchen. I made a fresh pot of coffee. We sat in the family room. "David's been gone for two months now," I said. "Missing him doesn't get any easier."

"I remember when you went up to Duluth," Augustina said. "I had to get a job at the bookstore. It was only from 10 to 1 but it got me out of the house."

"I never knew that," I replied. I tried to picture my mother twenty some years ago, putting on a print dress, doing her hair, going to work.

"I never told anyone but your father."

I listened to her complain about the housekeeper, how she didn't get the flecks of toothpaste off the bathroom mirror, that she didn't buy the right kind of bacon. How she had to wait for the paperboy in the mornings because kids today were too lazy to get out of bed when the alarm clock rang. I grinned to myself, thinking there wasn't a kid alive who used anything other than a radio alarm.

The house hadn't changed much in four years. There was a blue floral slipcover on the living room sofa. A newer and smaller microwave sat on the kitchen counter.

When Mother went to the bathroom, I circled the living room. David's high school graduation picture hung above the mantle. There was a photo collage Marlys must have made: Marlys, her daughter Jessie and Jessie's husband, Mike, their child Meg as a baby, a toddler, a little girl.

On the mantle was a picture taken at my wedding. I was holding Teddy's hand, my father beside me, Mother on Teddy's right. It was the most current picture of me on display. Apparently life stopped when I married Teddy. I felt my ears redden.

I resolved to send Mother a current photo. By myself, of course. I wondered if it would be put out for others to see. Then I remembered I had sent pictures taken around the time David graduated, realized Mother hadn't put up one of David and me which I particularly liked. Maybe it was in her bedroom. I took a puff of albuterol.

"What would you be doing if I weren't here?" I asked her.

"Knitting. Listening to public radio. Maybe dropping a card to your sister. Looking at the paper to see who Rosie's going to have on her show."

The consolations of a solitary old age, I thought. What would I be doing thirty years from now? E-mailing David at his busy job. Doing a crossword puzzle. Wondering what to get my grandchildren for Christmas. Planning a trip to the desert with Therese, some climate that would soothe our aching bones, Palm Springs maybe.

"What are you doing for Thanksgiving?" I asked.

"Your sister will come here early and do the turkey and stuffing. Jessie will bring a wild rice casserole and pies. I'll sit and talk to Jessie, play cards with her and Mike and Meg. Jessie's pregnant again."

"That's nice," I said. "I'm looking forward to David being home. And Therese—she's been traveling a lot."

"I don't want to hear about her," Augustina said.

I reddened as if I'd been slapped. "I should pretend I'm single because you're a narrow-minded bigot?"

"I'll never accept it. It's not God's will."

"Dad would have tried. He would have been interested in my happiness. You're too selfish."

"Your father was too lenient with you. God love him, he was a good man. And you, so cavalier about marriage, so wrapped up in your own importance at a job, let Teddy drift away."

"You're rewriting history, mother."

"Have you been reading those studies about what divorce does to a child? How children of divorce are less able to have a satisfactory marriage and family of their own? I hope you're satisfied."

I stood up. "Marlys' divorce hasn't seemed to slow Jessie down any. This is getting us nowhere. In your mind, it's still 1962. You live in a museum, mother."

"I pray to God every night, asking him what I did wrong. Begging him to let you come to your senses."

"Goodbye, mother," I said, grabbing my coat and slamming the door.

I turned the key in the ignition and drove down the block, out of sight of the house. I took a puff of beclavent. My chest felt tight. I took a half breath, coughed hard and put the car in gear.

I was still shaking when I got home. Changing into sweats, I cleaned the great room, the dining room, the kitchen, the den. I carried the vacuum cleaner up the stairs and dusted, then vacuumed the bedrooms, the hallway, the bathrooms. I sat gasping on the floor and used both inhalers. While rinsing out the tub, I sprawled on the tile and finally let myself cry. Christie came in and licked my face.

I ate a granola bar for lunch. I nebbed, coughed up mucus for half an hour and sprawled on the bed. Later I sat with chamomile tea, chasing the honey around the bottom of the cup with my spoon. I stared out at the rain falling onto the pond. What did you expect? She's not going to change.

I made comfort food for dinner, scrambled eggs and mushrooms, wheat toast with strawberry jelly. I coughed my way through the eggs and called Christie over to finish them. I rubbed the dog's head and tried to catch my breath. My chest was still tight. I went into the bathroom coughing and vomited mucus for twenty minutes.

I called Therese on her cell phone, gasping. "I can't breathe."

I could hear the edge in Therese's voice. "Brin, hang up. Call 911 right now. Can you do that or do you need me to do it?"

"Don't be ridiculous. I don't need an ambulance."

"Brin, you need to go to the emergency room. Now. You either have to call someone to drive you or you have to call 911."

"I'll call Alan."

"I'll call him for you and call you right back."

Alan was there in ten minutes. We sat in the ER waiting room for 45 minutes. I held Alan's hand for a while, then felt stupid.

They put me in a bay and hooked me up to a bigger, fancier version of the nebulizer. The doctor said my lungs were inflamed and wrote a prescription for prednisone.

"I hate prednisone," I protested. "When I come off of it, I get so depressed I want to die."

"Should I give you a prescription for Prozac along with it?" he asked.

I shook my head no.

Alan took me home and sat with me for an hour. By the time Therese called, I was calm. I said how good it was to have a clean house.

CHAPTER 37

Therese, November, 1995

When I walked into Paul's conference room, Don, Nate and Sandy were already there. We were making desultory chat about Thanksgiving when Paul strode in, looking purposeful and confident.

"We're being acquired," he said. I thought of Jabba the Hut, popping a small creature in his mouth, chewing, belching.

"How much?" I asked. I made it a point to ask the blunt, cynical questions now that Alan was gone.

"Who's buying us?" Nate asked.

"Ocean Health," said Sandy.

"$450 million," said Paul. Nate whistled.

"And the parachutes?" I asked.

"The parachutes are your stock. Ocean Health was trading at 50 1/3 yesterday. Stockholders get 1 share of Ocean Health for every 2 shares of Carepath."

"When does it vest?" Don said. I felt a perverse pleasure that he didn't seem to know any more than Nate or I did.

"Our ESOP said half the shares vest upon a change in control," I recalled.

"Good memory, Therese," Paul said. "Half your existing options vest when the deal closes, the rest on your current schedules. There will be a new round for management with four-year vesting."

Everyone did the math in their heads. I'd been exercising my options as they matured, then selling and investing the return in mutual funds so that my portfolio was sufficiently diversified. I thought I had about 10,000 options left. With half vesting, that amounted to a quarter of a million bucks. Not enough to retire, but I could certainly take some time off. Still, if I could hang on for another year, I'd have another 10,000 options vest in December of '96.

I thought about my weekend conversation with Alan. He came over to help me plant bulbs, gardening being the one outdoor individualistic activity permitted in condo-land. In the middle of burying four dozen hyacinths, bitching about work, I started to cry.

"What is this with you?" Alan said gently, putting his hand on my shoulder. "You're on some mission, trying to save somebody's soul. Your soul, apparently."

"I wish I knew," I said slowly. "I'm stuck in this Peggy Lee, is that all there is world. I want meaning and a feeling of family."

Alan held up his hand and ticked off one finger at a time. "Charity. Religion. Children. Nature. Poetry."

"What is this, the middle-aged woman's alphabet?" I asked, but I smiled when I said it. "OK, I think about the big questions even if I don't go to church. I'm doing my kids and computers charity. So that leaves nature and poetry."

"You're being rather literal, Therese. That is, if a computer scientist can call the kettle black. Take that exploratory, adventuresome, analytical mind of yours and put it in the service of something other than your employer."

"I must really be a pain in the ass to be around."

"Nothing a year at hard labor wouldn't cure."

Half listening to Paul give an overview of Ocean Health's lines of business. I flashed on Brin the earth mother tending raspberry bushes, mowing paths around lupine and lazy Susan. I could buy a cabin on Superior.

Paul blathered on about a process by which all management in both firms would be evaluated to ascertain their ability to contribute in the new world. I'm gone, I said to myself, trying on the words.

"I'm gone," I said to Brin, walking Christie after dinner. Snow flurries whirled in the wintry air.

"Good," she said. "What will you do?"

"I don't know," I said. "Find a new start-up?"

"Why? So you can relive the whole experience?"

I shrugged. "I have to do something until I retire." I paused. "I suppose I ought to wait and see what the consultants come back with."

"Right," said Brin. "You've been so excited about going to work already. Just think how much happier you'll be in a company twice your size."

"I await your brilliant insight," I said.

"Quit. Just quit. Give yourself time to figure it out. Sit still and stare out the window for a month. Or two. Go to a career counselor."

"Right," I said.

"The first step was admitting you're unhappy. Go on to step two. Find a new purpose."

Christie saw a rabbit streak toward the pond and nearly pulled my arm off. I ran with her, urging her on, holding tightly to her leash.

CHAPTER 38

Therese, November, 1995

My negotiations with the Minneapolis pacemaker company, Cardionics, intensified after they made the round of the vendors and decided to work with Carepath. Their president was a woman named Melissa Avery, a cardiovascular surgeon who got bored with the challenges of the operating room, and started Cardionics with Kevin Wright, a cardiology researcher from the University. Melissa had the authoritative manner of the Army lieutenant she once was. In our first meeting, she questioned whether Carepath had the necessary clinical expertise in-house to build a tracking system for congestive heart failure patients.

"Do you know Mike Nelson?" I asked.

"The Marlboro Man who rides into the OR on a white horse?" Nick looked at me, his careful-it-could-be-a-trap look.

I laughed. "That would be Mike. I thought I was the only one who pictured him on a stallion."

"We were in residency together. He used to smoke and fancied a cowboy hat on the weekends. I'd whistle the Marlboro theme whenever he walked into the doctors' lounge. Let's just say there was a bit of rivalry between us."

"Mike and Pro Heart worked with us to develop the patient profile software they're using. Mike consults with us from time to time when we need cardiology advice. We're pretty flexible in how we work with clients."

Melissa went on to grill Nick about fifteen provisions in the contract she didn't like and made him promise to change all but two.

"Jesus, she's obnoxious," he complained, as we walk to our cars.

I smiled. "She's just a small business woman looking out for her baby."

When we met the next week, Nick begged off at the last minute with a sick child. Melissa pushed me hard on the cost of the software licenses. When I didn't give on that, she moved on to the annual maintenance fee. I granted her an extra month on the warranty so that her maintenance fee started after 120 days rather than the standard 90. We debated the definitions of design sign-off for the custom work and she insisted on a pilot. She moved onto the response time of the software, which I told her depended on the speed of the workstations she bought and network bandwidth. She insisted on defining performance standards based on a Pentium 166-megahertz chip.

I requested a bio break. When I returned, she was on the phone. After she buzzed her assistant to bring in mineral water and we sat back down, I said, "I admire your persistence."

"This company is my life," she said.

"Is that good?" I asked. "Sorry, I didn't mean to get personal."

She laughed. "At least you came out and said it."

"I understand about small companies," I said, and gave her my history from the third employee view. She nodded and asked me about the public offering and the conversations with the financiers.

"You must be proud of the growth," she said.

"I am," I said. "Though it brings its own problems." I flashed on the Ocean Health due diligence team, who had taken over one of our conference rooms. After Thanksgiving I'd be off to Houston with Nate to review the sales picture with their management team.

She smiled. "Every situation does. The question is, do the business' problems fit with the way you want to be challenged?"

"That is the $64,000 question," I replied.

"Don't say that around Kevin. He'll give you a blank look and you'll feel old."

We laughed and shook hands. I hit her up for a contribution to

Kid CPU, my non-profit working with companies to donate computers to inner-city kids and pair the kids up with mentors.

"I'm on their board. It's my latest way of making myself believe I still have a mission at Carepath," I said.

"We're in," Melissa said. "Call Kevin to get the check."

Paul thought the Ocean Health deal would take another month or two to close. I mentally tripled his estimate from force of habit.

"We really need this Cardionics deal, Therese," he said last week. "It will give a big boost to the revenue projections."

"Paul," I said, "que sera sera. Remember, we're coming up on the holidays. I am doing my level best."

He smiled. "Then there's no reason for me to worry."

I went home to pick up Brin. We were trying to have a weekly date, a play, a concert, an immersion in art of some kind. Last week it was a graffiti show, local taggers' spray cans brought inside to canvas. Tonight it was "Love's Fire," a series of one-act plays based on Shakespearean love sonnets. As I smiled and pondered, I realized that I'd missed seeing many of the events I'd read about in hotel lobbies or on planes in USA Today. The run of "Angels in America" happened the year Carepath went public. I couldn't remember a year where I'd seen more than one of the movies nominated for best picture before it came out on video.

I awoke early the next morning to the pair of cardinals singing what-cheer, what-cheer. Don't wait, don't wait.

CHAPTER 39

Brin, December, 1995

December turned brutally cold, the temperatures plunging well below zero for a week. I moved from house to car to the clinic wrapped in a big black marshmallow of a coat, filled with down and leaking tiny feathers onto my black sweater dress. Life moved indoors, except for feeding the birds. I bought a Christmas tree, a Scotch pine, and wrapped it in popcorn strings, velvet ribbon and colored lights which flashed off and on.

I got home from work and plugged in the tree, plugged in the lights David had strung around the outside of the porch window when he was home at Thanksgiving. He'd be home on the 21st and didn't go back until the day after New Year's. I held onto this thought through days where the sky was the color of wet cement and the light vanished at four thirty in the afternoon.

When Therese was gone, I went from work to the mall to shop. I carefully stepped my way through the icy parking lot, feeling as though my legs were fragile branches rather than their usual tree trunks, watching teenagers streak by me in oversized Doc Martens. Weeknights at 5:30 the crowds weren't bad. I ate a chicken Caesar salad at Dayton's and consulted my list. Earrings and a new ski sweater for Therese. A fleece throw in Southwestern colors for Marlys. Flannel shirts and running shoes for David and a gift certificate so he could pick out his own CDs and computer games.

I stared at the word Mother on the list. I'd bought Augustina a black velvet top and a Santa Claus pin. They were easily mailed or slipped into a bag for Marlys to deliver. I had no other ideas.

Therese kept asking what I wanted for Christmas. A brain transplant for my mother. Maybe I'll get her a membership to PFLAG. I mustered a small grin at the thought.

Danny would spend Christmas Eve with Cathy and the girls and drive down for Christmas dinner. Carolyn and Shoney were going to Therese's parents in Tucson. Marlys and Meg's family would be with Augustina.

I wanted a day to sit in sweats, musing over the recipes cut out over the course of the year and flung in a basket on top of the refrigerator. To paste the keepers onto half-sheets of paper in a small spiral notebook divided into entrees, soups and salads, starches, vegetables and desserts. I'd make my grandmother's brown bread in cylindrical coffee cans and perhaps a batch of gingerbread men. I'd climb into the tub, light a gardenia-scented candle and read poetry.

I nibbled at the roll that came with the salad. Today I'd had lunch with a gay man at the clinic, a nurse named Phil. Occasionally I'd bring a patient from the pharmacy to the geriatric care unit where Phil did assessments and assembled family conferences. I'd write down recommendations on the patient's med list.

We'd walked to the Denny's down the frontage road from the clinic. I pushed the crusts of my grilled cheese sandwich around the plate. "The holidays suck," I burst out and he laughed.

"Isn't this just the most ambivalent time of year?" he said.

"You put it very well." I told him about David coming home, about Therese's depression and my mother's intolerance.

We were late getting back to the clinic. "Next time I'll let you talk," I said. "I promise," and he laughed again.

"It's OK," he said. "Life isn't meant to be even steven."

I finished my coffee and paid the check. Entering fine jewelry, I saw the 40% off signs. I blew my whole budget on diamond earrings for Therese. I held the studs in my hand and watched the light glint off their edges. I remembered my father's eyes, cornflower blue like my own. I was so lucky to have had him as long as I did.

The treachery of the holidays, I mused, driving home. You put up the tree and suddenly you're twelve again. You go shopping and settle in the lap of someone who's been dead for fourteen years. The arithmetic of Christmas, the simultaneous calculation of negative numbers and infinity.

I put a CD on and stared at the tree while I wrapped presents. At night, I liked a solitary instrument playing carols, no vocals. The carol of the bells played on the harp. Dave Brubeck's wistful solo piano on Jingle Bells. Acoustic joy and sorrow.

CHAPTER 40

Therese January 1996

I had another marathon negotiating session with Melissa Avery on January 2nd. We spent two hours arguing over the contract's termination clause, then another hour on succession rights if either of our companies were to be bought out or merged. We took a quick phone break and sat down to sandwiches and fruit catered from a restaurant down the street.

"So how do you and Kevin divide up the management?" I asked.

"It's getting harder," she said. "I'm the negotiator and chief marketeer—I go to trade shows, I get the financing, I buy the systems. He's the chief scientist—he supervises the researchers, writes the journal articles, schmoozes with the university types at conferences. We're up to thirty five employees now and he doesn't like management. Little things drive us crazy—we need to hire another secretary. Someone needs to create a human resource area: write job descriptions, compare our salaries and benefits to the market, develop a plan for stock options if and when we go public. We need project management and a way to evaluate staff performance. Et cetera, et cetera."

I smiled. "Sounds like you need a chief operating officer."

"Exactly. Someone to run the ship while I chart a business course and Kevin plays in the lab." She smiled at me. "How about you?"

"Me?"

"Would you ever think about coming to work for Cardionics? I have the sense you're restless where you are now."

"I don't know. I haven't thought about it."

"Think about it, Therese. Let's wrap up this contract so you can think about it without a conflict of interest."

We haggled with renewed energy over the appendices to the contract: the hardware needed for the pilot of the software, the service agreement defining Carepath's response time to system crashes, software performance and the final purchase price.

At four o'clock we agreed we could hand the contract over to the lawyers to finish the fine print. We shook hands and I put my suit jacket on. "I'm serious about hiring you, Therese," Melissa said. "When can we get back together?"

"Let's have breakfast next week."

I drove to Lake Harriet and sat in my car on the parkway. I watched the runners and the dog walkers maneuver along the icy path, a solitary skier glide across the lake toward the north shore. What did I know about Melissa Avery? She was smart, driven, and had taken her company this far. She seemed trustworthy. I remembered the year of Carepath's public offering—did I want to relive that? Did I want to be the one who created the infrastructure, which allowed the company to get big? Did I want to work for a growing company or should I go into consulting and advise them on how to grow?

When I got home, Brin had tuna steaks marinating in lime juice, sesame oil and ginger. I changed into sweats and a t-shirt and poured a glass of wine. While Brin added sliced mushrooms and croutons to salad from a bag, I sliced red potatoes, sautéed onions and put them together into the oven.

We sat in front of the fire with Christie and wine and pistachio nuts. I filled Brin in about Melissa.

"I thought you wanted to get out of management. Didn't you tell me you wanted to have less responsibility?"

"It's true. That's what we talked about." I sipped wine. "If I'm honest, I have to admit I'm a management junkie. I don't think I can give up being in charge."

Brin laughed. I looked at her indignantly. "I'm glad you're being honest. I'd rather have you managing other people than taking it out around here."

"Even I'm not that stupid. But here's the problem. When you get to this point in a management career, you can go out on your own and do something you're good at, or you can go to another company and do it. Sometimes you change industries to make it more interesting. Or do less of one thing and more of another. Say less project management and more marketing."

"That's a sad commentary," Brin said. "But there is another option."

"What?"

"You could change careers altogether."

"Yeah. If I knew what I wanted to do. But I'd have to start all over on the salary front."

"We'd get by." She laughed. "Though I don't know if you could get used to me making more money than you."

I sighed. "I hope I'm not that petty." But she was right.

"Didn't you say that your feelings about Carepath started to change after it went public? If Cardionics is going to go public next year . . .'"

Therese sighed. "Brin, I'm supposed to catch you in your logical inconsistencies, not vice versa. OK, I admit it, I'm going on a gut feeling here. I don't know if this is what I'd look for if she hadn't approached me. Or if Carepath wasn't about to get swallowed up by a very big fish."

We filled our plates and pulled a throw over our knees.

"You may be making this more complicated than it needs to be, Therese."

"How so?" I asked, through a mouthful of tuna.

"Doesn't day-to-day satisfaction depend on whether you're working with people you like, or at least respect, and whether you're in agreement about what you're trying to do? Whether it's road construction or state government or a software start-up."

"Maybe you're right. Maybe the problem at Carepath is your second condition. Paul's goal is to please the stockholders and that's not enough for me." I refilled my water glass. "How did Melissa put it?

Something about whether the problems of the business fit with the way you want to be challenged."

"Maybe you're bored with the day-to-day at Carepath and need the rush that comes with a start-up. But then you'll complain about the intensity of it, like the year we hardly saw you while Carepath went public. And you ought to talk with Melissa about how the company can change once shareholders come into the picture."

"OK, there's no career nirvana. I hear you."

"I don't know if you do, Therese."

I sighed. I looked at her and reached inside to hold on to my temper. "I know I've been pretty self-absorbed lately, Brin. But you're not the only one who misses David."

"What do you miss, Therese?"

"I miss him teasing me, him telling me to work harder not smarter. I miss the walks he and I would take Christie for. I miss my golfing partner. I miss seeing his big feet on the coffee table and him taking them off when one of us walked in."

Brin laughed at that.

"What do you miss the most, Brin?"

Her eyes got misty. "I miss feeding him cookies and milk after school. I miss him coming into my room in the middle of the night during a thunderstorm to see if I'm awake too. I even miss him picking me up and giving me noogies."

"You're missing all your years together."

She started to cry. I took her inside and cradled her on the couch. I stroked her hair until we both dozed off.

*   *   *

Instead of meeting Steph at the bagel place, I went to a new coffeehouse she liked. A fountain trickled over a rock waterfall in one corner. Norfolk pines and maidenhair ferns sat on a window ledge. Fresh carnations and roses graced tables and booths. Cell phones were banned.

"Nice place," I said, looking around.

"It's peaceful," Steph said.

I talked about Melissa Avery and the dilemma of whether to leave Carepath, the 10,000 stock options right around the corner.

Steph shook her head. "Honestly, Therese, aren't you bored of this topic? Aren't you making a mountain out of a molehill?"

Stung, I said, "I'm not as spiritually advanced as you are, Steph. I don't have a roshi I study with. My knees aren't good enough to sit zazen every morning."

"You complain that you need something else in your life besides work and you sit around and obsess about whether you have the right job? You pretend these so-called options aren't a corporate bondage outfit?"

"I feel like maybe if I start over, I'll have a chance of getting a grip on my work obsession. If that makes any sense."

She shrugged. "Maybe. Hold on to the idea that you need more than a job to find meaning. And that options are about choices, not strings."

*   *   *

I stopped at the library and picked up a book on Thomas Merton, the Trappist monastery in Kentucky where the monks could speak to each other only in sign language. They were permitted to sleep five hours a night, ate meager meals of soup and bread and wore white robes and the same heavy underclothes in summer and winter. They made public confessions of their lapses and received punishments such as kissing the feet of the other monks. The monks believed that their willed suffering, their practice of medieval routines in 1942, could diminish the agony of the world. I did not see myself as an ascetic. The pleasures of self-deprivation were lost on me.

Merton received acclaim for his autobiography, *The Seven Storey Mountain*, royalties from which were turned over to the monastery. Perhaps this was the point, I mused. How to have success in the world, and still be grounded in spiritual beliefs and routines. Not to complain about our hardships, our choices. I could fund something meaningful with the money from those options.

Passion had taken me this far. It had mellowed with Brin into the long glow of an October afternoon, the honey-colored light of autumn. Sweet in the moment, bittersweet when contemplating the inevitable. It had slipped out of my grasp at Carepath and I couldn't call it back. Passion required an innocence I seemed to have lost.

Steph continued to be impatient with me. "You've got a wonderful woman and a good, high-paying job. Your worries are a luxury."

"I know you're right," I said. "But they're still my worries. Am I supposed to ignore them?"

"No, you're supposed to keep them in perspective."

What comes after passion? I wondered, as I gradually fell towards sleep. Everything else seemed dull by comparison.

CHAPTER 41

Brin, March, 1996

The call from Marlys came while I worked the pharmacy window. "Mom fell and broke her hip," she reported.

I groaned and looked at the line of patients. "Make it quick, Marlys. When's the surgery?"

"Tomorrow at 7:30 AM. Will you be there?"

"I'll see if I can get off. Otherwise I'll come after work."

All day I wondered, replaying the scene of the walker skidding and Mother toppling over, in various locales. In the bathroom—it was so small, surely she would have hit her head. In the kitchen, standing at the stove. I winced. The poor woman. She must have been so afraid. I called the health plan and told them I wouldn't be in tomorrow.

I called Therese.

"Are you sure you want to go?" Therese said.

I sighed, grasping my temper with both hands. "Therese, she's my mother."

"She certainly is," Therese replied.

The next morning I brought two lattes to the waiting room. Augustina had been taken directly into surgery on a gurney. Marlys looked tired. Marlys was fifty, of course she looked tired. And Mother was 80, twice as old as I was.

"Marlys," I said. "How is fifty different than forty?"

Marlys laughed. "The forties are a great decade. As you approach menopause, your memory disappears. Every calorie sticks to you like flypaper. The good news is just as you're feeling really stupid, your kids think you might actually know something, at least about babies. They call you up in a panic about fevers or croup or diaper rash."

I smiled. I wondered if David and Maris would stay together, get married after college, have babies. Maris was thinking of changing her name back to Marianne, David had confided. "Frazier" was still big but the name didn't seem quite so hip anymore. Now a show called "Friends" was all the rage.

"Where did Mom fall?"

"She tripped on the rug in the entryway after she got the paper. Fortunately she had the cordless phone in the pocket of her robe."

We sat and flipped through the photo albums each of us had brought and waited for the report from surgery.

After a couple of hours, the surgeon emerged in his green scrubs. "We reset the hip as best we could. She's got quite a bit of osteoporosis so it will take a while to mend."

"What are her chances of surviving this, doctor? I've read that a lot of elderly women never recover from hip surgery."

I stared at my sister.

The surgeon shrugged. "If she can leave the hospital quickly and work hard in physical therapy, her chances are good."

After the surgeon left, I said, "You never told me that she might not walk again."

"What was her other choice?" Marlys responded. We got in the elevator, headed up to Augustina's room. She was still asleep from the anesthesia.

I took a walk on a path behind the hospital. The sun was a pale yolk in the sky. The wind was icy. I called Therese's cell phone and got voicemail. I left a message for her and one for David at the dorm to call me on the cell phone.

Mother was 80 years old. Even if she survived this operation, the odds were pretty good that she would not make it to 90; none of her siblings or first cousins had lived that long. It was likely that before I turned fifty and Marlys sixty, our mother would die. I looked at the bare trees, the gray snow and tried to comprehend this idea.

Suddenly I saw my father's blue eyes, his smile and I seized up, began to sob.

I took the elevator back upstairs. Marlys leaned over the bed, adjusting Augustina's pillows. I took my mother's hand. "How are you feeling, Mother?"

Augustina opened her eyes. "Woozy. It knocked all the whoop out of me."

"Then we'll just have to get you a whoopie cushion," I said. Feeling stupid, clueless about what to say, how to behave in this situation I did not, stupidly, anticipate.

Marlys rolled her eyes at me. "How about some cracked ice?"

Augustina sucked on an ice chip. She fell back to sleep.

CHAPTER 42

Therese, April, 1996

I stumbled through my days reading e-mail and trade magazines on-line, chairing meetings where we discussed the settlements we'd give customers when we discontinued the cardiology product, diabetes, formulary. How we'd move others to the new Perspective series.

Every two or three weeks I forced myself to go to the new company headquarters in Houston, where I was reminded all over again that I was now consigned to a backwater. That the action was here where people drawled, hung cowboy hats on the back of their doors and sported "Don't mess with Texas" bumper stickers and mugs.

"Call in sick," Brin said.

"I still have people who work for me," I protested. "Hopefully I can save some of their jobs."

Brin snorted. "You're still acting like you're in charge."

"No," I retorted. "I'm acting like I have responsibilities."

Half of our staff was cut the day after the merger became effective, March 1. Paul, Nate, Sandy and I spent the month of February locked in Paul's office. Reading Excel spreadsheets with all the staff listed. Arguing over which column heading—0 days, long term employee— each name belonged under.

We were supposed to go to Italy in February, but I insisted we cancel. "I can't afford to be gone right now," I told Brin. "There's too much uncertainty, for myself and my people."

She snorted. "The best thing that could happen is that they'd lay you off. Don't trouble yourself, I got trip insurance. I'll never plan a trip with you where I don't."

I went back to my office and worked on the go-forward plan, listed the accounts we thought we could move into the new products, the amounts we were liable for under the terms of existing contracts. An appendix with each of my employee's salaries listed and the column where the salary was divided by twelve.

"One month's severance?" Brin exclaimed. "That's obscene."

"That's the minimum," I replied. "For people that have been there less than two years. Everybody else gets two weeks a year."

"So you'd get 22 weeks," she said.

"If I were leaving now," I said. "They want me to be there for a year to lead the transition. That's worth 6 months salary."

She stared at me. "You think one extra month of salary is worth it for the pain and suffering of the next year?"

"I've got all this stock vesting," I said. "In December. That's why it's worth it, not the salary."

Brin gave me her hardest look. "Then quit your whining. Decide the cabin and financial security are a price you're willing to pay."

Bound in parachute silk.

I called Melissa Avery once a month. Business had fallen off. She said she still wanted to bring me on board. She told me to be patient. She also worried that the project we contracted for would slow down in the new mega-world of Ocean Health.

"I couldn't say anything," I told her. I'd felt badly about it.

"Of course you couldn't," she agreed.

*   *   *

Packing for a business trip the night before. Feeling that familiar ache of having to leave home before you're ready, before you planted the twelve-packs of pansies sitting on the four-season front porch waiting for the weather to be warm enough. Putting into the black bag on rollers a navy dress, a two-piece floral print, a tan pants suit, a blouse, nylons, underwear, a slip, earrings in a small white gift box secured with a rubber band, the pre-packed toiletries case, bathing suit, gym shorts, t-shirts and socks, two pairs of shoes. A travel alarm in case waking up in today's planes, airports and hotels isn't alarming enough. A sweatshirt and sweatpants in case the hotel room is cold or the neighborhood appears safe enough to go for a walk.

Wondering if the first plane will be delayed long enough that you'll miss your connecting flight. Tucking a book and a magazine into your brief case for the moment on the plane when you absolutely cannot look at another prospectus or report or journal article. Putting a length of phone cable into the computer carrying case so you can lie on the bed to log on and read your e-mail. Leaving the photocopy of your itinerary under a refrigerator magnet so the others will know where you are. Hoping that the hotel will have a decent movie on pay-per-view that you haven't already seen if the dinner meeting ends early or you wake up in the middle of the night.

The feelings that travel stirs up. Waking up early, spooning yourself around the sleeping body beside you, seeking warmth, silently telling the sleeper the things you don't say often enough. Your mind flipping between what you're leaving and what you're going to. Hating that you're traveling alone and will have to do all the relationship building by yourself, or bemoaning your partner's shortcomings and how you'll have to cover for him.

In the early dawn, hair still wet from the shower, blowing a kiss to the sleeper, checking on the whereabouts of the dog, who rolls over on her mat at the foot of the bed and gives you a sad, resigned look. Patting your ticket and wallet once more, you trudge to the garage with your burdens and hope that the sleeper remembers to water the petunias.

CHAPTER 43

Therese, December, 1996

I must have seen every hour pass on the clock face. I punched the radio alarm three times, listening to Brin's soft snores beside me, then dragged myself into the bathroom. I stood in the shower for 15 minutes waiting for the warm water to wake me, then climbed out and put on black pants and a sweater set.

Sitting on the sofa in Paul's office, I clutched a notebook in my hand. I hadn't seen him for several weeks. I'd been sitting in a conference room in Houston giving status on a series of clinical projects when he walked by with a group of Ocean Health execs and waved. He looked like a prisoner with an escort. I waved back.

The last time we'd talked had been in the fall at a corporate charade called "Celebrating Change." The five of us who remained from Carepath's first year of existence stood on stage and performed a highly scripted piece called "I Remember." My job had been to recall our first office and our first piece of software. I'd held up a copy of "Mental Fitness" and said, "I could use a refresher course on this topic," and got a few laughs from the crowd. Then the music kicked in, David Bowie stuttering "Ch-Ch-Changes," and Paul walked out to prolonged applause.

And why not? The company had grown to 1400 employees in twelve years, now down to 750. Most of the people left had seen their stock double in value and half of their options vest.

When Paul had finished his spiel, I walked off stage with him. "In 1984, could you have imagined this event?"

He laughed. "In 1984 I couldn't imagine how I was going to write out paychecks without them bouncing."

I heard Paul's voice outside, conferring with Dorothy. I took a deep breath.

He closed the door and said, "The last time you were on my schedule without a meeting title wasn't a whole lot of fun."

"I'll make it brief," I said. "Vice President of Strategic Contracts announces, 'I Quit.'"

"Really," he said. He smiled. "You hung in long enough to get that big chunk of options. Congratulations."

"Thanks," I said. "I kept a picture of a cabin on Lake Superior as my screensaver to keep me going. It was hard. I can't stand feeling this irrelevant." Going from prime time to a bit player on a soap. I felt my stomach coil and uncoil as though it held a trapped snake.

"Have you got another job?"

I nodded. "I'm joining Cardionics."

He whistled. "Didn't see that one coming."

"It's all on the up and up," I said. "We didn't start talking about it until after the contract was signed." It hadn't been easy. Melissa had been ready for me in September. I'd told her there was one final deal I had to get done before I could leave. I'd finally figured out that job one was taking care of myself and Brin.

Paul ran his hand through his hair. I winced involuntarily. He looked very tired. "What will you be doing for them?"

"COO," I said. "You remember that phase. No policies. No procedures. No HR department. 35 employees."

"The second stage of a start-up," he said. "Should be fun."

"Fun is my middle name," I said. I started to cry. Shoulder-heaving sobs. I took my glasses off and put my head on the table, my hand over my mouth so I wouldn't shriek.

He offered me the box of Kleenex.

"I thought maybe I could get through this in one piece." I sat up. My head hurt. I blew my nose.

"Nah," he said. "You love this place. You always have."

I opened my notebook and handed him my letter of resignation. The photo of Paul, Alan and I fell out onto the table.

He picked it up and shook his head. "Man, we were young. How's Cold Fusion doing?"

"Fine," I said.

He read the letter and set it on the table. "I'm going to miss the heck out of you," he said.

"It was a hard decision to come to," I said. Waking up at 3 AM every night for the past three weeks. Sitting in the den with a magazine, crying. Wondering how my staff would fare. Wondering if Cardionics would be any better. Having Brin finally explode. "Just do it! Quit being such a martyr!"

"You've been the heart and soul of the place, Therese. You'll be missed big-time."

"What will you do?"

He shrugged. "Hang around until I feel like a fifth wheel. Until they stop inviting me to Executive Committee meetings."

"That ought to be good for the next chunk of stock," I said.

He smiled. "We'll see. We'll have Dorothy plan your party. You deserve a blowout. Does Nate know?"

I nodded.

"I figured." He sighed. "This is a memo I don't want to write."

I opened the notebook and handed him another piece of paper.

He grinned. "Still the model employee, Therese. To the bitter end. You're a class act."

I stood up. He said, "Now that you don't work for me anymore, do I get a hug?"

"Sure," I said. "You're the only boss I've ever had, Paul. That must be some kind of a record in corporate America."

When he put his arms around me, I started to cry all over again. "It felt like family," I said. "For a long time. Like the good part of family. People who cared about each other doing something important. Backing each other up."

"Yeah," he said. "That was back when we knew everybody by name." He laughed. "Then you went and bought Chronicom."

"I'll miss you, too, Paul," I said.

He squeezed me hard. "Yeah. I know."

When I got home, Brin asked, "How'd it go?"

"It was hard," I said. "I cried with Paul. Then I had to tell my staff."

"Then they cried," she said.

"Yeah," I said. "They did. Even the guys got a little misty-eyed."

Brin said, "Promise me you won't automatically turn your soul over to Cardionics."

"I'll do my best," I said. "I'll come home every night and write 100 times on the blackboard, "There is no career Nirvana."

"You think you're funny," Brin said. "On this topic you are still stuck in the second grade."

"Yes," I said. "I am." I paused. "I'm going to buy a cabin. On Lake Superior. Steph's going to look with me. It will help me balance things."

"Good," Brin said. "I'm going to quit my job. At least for a while."

I stared. "I thought you were enjoying it, on the whole."

Brin shrugged. "For the most part. I've been tired lately. I also need some flexibility to deal with my mother."

I said, "Take all the time off you want."

Brin nodded. "I will."

Brin, February 1997

I went back to work and gave notice. The clinic said they'd hire me back anytime. The health plan asked me to keep in touch.

Marlys and I moved Mother to an assisted living facility. The two of us went through her house, the clothes, the papers, the personal keepsakes. I kept some photographs, my Christmas stocking and ornament from 1956, a couple of vases, the Hans Christian Andersen book, a music box, a bowl my mother had set oranges in and a Raggedy Ann. I took one of my father's pipes and the globe that sat next to his easy chair on a stand, a spherical map of the world as it was in 1960. For David I saved his Christmas stocking, several photographs, the Minnesota Twins pennant and the cards he and his grandmother used for games of hearts.

I had lunch with Therese, who recounted a conversation with Melissa. "I was talking about the year that Carepath went public," Therese said. "The way the pressure ratcheted higher under the spotlight of quarterly earnings, how the stakes went up.

"Melissa challenged me. 'Let's get in on Internet IPO fever. We'll become Cardionics.com. We'll lower the pressure to produce earnings right off the bat.'" Therese laughed. "She talked about an employee stock ownership program that she felt would help to balance the pressure from other shareholders."

"Sure," I said. "It made such a difference at Carepath."

Therese raised her eyebrows. "Then I said there will be times when we're going a hundred miles an hour where we may need to slow down". She held up her hand in a stop sign. "And Melissa said I haven't found my brakes yet. But I promise I'll listen."

I patted her hand. "You just be sure your brakes are in working order."

Carepath gave Therese a going-away party that Paul missed because he and Sandy were called to Houston at the last minute. Nate presented Therese with an anniversary clock and a platinum disk on a plaque that proclaimed her as the chief songwriter on Carepath's top 40 greatest hits.

Alan, June and I took her out for a first, Friday night meeting of the Carepath alumni club at a wine bar where we told stories, drank Merlot and ate June's butterscotch brownies until the bar closed. I felt an overwhelming sense of relief. As though Therese had finally, voluntarily swum out of shark-infested waters.

I bought a series of coffee table books: Michelangelo's David, portraits from the Uffizi Gallery, a collection of frescoes on church ceilings and walls. I painted a series of Madonna and child portraits on chilly Saturday mornings and the evanescent light of Sunday afternoons.

For Valentine's Day I gave Therese a watercolor of two women lying together, naked, in rumpled sheets. The woman in the rear had her head propped up on one hand and the other hand resting on her lover's hip. The woman in the foreground was curled up, her head propped on pillows, gazing blankly ahead. I titled it "Surviving Passion."

Passion is the torrent of water that erodes rock and sculpts cliffs. It is also the steady drip of water on stone that hollows out a curve, a space where the arc of one body can fit against another. Careening through the waterfall, if we can avoid the rocks and keep our heads above water, we reach a pool in a glade, before the river carries us downstream. A rock juts out of the pool and a solitary woman, her back turned to us, lies atop it, staring into the depths below. The glade of trees forms a semi-circle around the pool which encircles the rock. There is air and water and light, definition and shadow, renewal and decay. There is the illusion of permanence, and it is enough.